SILENT NIGHT

Tamara von Werthern

SILENT NIGHT

TAMARA VON WERTHERN

Para-Site Publications

Para-Site Publications

Silent Night first published in Great Britain in 2024 as a paperback original by Para-Site Publications

Translated and adapted from the German novel *Ach Du Liebe Zeit! Ein Hofheimer Lokalkrimi in der Philipp-Reihe* by Tamara von Werthern

1 edition

Editor: Robin Booth

Typesetter: Brighton Gray

Cover image: Sam Green Studio

Series Design: Andrew Davis Designs

ISBN: 978-0-95595-115-2

For my father Philipp,
who is imitating art and has started playing the detective,
and for his dog Maschka

PROLOGUE

I love sitting on that little bench in the old town centre, watching the world go by. You know the one I mean? Between the Catholic church and the river, on the cobbled street with all the shops. People don't really do their shopping there any longer – they go to the big new out-of-town place where you can park. But still, there are cafés, restaurants, a bank or two and some bookshops. At the weekend there's a market that sells fruit and vegetables, cheese and wine and flowers. People come just to get out and about, do some window-shopping, bump into old friends. The youngsters like to get an ice cream at Venezia. Often there's quite a crowd.

I like sitting there, knowing that none of them have an inkling who I really am. They've got no idea what I'm thinking, or the things I get up to. Nobody knows, not even my friends. Won't they be surprised when they find out!

That day is coming. It'll all come out in the end. It will be a glorious day when everyone realises what I've done, how many lives I've changed. No one will accuse me then of hiding my light under a bushel. When all is said and done, I'll know my life has been worth living. Not everyone can say the same.

It's getting colder now. Christmas is coming. But I still come and sit on this bench, at least once a week. I make a point of it. I wrap up warm and I just sit here, smiling and nodding to anyone I know. And if a dog stops to sniff at me, I smile at it too and pat its head. Good boy, I say. There's a good boy. Now on you go.

ONE

It came upon a midnight clear

Darkness had descended on the little town of Hofheim, nestled into the Taunus foothills just west of Frankfurt. It rolled through the narrow cobbled streets, swallowing up the onion-domed tower of the Catholic church and lapping at the windowpanes of the half-timbered houses. Apart from the orange glow of the streetlamps and the occasional car driving along the Rheingauer Road looking for late-night entertainment, everything was dark and silent. It was nearly midnight, one Monday the week before Christmas. The Hofheimers were asleep in their beds.

Over on the Zeilsheimer Road, the darkness was broken by a lonely square of light, one of the very few windows still lit in the town. It illuminated a patch of untended lawn at the front of the house, painting shadows across the overgrown grass and picking out a rusty old tractor that had been parked there for years.

Inside, a man in his early sixties wearing a woollen jumper and jeans, and with untidy curly black hair that had a touch of grey in it, was walking back and forth between the kitchen and the living room, watched over by a patient Golden Retriever lying in her basket. The man seemed unable to keep still. One minute he was putting more logs into the wood burner, filling his glass with some Grauburgunder wine, and then lying down on the couch with a paperback crime novel; the next he was up again, topping up his glass and opening his laptop at the kitchen table. For a minute or two, he stared at a spreadsheet that recorded the various garages that he owned and rented out across Hofheim. Then, snapping the laptop shut, he was on his feet again, pacing up and down, turning night into day.

Philipp had long since come to terms with the fact that there were nights when sleep simply wouldn't come, when his thoughts would go round and round in his brain as if on a carousel, and the darkness of the night only made them shine brighter. On nights like these, all he could do was get up, get himself dressed, and crack on with the things that needed doing.

With Philipp, there was always something that needed doing. If he wasn't busy renting out his garages, he was arranging insurance cover for his roster of private clients, or managing his small removals firm, or assisting people who needed their car registering at the Vehicle Registration Office. He'd somehow acquired a bit of a reputation as a private detective, too, but as he had no credentials for that sort of work (other than some notable successes in one or two local cases), he didn't go about looking for it, and demand for his services had rather tailed off lately. There was, in any case, plenty to do about the house: he had his chickens to look after, his dog Maschka to take for walks, his horse Schimmi to feed and groom, and a whole fleet of classic cars and motorcycles that needed perpetual care and maintenance if they weren't to fall into disrepair or succumb to rust in the long grass at the back of the house.

As if all of that wasn't enough, he also took on occasional catering jobs whenever they came his way. In fact, he still had to source the wine and a selection of canapés for a gallery opening at the Museum of Modern Art in Frankfurt in a few days' time. He mustn't forget! This Grauburgunder was rather good. He tried to remember where he'd got it from. Oh yes, it was from his cousin's vineyard in Castell. He'd picked up a few cases when he was there for a party in August. This was the end of it, the very last bottle. What a pity. He raised the glass to his lips and knocked it back.

'Ah, farewell then, summer! It's all gloom and dreariness from now on. That's life.'

There was a whimpering cry from Maschka in her basket, where she now lay curled up asleep. Was she protesting at his melancholy mood, or was it just some dream of canine adventure she was having? Her tail thumped twice against the rim of the basket, and she whimpered some more. He was tempted to wake her for some company. But no, it wouldn't be fair. A dog needed her sleep.

Usually, if he had work to do, he went down to his office in the basement, where he could get on with it without disturbing any of his housemates. But right now the house was unoccupied except for him and Maschka. Michi was away on holiday in Lanzarote, in search of some winter sun. His other housemate, Youssef, had moved out not long ago, leaving a vacant room, a yawning chasm on the upper floor. The sense of emptiness all around him was probably the very thing that was keeping him awake. He couldn't settle on anything. There was nothing he could do about it. No point even doing any cleaning, though the house was in its usual state of total disarray; there was nobody but him to appreciate the difference, and in any case he had a high tolerance for disarray.

How things had changed since the summer. Back then, when he'd still been living with Annelie and their baby daughter Emma, his life had been full to the brim. It had been a whirlwind romance, the result of an adventure he'd been accidentally drawn into in his capacity as a private detective. When Annelie had fallen pregnant soon after the conclusion of the case, he'd been seized by a sudden onrush of delight and joy. How unexpected, to become a father again at his age! He'd embraced it wholeheartedly, the chaos and the wonder and the sleepless nights. He'd moved in with Annelie in her spick-and-span house in Langenhain, where he thrilled to every little thing that Emma did. She seemed to transport him back to when he was nineteen, bringing up his first daughter when he was barely out of school himself, learning the ways of fatherhood on the job. It all came pouring back to him, and he felt like his heart was about to burst.

It didn't last. Philipp shook his head mournfully now at the memory of it. Perhaps nothing that good could outlast the summer.

The cracks had appeared almost as soon as he'd moved into Annelie's house. It started with her insisting that he leave his shoes by the front door. It was a rule she had for any visitors, and it made Philipp feel like he too was a guest in the house. In fact, he found nothing so *ungemütlich* as having to walk barefoot around his own home. It put him on edge. A house was there to serve its occupants, not the other way around. He liked to have his Danish leather clogs on his feet at all times, inside or outside the house. They were simply a part of him. He could never get used to leaving them in the shoe rack by Annelie's front door.

'Philipp!' she'd cry, as he came back from a long walk through the fields in the rain with Maschka and baby Emma. 'Shoes!' And he'd do an about-turn and shuffle his way back to the front door to take off his clogs.

Incrementally, the cracks between the two of them grew, and before long there were chasms. It wasn't simply the shoe rack by the door. It wasn't even the spices that had to be kept in alphabetical order in the cupboard, or the dishes that had to be stacked in a particular way in the dishwasher, or the clean socks that were always to be put away carefully in matching pairs. It was none of these things, and it was all of them. Living together, looking after Emma, it became apparent that the two of them had entirely opposing ideas about life. Cleanliness and order were the air that Annelie breathed, whereas Philipp went about everywhere in a billowing cloud of chaos. To her, he was infuriatingly messy and inconsiderate, always leaving his things lying about the place, never putting them away when he'd done with them. Whereas to him, her habit of tidying things away before he'd finished with them was infuriating and counterproductive.

'I'm going to need that number plate tomorrow,' he'd say. 'Herr Krüger's Passat needs registering before the weekend.'

'Well, when you do need it,' she'd reply with a barely suppressed air of indignation, 'It'll be in the cupboard with all the others you left down the back of the sofa.'

Really it was a mania with her, this compulsion for tidying. It bordered on *Spießigkeit*, that narrowminded parochialism that took pride in superficial things, in highly polished surfaces and decorative knick-knacks arranged in height order along the mantelpiece. He couldn't abide it.

These fundamental differences between them made life as a couple ever more complicated. The love they felt for each other was undeniable, but it was under constant attack from everyday life. They were always being ambushed by arguments. Petty disagreements peppered their days. Minor resentments detonated subterraneously by night. And this is how it came about that Philipp spent more and more time back at his own house on the Zeilsheimer Road – and eventually, by mutual consent, he moved back there completely.

Despite this calamitous reversal of fortune, the two of them had managed to maintain a cordiality in all their dealings. They were in fact, despite everything, the best of friends. But still, Philipp had to admit he was more than a little sad that it hadn't worked out. He still cared a great deal about Annelie. And their daughter Emma – who was now one and a half, and came to him for part of every week – was truly the light of his life.

'Ah, Maschka,' he said to the sleeping dog, 'You can only play the hand you've been dealt.' And with a mournful expression he poured the dregs of the Grauburgunder into his glass.

He was beginning to think he was going to have to sit out the rest of the night without a wink of sleep. He got up and put another log in the wood burner. It was cold in the house, but he wasn't about to turn the central heating on, not with everyone away. His thick woollen jumper kept the worst of the cold at bay, and there was a grubby blanket he used for removals lying on the sofa. He grabbed it now and pulled it up over his knees. Half past four. Soon it would be daytime, and then he'd no longer feel like the only person left awake in the whole wide world.

The blanket brought a little warmth. Miraculously, his eyelids began to feel heavy. Ah, blissful sleep, at last!

Suddenly he was awake again. The clock still said half past four – he'd hardly even dropped off. A moment ago, there'd been an almighty crash from somewhere outside. Had he dreamt it? He must have done. What a nuisance! Even his dreams were conspiring against him. He pulled the blanket up over himself and tried to block out the thought.

It was no good. Something was tugging at the blanket. He sat up, dazed, and saw that it was Maschka who had a corner of the blanket between her teeth, and was giving it a determined pull.

'What is it, Maschka? What's got into you?'

The dog let the blanket drop, gave a couple of loud barks, and ran to the front door. Philipp could hear her yelping in the hallway. This wasn't like her! She always went out just before bedtime, and he rarely had to let her out again before morning. What was the matter with her? He stood up blearily, his legs getting tangled in the blanket as he stumbled his way into the hallway to investigate.

Maschka was lying flat on the doormat with her muzzle pressed against the crack under the front door. She was making loud snuffling noises, her tail batting from side to side. When she realised that Philipp was on his feet at last, she gave another enthusiastic bark.

'Quiet, Maschka! You'll wake everyone up,' he chided, before remembering that they were the only ones in the house. 'All right, then. You win. Let me open the door.'

Maschka backed away, and as he pulled open the heavy wooden door, a wave of icy cold air rushed in, making him shiver violently. He peered out at the darkened street.

For a moment, he didn't recognise it. The Zeilsheimer Road was a respectable street with houses that were large and well-maintained, set back behind neatly tended front gardens – with the one exception of his own, which was gloriously overgrown. It was the sort of place people took pride in, and normally you could tell this from the neat fences and the great variety of shrubs and outdoor ornaments, including, here and there, one or two garden gnomes.

But something wasn't right. In front of the house next door, which was currently vacant and for sale, there was a large black rectangular shape right across the pavement. It was as if they'd put up a huge extension overnight. It was difficult to make out its proportions straight away, because everything seemed so much darker than it usually was. In fact, Philipp realised, this whatever-it-was had taken the place of the streetlamp that normally lit up the street in front of his house. There were now two brilliant shafts of light that pierced the neighbours' fence, making jagged patterns up the white pebbledash. He found himself wondering how on earth they'd got planning permission for such a monstrosity – and then realised that what he was looking at was in fact a lorry. It was standing slantwise across the pavement, with its front end projecting right through the metal fence. It must have ploughed right across the pavement, taking out everything in its path, including the streetlamp. The beams of its headlamps were still blazing through the fence.

There was an eerie stillness lying over the whole scene, as if some violently thrashing creature had just collapsed and died. The crash that Philipp had heard in his sleep now echoed through the silence.

Maschka, beside him on the doorstep, let out a fearful whimper. The sound stirred him into action. He dashed back into the house to fetch his jacket and his glasses and to put something on his feet – his clogs must have fallen off while he was having his doze. He snatched up his mobile phone too – he'd better call the emergency services straight away – and then clattered out through the porch and into the street.

TWO

The weight of the world

'Yes, there's been an accident on the Zeilsheimer Road. A lorry's gone into my neighbour's fence. I'll see if there's anything I can do, but you'd better send an ambulance. And the police. In fact, send everyone!'

As Philipp hung up, he felt Maschka's warm flank against his leg. She was pressing herself against him, shivering. He took a deep breath to steady himself.

He was standing right beside the lorry. It was a big one, probably a thirty-tonner – much bigger than the six-tonne truck he used for his largest removals jobs. This was a different beast entirely. It had a separate driver's cabin high up at the front, too high for him to be able to see inside without climbing up. And he couldn't do that on this side of the lorry because most of the cabin, along with the driver's door, was embedded in the neighbours' fence. Its solid steel panels had crumpled like cardboard under the force of the collision.

He had a bleak idea of what he'd find if he did look inside. It felt like he was standing on the edge of a precipice, unable to see what lay beyond, but still compelled to take the plunge. He looked down at Maschka, who had her tail firmly wedged between her hind legs.

'I know, Maschka. It doesn't look good at all.'

Together, they went round to the other side of the lorry. He took hold of the handle and pulled himself up onto the metal gridded step by the cabin door. He peered in through the window. It was dark inside, and difficult to make anything out. Perhaps there was a figure huddled over the steering wheel. He yanked at the door handle, but it was locked. There was no obvious way to get in. Down on the pavement behind him, Maschka let out a high-pitched whine.

'I'm trying, Maschka. Be patient.'

He jumped down. There must be something he could use to break the window. There was a twisted piece of steel panel hanging off the fence – maybe he could use that? He took hold of it and tried to yank it free, but it was stuck fast. No good.

Maschka gave a quick, sharp bark. He turned and saw that she was standing over something lying in the road. What was it? Rushing over, he found it was a large section of metal pole, probably part of a road sign knocked over in the crash. Could he use that, perhaps? It was certainly heavy. He carried it in both hands over to the side of the lorry, heaved it up into the air, and brought it crashing down in the middle of the passenger-side window. Instead of shattering into tiny pieces as he'd expected, the glass simply dented, forming an intricate pattern of filigree cracks radiating out from the point of impact, like a spider's web. He dropped the pole and climbed up once again onto the step. This time the glass gave way as he pushed at it with his hand, wrapped in the sleeve of his jacket. He reached in through the window and unlocked the door.

Inside, the driver's body was slumped over the steering wheel. He felt for a pulse in the man's neck. He couldn't be sure, but perhaps there was a weak fluttering there. Best not to move him, in case it did some further damage. He could hear sirens now, coming from the direction of Zeilsheim. Help was on its way.

He took out his mobile phone again and used the torch function to illuminate the cabin. There might be something to indicate why the driver had lost control of the vehicle, and it would help the police if he could point it out to them. The windscreen was intact apart from three larger cracks zigzagging across it, converging in a point that would have been right in the driver's eyeline. It looked very much like a bullet hole. Philipp had the sudden thought that this would have been the last thing the driver had seen as he ploughed off the road into the fence. He touched the jagged edges of the small hole. Had the man been shot? He shivered and turned his light away from the windscreen.

There was little more to be seen. An air freshener in the shape of a pine tree, dangling from the dashboard. A half-empty bottle of mineral water in a compartment in the door. And there, down in the passenger footwell, covered in shards of glass, a road map of Europe.

The siren, which had been growing steadily louder all this time, now fell silent and the driver's cabin was lit up by a flashing blue light. The ambulance had arrived.

As Philipp climbed down from the cabin, two paramedics in hi-vis came running towards him.

'Don't worry about me,' he told them wearily. 'It's the guy in there you want to take a look at.'

As they clambered up into the cabin, he turned to look for Maschka. There she was, sitting quietly on the pavement. She was clearly unsettled, barely glancing at him as he approached, looking this way and that, up and down the road, trying to work out where the danger was coming from. He sat down on the pavement beside her and gave her a stroke.

'It's okay, Maschka, old girl. It's out of our hands now.'

He looked glumly across the street. A few lights were on, here and there, and some curtains were twitching, but nobody else had come out of their house. A sign of the times. People heard a bang and they stayed inside. There'd been stories in the newspapers about bomb threats and terrorist cells – clearly a load of bunkum, but it was bound to have an effect. Safety first. Stay inside and hunker down. Don't take any risks. Let the authorities deal with it. He understood it all perfectly well.

The two paramedics were lifting the driver down out of the cabin. Philipp offered to help, but they ignored him and just got on with their job, doing it with precision and care. They carried the limp body over to the pavement and laid him down gently on a foil blanket. One of them immediately started doing chest compressions while the other administered mouth-to-mouth.

Philipp felt a bitter chill pass through his own body and pressed himself up against Maschka's warm flank. The man on the ground looked like he was in his forties or fifties. He was dressed in jeans with a fleece jacket stretched tightly over a bulging belly. It may have been the effect of the flashing blue light from the ambulance, but the man's skin seemed to have taken on an ashen pallor. There was an awful slackness about his body. The paramedic doing the chest compressions kept on working away, but he seemed to be losing hope. Philipp felt his whole body vibrate with mounting tension. He found himself moving his lips in a silent prayer, one he didn't even know he remembered. Something from his childhood. Time seemed to float and bend, and he lost all sense of where he was and what he was doing.

When he rallied, he saw that the paramedics were no longer bending over the body. It was still lying on the pavement, now covered with a blanket. A feeling of immense heaviness came over Philipp, as if his entire body had been filled with bitterly cold water, right to the brim. He could barely move. With a great effort, he checked the time on his watch. It was nearly five. What had seemed like an eternity had lasted less than half an hour.

One of the paramedics – a man with long blond hair tied at the nape of his neck – came towards him. 'Are you the neighbour who reported it?'

'That's right,' Philipp said dully. 'Is he dead?'

The paramedic nodded. 'Nothing we could do. Heart attack, most likely.'

'Wasn't he shot?'

'Shot? No. What makes you think that?'

'There's a hole in the windscreen.'

'Is there? Well, no sign of a bullet wound. The coroner will find it, if there is one. I'd say he had a heart attack behind the wheel and lost control of the vehicle.'

Philipp nodded. 'Do you think he was dead before the impact, then?' He'd begun to hope so. It's a terrible thing to see your death come at you through the windscreen.

'Hard to say,' the paramedic shrugged. 'Most likely it was the crash that finished him off.'

As the man went over to the ambulance, Philipp realised that a police vehicle had pulled up next to it. He'd been distracted and hadn't noticed it arrive. Two uniformed officers were already taping off the scene. One of them, the large, portly one with a squat neck, he recognised straight away: it was Hannes Schnied. Oh yes, he'd had run-ins with Schnied in the past. There was no love lost between them. He knew the other one by sight too, though he didn't know his name. He was familiar with most of the Hofheim Police Force, and they were all too well-acquainted with him.

Schnied caught sight of him and came marching over. 'You, is it? I might have known you'd be sniffing around.'

'It's right on my doorstep,' said Philipp, with as much civility as he could muster. 'I thought I'd make myself useful.'

'It would be more useful if you went back inside and never came out,' said Schnied. 'The last time you got involved in police business, a young woman lost one of her toes.'

So Schnied wasn't going to play by the rules. The reminder was a painful one – Philipp still had pangs of conscience about Annelie's toe. She'd lost it during a bungled kidnap – a kidnap that he hadn't been able to prevent. He felt himself going crimson with rage and indignation.

'What's all this about a toe?' came a voice from behind him. A woman's voice.

Philipp turned to see an unfamiliar figure in jeans and a leather jacket, with a motorbike helmet under one arm. She had strikingly curly, jet-black hair and dark eyes in a face that seemed to radiate warmth and good humour. He thought she might be in her mid-forties perhaps, though he wasn't good at telling people's ages, despite all the practice he'd had. He glanced further up the road and saw a Yamaha SR400 propped on the roadside. So he'd missed her arrival too.

'Sergeant Bernstein,' muttered Schnied. 'I was just questioning one of the neighbours here.'

'Were you, Officer Schnied?' said the woman, rather sharply. 'Then where is your notebook?'

Schnied patted his chest pocket, then frowned. 'I must have left it in the car.'

'Better go and fetch it then, hadn't you?'

Schnied scuttled off, and Philipp, feeling a glow of satisfaction, turned to smile at the woman. Maschka, who was standing at his side, began wagging her tail for the first time since they'd left the house.

'Sergeant Bernstein,' said the woman, flashing her badge and holding out her hand. 'Hofheim Police.'

So this was Schnied's superior officer! She must be new to Hofheim. He shook her hand warmly. 'Philipp von Werthern.'

At the mention of his name, a smile flickered across her face. She looked down at the dog at Philipp's side. 'Then this must be Maschka,' she said, giving her a friendly stroke. 'I've heard about you.'

'Only good things, I hope,' said Philipp, unsure if she was talking about him or the dog now, and hoping it was both. He could well imagine what Schnied might have told her about him.

'Mind if I ask you a few questions myself?' she said, her voice sounding suddenly businesslike.

'Please, go ahead.'

She reached into her leather jacket and brought out her own notebook. 'Did you witness what happened here?'

'I'm afraid not,' he replied. 'I heard the crash and came out to see. But it was all over by then.'

'You were in bed?'

'No, not exactly. I mean, I have trouble sleeping. I wasn't sure what I'd heard, but Maschka here knew something was wrong. Didn't you, girl?'

Sergeant Bernstein looked intensely serious now. 'Did you

happen to note what time the crash occurred?'

'As a matter of fact, I did. It was on the dot of half past four.'

She jotted something in her notebook, then checked her watch, and made another note. 'And this is your house?'

'No, I live next door. This one's vacant. They moved out some time ago.'

'I see. And is there anyone else at your address who might have witnessed the crash?'

'No one,' he said. 'It's just the two of us at the moment. Maschka and me, that is.'

'Very good.' She looked thoughtful for a moment, sucking on the end of her pen. 'Well, now that I know where you live, I can call on you if I have any more questions.'

'Please do. Any time.'

'You'd better try and get some sleep, Herr von Werthern. We insomniacs carry the weight of the world on our shoulders, do we not?'

He smiled. The severity had slipped from her face, and he thought he saw a twinkle in her eye. 'Please, call me Philipp. No need for formalities.'

A shadow passed again over her features, making him feel like he'd spoken out of turn. 'If you do remember anything else, Herr von Werthern, you'll find me at the police station. Ask for Sergeant Bernstein. I'm the one in charge.'

He nodded, pleased to see that Schnied was within earshot. He must have heard every word she said. 'Good morning to you, Sergeant Bernstein.'

She turned away briskly, and went over to the paramedics, who were busy loading the dead body into the back of the ambulance. Philipp heard her issuing precise instructions to them about a forensic autopsy. The one with the ponytail was nodding grimly.

There didn't seem anything more he could do. He might as well go to bed, as she'd suggested.

'Come, Maschka,' he said.

The dog wagged her tail, and trotted happily alongside him, back to their front door. He'd left it open all this time, and light was blazing out from the hallway. It would be even colder now inside. Never mind, it couldn't be helped. Someone had lost their life tonight, and he'd been unable to do anything about it.

From the porch, he turned back for one last look. The whole street resembled the set of a TV cop show. Schnied and the other police officer had forced open the rear door of the lorry and were flashing their torches around inside, following Sergeant Bernstein's instructions. He wondered what they'd find in there. No matter, it was none of his business. He saw the sergeant standing on the edge of the circle of light, speaking to someone on the phone. She clearly took her job more seriously than they were used to at Hofheim police station. If he knew anything about Hannes Schnied, he was certain that he'd be gritting his teeth and cursing her arrival. Hannes didn't like taking orders from anyone, least of all a woman. Maybe a new broom was exactly what was needed in this town. Good luck to her. He heard the roar of her motorbike and watched as she sped off down the road. A Yamaha SR400!

There were more lights on now in the neighbouring houses. A little group had gathered in the street, mostly in their nightgowns and slippers, with thick winter coats pulled on over the top. People couldn't help being curious, once the police had turned up and it was safe to come out of their burrows. Death was always entertaining, so long as it wasn't someone you cared about in the body bag.

He let the front door close on the whole sorry scene, turned out the lights in the house, and went up to bed.

THREE

Roadblock

Philipp woke bleary-eyed and hungry, the sun pouring in through his bedroom window. The clock said it was eleven thirty, and he had no reason to doubt it.

Gradually the events of the previous night pieced themselves together. He got up and looked out of the window, half expecting it all to have resolved itself back into a dream. But the lorry was still there, slewed across the street with its front end buried in the neighbours' fence. It looked even larger and more shocking in the daylight. From up here he could see the long tyre tracks left in the tarmac, extending far up the street.

The road had now been closed to traffic, and a large section of it – about twenty metres on either side of his house – was marked off with yellow police tape. An officer was stationed at each end, turning traffic away and making sure the little gaggle of onlookers didn't trespass into the no-go zone. One of the officers, he noticed, was Hannes Schnied. He must have put in a shift! Had he been there the entire time Philipp had slept? He almost began to feel sorry for him. They must all be working overtime in the Hofheim police force in the run-up to Christmas… But then he remembered that comment about the toe, and suddenly he felt just the same as he always did towards his old adversary. He stuck out his tongue at the back of Schnied's head and made a very satisfying childish noise. Seeing the other police officer glance up at him, he styled it into a yawn and a stretch, and ducked away from the window.

Downstairs, he let Maschka out into the garden and then set about making the two of them breakfast: rye bread, toasted, smeared with butter and spread very thickly with some garlicky Mettwurst straight from the fridge; and a pouchful of dog meat with some biscuits alongside and a bowl of fresh water. Maschka returned from her ablutions and they both settled down to eat, Philipp's coffee percolating busily by the stove. They were both famished. Every now and then, Maschka gave him a look, one eyebrow raised as if to say, 'What time do you call this?', and he took another bite of his toast to avoid having to reply.

He tried very hard not to think about the body of the driver, lying out there on the pavement. A death like this, behind the wheel, could happen at any time. It could just as easily have been one of his removals team. Or one of his children, even. But he mustn't think like that. Life was short. He sincerely wished that, when his time came, all five of his children would be there at his graveside. He'd known since becoming a father in his twenties that it was any parent's deepest fear that they would have to bury their own child one day. Fortunately, he was not in the habit of dwelling on it. He was generally too busy for that.

He was just beginning to think about his schedule for the day when his mobile rang.

'Philipp, where are you?' It was Annelie. Clearly she was in one of her moods.

'I'm at home. Why?' He could never quite keep the defensiveness out of his voice.

'You were supposed to pick Emma up an hour ago. I need to go out. Are you on your way?'

'Just leaving!' he cried, snatching up the rest of his toast and the car keys. 'I'm walking out the door right now.' Where had he left Maschka's lead? It was nowhere to be seen. He'd better just go without it. 'Come, Maschka.' The dog, still only halfway through her breakfast, looked up at him, bemused. 'Sorry, Annelie. It's been a difficult morning.'

'Aren't they all,' she said, with her customary irritation.

'I'll be with you in ten minutes,' he said, grabbing his coat and opening the door.

There in front of him, clear as day, was another problem. The street was cordoned off. He was barricaded in behind the police tape, along with every vehicle he owned. To one side, Hannes Schnied. To the other, a police officer he didn't know, probably no more friendly towards him than Schnied was. That man had poisoned his name to everyone in the police force.

'Annelie, I'm going to have to call you back,' he said. He could hear her opening salvo as he hung up.

What to do? His motorbike – the one with the sidecar – was in the back garden, along with the MG and the Opel, and of course his horse Schimmi and the chickens. But it was no use. The access lane went down the side of his house and opened out onto the part of the street that was barricaded off. There was no way out. Even the Porsche, parked at the front, was in the no-go zone. And there was simply no conceivable way that Hannes Schnied was going to let him through.

He slouched back into the house and closed the front door. Maschka, who had followed him out and then back in again, sloped back into the kitchen to finish her breakfast. Philipp caught a glimpse of himself in the hall mirror. He was still in his pyjamas. He took off his coat and hung it back up.

In the kitchen, his coffee was just coming to the boil. He poured himself a large cup and scooped several spoonfuls of sugar into it.

His phone bleeped. He ignored it. He had to think. If he let Annelie down this time, she might think twice about coming over for Christmas. It was a delicate agreement. They'd discussed it for hours, like grown-ups – and then for several hours more, when perhaps he hadn't been quite so grown-up about it. And in the end, she'd reluctantly agreed that they would both come over to Philipp's and celebrate Christmas with the rest of the family. All of Philipp's children were coming, every Schlumpa, with all their various clans. The house would be full – but not so full that there wouldn't be room for Annelie and Emma. And it was out of the question to have everyone over at Annelie's – her house was far too small, and also just think of the mess, everyone trooping in and out with their shoes on, mud all over the carpet! No, it had to be at Philipp's. And surely Annelie wouldn't deprive Emma of being a part of it, Christmas with all the family, the centre of attention as always? Emma had gurgled merrily in her highchair at hearing the word *Schlumpa*, and the matter was finally settled.

But not so settled that Annelie couldn't change her mind. And this little predicament was putting it all in jeopardy.

'Maschka,' he moaned. 'What are we going to do?'

And as always with the two of them, an idea soon came to mind.

Philipp rushed upstairs to throw some clothes on, and then grabbed his bag and thrust everything he needed into it, including the baby-sling. All set. He said a hurried goodbye to Maschka, who was going to stay at home and hold the fort. Then he dashed out through the back door, into the garden.

Fortunately, Hannes Schnied was standing all the way over by the police cordon with his back turned, and so didn't hear the horse's hooves until Philipp had made it all the way down the access lane at the side of the house on Schimmi, and out onto the street.

At that point, the horse's hooves made a loud clatter on the tarmac, and everyone turned to look – not only Schnied, but twenty or so passers-by who had come to gawp at the scene of the crash. Well, let them gawp, thought Philipp, steering Schimmi into the street and to the left, in the direction of Annelie's house in Langenhain. He gave the horse's flanks a firm prod with his heels.

Schnied was coming towards them now, waving his arms. 'Stop! Stop at once! You can't ride through here!' He'd gone very red in the face.

'Whyever not?' called Philipp, as Schimmi shied a little at the strange man with the windmilling arms and drew to a halt.

'This is a police control zone. Get down off the horse!'

'I will not,' said Philipp. 'A horse has as much right to exercise as anyone else.'

'You're interfering with the scene of an accident,' cried Schnied, who seemed very close to bursting a blood vessel.

'I'm not interfering with it, I'm simply passing through it.'

There was a soft crumpling noise from behind and Philipp turned to see a heap of manure had landed right on top of one of the tyre tracks.

'Look what it's done! Look!' screamed Schnied.

'Yes, well, if you hadn't scared him like that...' began Philipp, though he could see that Schnied had a point.

'Wait until Sergeant Bernstein hears about this!'

'Come on, Schimmi,' Philipp said, trying to keep a reassuring tone in his voice. 'Let's leave Officer Schnied to get on with his job.'

But Schnied came at them again. 'Get down off the horse!' he cried, making an ineffective lunge for Schimmi's bridle. The horse backed away, panicking a little, and bolted towards the lorry, then swerved and began to head for the police cordon at speed.

'Woah, Schimmi!' Philipp called, trying to pull back on the reins. But in truth he'd never been a particularly assertive rider. As a general rule, it was Schimmi who decided which way to go and how fast. And it was no different today.

Philipp found himself clinging on as Schimmi accelerated into a canter, sped towards the cordon and, in one swift, gravity-defying leap, flew into the air.

For a few seconds that seemed like minutes, all four of Schimmi's hooves parted company with the tarmac, and Philipp found himself slipping backwards, aware of the astonished faces of the bystanders beneath him. He held on for dear life with trembling knees.

And then he shot forward again as Schimmi landed on the far side of the cordon, and continued without breaking stride, flat out, along the street. The clattering of the hooves rang loud in his ears, but he could still hear the jubilant cheers that broke out behind, and – perhaps he imagined it – the high-pitched wailing of a furious Schnied.

After a while, as the traffic grew busier, Schimmi decided to slow up, and settled into a trot. And then, after crossing the junction, into a walk. At that point, having caught his breath a little, Philipp risked giving the horse a little pat on the neck, to show his approval. He'd survived. And they'd be at Annelie's house in no time at all.

Feeling more secure now, Philipp swung his backpack round to the front and extracted his phone. He could see he had eight missed calls and a text message. All of them from Annelie. The message said: *Don't bother. I'm leaving now, and I'm taking Emma with me. Come and fetch her tomorrow by 10.*

He stuffed the phone back into the bag. Damn. Damn and blast.

For a while he let Schimmi carry him on down the road, hardly caring where they ended up. It was a Quixotic quest after all. Perhaps he ought to turn back? But no, he couldn't contemplate facing Schnied again so soon. He might as well continue into town. There would be people there, hustle and bustle, pleasant distractions. He even had his Christmas shopping to do. Why not do it on horseback?

FOUR

Ding dong! Merrily on high

'Have we got an ID on the lorry driver yet?'

Nadja Bernstein swung round on her swivel chair and looked Bremsberger square in the face. She had to do this a dozen times a day or more, since the desk they'd given her was tucked into the corner of her cubicle. Whenever she sat down, the rest of the office disappeared from view.

'Yes, Sarge,' replied Bremsberger. 'The driver's name is Jürgen Fischer. Fifty-three years of age. Local man. Lives over in Diedenbergen, just behind the Grillrestaurant…'

'Any police record?' Nadja cut in.

Bremsberger shrugged. 'Not that I know of.' He looked down at his notebook and began flicking through a few pages. They were all blank.

Nadja sighed. 'Well, hadn't you better go and check, Officer Bremsberger?'

'I didn't think, in a case like this… an RTC basically…'

'All the same, let's dot the i's and cross the t's. And then, when we file our report, Commissioner Rabbinger will see we've done more than check out which burger joint the guy liked to eat in.'

'It's actually a nice little place, Sarge. I've eaten there myself…'

'Bremsberger, just check if this Fischer guy has a record, will you? And then find out who the vehicle's licensed to, and where it was going. Has it been towed to the pound yet?'

'Not yet, Sarge.'

'You mean it's still sitting out there in the street?'

Bremsberger went back to flicking through his empty notebook.

'Will you stop doing that,' she snapped. 'What time is it now? It's after midday. What on earth have you been doing all morning?'

She knew the answer to this. He'd come in late and had spent the best part of two hours over by Officer Schröder's desk, helping to devise some kind of Christmas quiz. He stood gaping at her now like he was facing a tiebreaker, and the answer was on the tip of his tongue. His jaw went up and down like he was a human PEZ dispenser. He was a moron, she knew, but no more useless than the rest of them.

'So the road is still closed to traffic, is it?' she said through gritted teeth.

'The recovery team turned up at nine thirty this morning, Sarge. But the photographer hadn't attended yet, so Officer Schnied sent them away.'

'For goodness' sake. What happened to the photographer?'

'Apparently he went to the wrong address.'

'How could he get that wrong? It's the Zeilsheimer Road. All he had to do was walk out the door and turn right!'

'He went to Zeilsheim.'

'Well get him back from Zeilsheim, Bremsberger. Immediately. This is a shambles!'

'Right, Sarge.' Bremsberger turned to go.

'And Bremsberger?'

'Yes, Sarge.'

'When Officer Schnied comes in, tell him I want to see him before he clocks off.'

'Will do, Sarge.'

As Bremsberger sloped out of her cubicle, she swivelled back to her desk. There was an open file on top of it, which she pushed aside. Underneath lay a textbook, open at the module she was working on for her Police Commissioner exams, which were fast approaching. Those exams were her ticket out of here – right out of this cubicle, down the corridor, and who knows, into Rabbinger's office. Or, even better, some Commissioner's job a long way away from Hofheim. Frankfurt, maybe? Düsseldorf? Berlin? Anywhere but here.

She'd taken the job in Hofheim just two months ago. It was a step up from her last position in Frankfurt, but not where she'd hoped to be, this far into her career. Not what she'd expected after acing the fast-track scheme back in Hamburg when she first joined the Police Force. If you'd told her then that she'd be managing road closures in a small town in Hesse at the age of forty-six, she'd have laughed in your face.

She bent over the textbook, and a thick strand of her black hair came loose. It was always doing that. No matter how carefully she tied it up in a bun each morning, her hair always came loose. She twisted it back behind her head and, with her other hand, opened the desk drawer to find something to fix it in place. A pencil, a ballpoint, anything. She glanced down into the drawer and there was Sven staring up at her. His thin, angular face. Dark, puppyish eyes. She closed the drawer again.

Breathe, Nadja. Breathe. Forget about Sven. Sven's gone now. It's over. It's done with.

Sven had moved out of her flat in Kelkheim just the week before. It had been awful. He'd apologised endlessly, even though it had been her who broke it off. It had taken him the entire afternoon to pack up his stuff, and he'd cried the whole time. It had been the worst four hours of her life. And then, once he'd gone, she felt that familiar weightless sense of remorse, the feeling you get when suddenly you're on your own again. Simultaneous relief and utter desolation. She'd ordered a takeaway and opened a bottle of wine and, for the first time in two years, polished it all off by herself.

She couldn't quite bring herself to ditch the photo. It had taken up residence in the desk drawer, along with a stapler she never used and a fraying mousepad. The pot plant he'd bought her, a miniature aspidistra, was still on her desk. Really, she ought to throw it away, but it was useful cover whenever she was doing covert work for her exams. She drew it close over the open pages of her book, in case anyone sneaked up on her.

She pored over the textbook. None of it would sink in. It was impossible to concentrate. Her exams were only weeks away and all she could think about was Sven and the sound of his snivelling.

She picked up a highlighter pen and began highlighting words more or less at random in her textbook. *Legality, mitigating circumstances, faith-based practice* and *disciplinary procedures.*

The telephone on her desk began to ring.

'Sergeant Bernstein,' she said briskly into the receiver.

'Nadja, is it okay, I just wanted to…'

'Sven? I said not to call me at work.'

'I know, Nadja. I know you did. I'm so sorry about this.'

His voice still had that tremulous quality that, in the early days of their relationship, Nadja had found irresistibly endearing. It had seemed to her so charming, so sure a sign of his superior nature, his profound and unusual sensitivity, that she had wanted to clasp him to her breast and offer him protection from the buffetings of the world. Now it irritated the hell out of her. It was the sonic equivalent of a cute little kitten digging its claws into your soft, unprotected flesh.

'What do you want now, Sven?'

'I loaned a book to your mother, *The Sorrows of Young Werther*. Would it be a great deal of trouble to ask for it back?'

Nadja sighed. 'No. I'll get it from her next time I'm there. I'll send it on.'

'Really? You'll do that? Nadja, that's really… I'm so so…'

'It's fine.'

'Or if you want, I could call on her myself…'

'No, don't do that.' Sven had always got on famously with her mother. It was one of the reasons she'd stuck with him longer than she should have: she hadn't wanted to break her mother's heart. If he struck up an independent relationship with her now, she'd never be shot of him. 'Please don't bother her about it. She's not been well.'

The lie came out of her mouth before she'd given it any thought, and suddenly she saw that he might think her mother was ill because of him. Because of their breakup.

'Really? Not well? I'm so sorry. I'll send her some flowers.'

The man really was a paragon of chivalry. She had a brief, terrifying vision of him and her mother snuggling together under a blanket, reading Goethe.

'I've got to get back to my work now, Sven.'

'Of course. I'm so sorry to bother you. Sorry, Nadja. Sorry.'

She hung up before he could apologise again. Was there, she wondered, any chance that Sven was being sarcastic? No, she didn't think so. Sadly, he meant every word.

She looked down at her textbook and found that she'd doodled something indecent alongside the words *Designated Adult Safeguarding Manager*.

'Sergeant Bernstein.'

The voice came from somewhere above her. She looked up and there, looming over the cubicle screen, was the face of Commissioner Rabbinger.

'Sir!' she said, springing to her feet. With a deft movement of her left hand, she slid the case file back on top of the open textbook. He probably hadn't seen it – the aspidistra was perfectly positioned.

Rabbinger twitched his moustache like a man weighing up a delicate matter. 'This incident on the Zeilsheimer Road. You've got it all under control?'

'Yes, sir. Absolutely. Officer Bremsberger is tracing the haulage company right now, sir, and we'll have the vehicle towed away as soon as we've got some shots of the scene.'

Rabbinger began to mobilise his moustache again, and Nadja wondered if he was chewing some remnant of his lunch.

'It was the incident with the horse that concerned me, Sergeant. You're dealing with that, I take it?'

Nadja gulped. 'The horse, sir?'

'Some idiot on horseback, riding about and threatening our

officers. I suggest you get onto it right away.'

'Yes, sir!'

'I want a full report on my desk, first thing tomorrow.'

'Right, sir. You'll have it. First thing tomorrow.'

The Commissioner, hoicking his moustache so far up his face that it threatened to merge with his eyebrows, turned and stalked off down the corridor to his office.

Nadja looked across the office for Bremsberger. He was over by Schröder's desk again.

'Bremsberger!'

'Yes, Sarge?'

'Come here.'

She watched as Bremsberger threaded his way across the office, between the deserted cubicles, many of which were festooned with tinsel.

'What's this about a horse?'

'Yes, Sarge. One of the residents on the Zeilsheimer Road, by the crash site… I believe he emerged from the back of his property on horseback. He proceeded to despoil the scene, and nearly caused an injury to Officer Schnied. He then made off in the direction of town.'

'On horseback?'

'Yes, Sarge.'

Nadja found herself wrinkling her upper lip, conscious of her lack of a moustache.

'Do we have the name of this resident?'

'Yes, Sarge. Von Werthern. Philipp von Werthern.'

'Oh, yes.' She nodded. 'Well, in that case, whatever Officer Schnied says, we must take with a pinch of salt. They have a history, those two, I believe.'

'He's a troublemaker, Sarge. A pain in the backside.'

'Where is Schnied now? Is he still at the scene?'

Bremsberger shifted uneasily. 'He clocked off twenty minutes ago, Sarge.'

'Clocked off? Why didn't he come to see me, as I asked?'

'He had to go home, Sarge. He was in a state of shock, because of the horse.'

'Right. And why is it that everybody, from you all the way up to Commissioner Rabbinger, knows about this horse before I do?'

Bremsberger shrugged his shoulders.

'From now on, if there's so much as a fart directed at one of my officers, I want to know. Is that clear?'

'Yes, Sarge!'

'And Bremsberger. Has the lorry been towed yet?'

'We're trying to contact the recovery team. They've gone AWOL.'

'Well find them. It's got to be towed by the end of today, you understand?'

'Right, Sarge. Got it. End of the day.'

She watched as Bremsberger wended his way across the office, through the forest of gaudy decorations, back over to Schröder's desk. This was going to be a long day.

FIVE

All wrapped up

Philipp was sitting on the bare floorboards in his bedroom, surrounded by glittering silver packages of all different shapes and sizes. He surveyed the scene with quiet satisfaction. It was a job well done.

It had long been his habit to wrap all his Christmas presents in tin foil. He found it much preferable to the endless fuss with wrapping paper and sticky tape – all you had to do was place what you wanted to wrap in the middle of a sheet of foil, fold the sides up and over, then press the edges down tight. And hey presto, another one done! Even better, he could use the same sheets year after year.

Besides which, the results were infinitely pleasing. The parcels gleamed under the lights like outsize baubles. The foil itself got better and better with reuse, all the little folds and creases that accumulated over the years adding sparkle and lustre, producing a dazzling, kaleidoscopic effect. It made Christmas feel like an annual convention of mirror balls. It never failed to make the children gasp when, running in from the hallway, they came upon the heap of sparkling presents under the Christmas tree!

Best of all, he'd bought and wrapped all his presents in a single afternoon, and still it was not yet dark. He piled the precious items up in a corner of the bedroom, where the fading light from the window made them look like a pile of jacket potatoes ready to be tossed on the glowing embers of a campsite fire. In due course he would carry them all downstairs and place them under the tree – but first the tree itself would need to be brought in from the terrace outside, where it spent most of the year in a sizeable pot. It had grown substantially since last Christmas, and Philipp wasn't at all sure if it would fit inside the house. He might have to lop a bit off the top.

As he came downstairs, Maschka was pawing gently but insistently at the front door. He ought to take her out before it got dark. She'd been very patient with him after all the turmoil of the previous night, and then putting up with his sudden disappearance earlier on Schimmi, just when she'd been promised a walk. Really she was a very understanding dog. But there was a limit even to her tolerance, and right now she was making it perfectly clear.

'Sorry, Maschka. I know. Let's go for a nice long walk.'

He grabbed his coat and her lead and opened the front door. He hadn't dared look out at the front of the house since he'd returned on Schimmi earlier in the afternoon. At that point, he'd been glad to see that Schnied had been relieved on the front line by someone unfamiliar and altogether less hostile to him. The officer had even allowed him back through the cordon without making much of a fuss. Philipp had asked politely if they'd any intention to move the lorry and reopen the road. He'd been given a cursory reply: 'Search me, mister. It could be here until Christmas now.'

Philipp hoped with all his heart that this wouldn't be the case. Not only would it be a difficult thing to explain to all his guests, but more pressingly, he simply had to be able to drive to Annelie's tomorrow morning to collect Emma. It was do-or-die.

So when he looked out onto the street, he did so with his heart in his mouth.

Disappointingly, the lorry was still there. But then he would surely have heard them if they'd come to tow it away. On the plus side, the cordon had been repositioned and one lane had been opened to traffic, which was now being controlled by temporary traffic lights on either side of the crash site. There was no sign of any police officers in attendance. He could see long lines of cars building up behind the lights, mainly from the direction of town – people were heading home from work, or maybe from doing their Christmas shopping. There was, after all, an advantage to doing it on horseback, and parking was so much easier.

'Come on, Maschka. The coast is clear.'

Together they bounded out onto the pavement. Dusk was setting in, but there was still a good hour before dark. Enough time to stretch the legs. He wanted to give Maschka a really good walk, out onto the fields at the edge of town. He'd noticed that she'd put on a bit of weight recently – he hadn't been able to get out with her as much as he used to, not since having Emma every week. His daughter loved going for walks with her beloved Maschka, but she quickly tired and they'd have to head home before they'd got very far. He could at least give her a proper walk now.

He hadn't gone far when he realised that Maschka was no longer at his side. He turned and saw that she'd gone the other way. She was inside the police cordon, sniffing around by the lorry.

'What are you doing, Maschka? We're going for a walk. Let's go!'

She ignored him, too busy exploring whatever smells there were to be found, and he had to duck under the police tape and put her lead on before she'd come away.

'Just you wait till we get to the fields. There'll be all sorts of things to sniff there.'

Still, she didn't come willingly. It wasn't until they were a good way down the street that she finally lost interest in the lorry. However, by the time they reached the pedestrian walkway past the animal hospital, she seemed to rediscover her enthusiasm. There were a couple of canine patients on the other side of the hospital fence, taking the afternoon air in the hospital garden. One of them, a black Labrador, had a bandaged leg and was wearing a big white conical collar. He looked rather miserable about the sad state of affairs, and Maschka gave him a little sympathetic whine, then marched on, ready now to give the fields a good run for their money.

Once they were out in the open, he let her off the lead and she raced off, running a huge circle around him, then zigzagging ecstatically through the little apple orchard. He lost sight of her for a while, then saw her again, pricking her ears at some birds she'd seen landing in the ploughed field. She revelled in the clear cold air and the wide expanse of the horizon, out here on the edge of town. And Philipp too felt a sense of relief after the stresses of the day, and the upsetting scenes of the previous night. He kept thinking about that lorry with its cracked windscreen, the driver slumped over the wheel – and then his body lying prostrate on the pavement, turning blue from the cold night air. Or from something even colder than that. Death. A shiver went down the whole length of his body. That was another reason he hoped the lorry would soon be gone. As long as it stood there, outside his house, he would struggle to forget what he'd seen.

Darkness was falling. It was time to head home. He whistled for Maschka and called out her name. Where was she? In the deepening gloom he didn't spot her at once, but she couldn't be far away.

There she was, her head down hunting for voles. She knew where their burrows were, along the edge of the field. Her hindquarters were up in the air, tail twitching frantically as she sank her head deeper and deeper into the cleft in the soil. No wonder she couldn't hear him! She was deaf to everything above ground. He went over, took hold of her back end and gave her a tug. But she resisted his efforts, intent on catching her prey. Goodness me, she was getting even chubbier than he'd thought! Was it all the voles she was eating, or was his housemate Michi secretly giving her snacks between meals? He'd have to have a word when Michi was back from his holidays.

'Maschka! Come on, girl. Leave it alone!'

It took a while to persuade her to give up the hunt. When she eventually agreed to call it a day, her head came out of the hole so caked with mud that, for moment, he thought she was an entirely different dog. But after a good sneeze and a shake of the ears, she was Maschka again, and they set off for home.

She stayed by his side now, and he didn't have to attach the lead, even as they walked past the animal hospital. It was so dark, all they could see was the Labrador's white conical collar in the middle of the lawn, moving slowly and silently as it tracked their progress along the path.

They crossed over by the traffic lights and walked on past the police station, which was still brightly lit. Philipp wondered if that sergeant with the motorbike was working late. Bernstein, wasn't that her name? She'd told him she was an insomniac, thinking he was one too – though he wasn't, not really. He had sleepless nights from time to time, that was all. Often he slept like a baby.

As they were passing the outdoor football pitch near his house, he spotted a ball that had got wedged in the branches of a tree on the side of the road, and stopped to see if he could reach it. He might, if he climbed up. He considered it for a moment. No, Philipp, don't do anything stupid. You're too old for climbing trees. When he turned back from the tree, he saw that Maschka had gone.

'Maschka!' He whistled for her. Where'd she got to? Perhaps she'd just gone on ahead, ready for home.

Then, as he drew near the house, he saw her. She was over by the lorry again, a soft pale blur in the dwindling light.

'What are you up to, girl?'

He ducked under the police tape again. This was becoming a bit of a habit, he thought. Schnied would be hopping mad.

Maschka was busy sniffing away at the side of the vehicle. He could hear a low-pitched whining coming from her. It didn't seem to be her usual curiosity about things, it was something much more intensely focussed than that. It was all directed at one particular spot on the lorry, just above the wheel arch. As he came up alongside her, she ducked away and began running up and down alongside the vehicle in great excitement. He was worried she might run out into the road, where cars were moving at speed along the single lane.

'Maschka! Heel!' Immediately she came back to him, tail between her legs. 'Good girl. What's got into you?' She gave another pitiful whine, and then took hold of his trouser leg with her teeth and began to tug him towards the lorry.

'OK, enough. That's enough Maschka! Let's go home.'

He snapped the lead back onto her collar and began to haul her towards the house.

Then he stopped.

Something had made him stop. Not Maschka this time, she'd fallen silent. There was no traffic driving past either, the lights must be on red. There was very little noise, in fact.

Just a quiet, steady knocking. Coming from inside the lorry.

SIX

A discovery

Philipp went back over to the lorry, keeping Maschka close. He pressed his ear to the cold metal, just above the rear wheel. Silence.

Then it came again, muffled but undeniable. Knock-Knock-Knock.

He looked down at Maschka in amazement and met her eyes looking up at him. She was giving him a questioning look. Or was it more, 'I told you so'?

'Okay, yes, I see now.' He gave her an apologetic stroke. 'You're right, and I should have listened to you before.'

The knocking came again, and they both swung their heads to look at the lorry. Philipp felt the hair stand up on the back of his neck.

'Maschka, do you think there might be someone in there?'

She gave a loud whimper and put her forepaws up on the side of the lorry to get a better sniff at it.

'We can't get in that way, can we? Let's have a look round the back.'

He went to the back of the vehicle, where it was sticking out into the road, and peered at the two massive doors. There was some kind of locking mechanism, but it had been taped over with reflective tape: *Police – Do Not Enter*. It was difficult to tell if the doors were still locked.

He took out his phone and used the torch function to take a closer look. The doors were secured by two thick metal rods running the full vertical height of the lorry, slotting into a socket at the bottom and operated by a solid-looking lever. He took hold of the lever on the right, but it wouldn't budge. The rod on the left, he noticed now, was slightly buckled – perhaps where it had been forced open by the police. The end of it, instead of sitting securely in the socket at the bottom, was only resting on the rim. He grabbed the lever and gave it a firm tug, and the rod sprang out of the socket. The door creaked open a crack. Bingo!

But wait. What was he doing? He was breaking into a crashed lorry, the scene of a possible crime. There was police tape all over it. *Do Not Enter*. Shouldn't he call the police station and let Sergeant Bernstein know there was someone inside?

But she might not even be there. And what if he got Hannes Schnied or one of the others? They'd probably take ages to get here, even though it was just down the road. This was an emergency, he had to act now. Who knew what he was going to find in there!

He took hold of the door and heaved it open, snapping the police tape as he did so. Luckily, the side that was unlocked swung open towards the pavement, not into the road where it would have blocked the traffic. He was aware, all the same, of the cars that came whizzing past, inches away from his heels. He wondered if anyone would stop and ask what he was doing?

With Maschka looking on from the pavement, he secured the door against the side of the lorry, and then went back and shone the torch on his phone into the cavernous interior. Its beam didn't quite reach all the way to the far end, but even so it looked like the lorry was empty. Perhaps the police had removed whatever contents it had been carrying? It was impossible to tell.

He climbed up, using the ridged step that jutted out under the lip of the doors. As he took the first cautious step into the dark interior, his clogs ringing out on the metal floor, Maschka came leaping past him and ran straight over to the wheel hub on the left-hand side. She began to yelp excitedly.

With all the noise Maschka was making, it was impossible to hear if there was any knocking still, or if it had fallen silent. But one thing was for sure: there was nobody lurking in the shadows.

The whole inside of the lorry had been stripped clean.

Had he been mistaken about the knocking?

He looked again at the wheel casing on the left. Wait a minute! Yes, it was much bigger than the one on the other side. Someone had built a crude box over it with plywood and painted it black so that it was almost imperceptible. No wonder the police hadn't noticed it. Still, Hannes Schnied couldn't see a piece of evidence if it poked him in the eye…

At that moment there came another Knock-Knock-Knock. It was weak, but it did seem to be coming from the wheel casing. Maschka heard it too, and she began pawing at the wooden casing with frantic scrabbling movements.

'Easy, Maschka. Let me see!'

But she wouldn't let him near it. She got her front paws up on top of the casing and began sniffing her way along the entire length of it, inch by inch. Suddenly she gave a pitiful yelp and jerked herself away, tail between her legs.

'What is it, old girl? What's bitten you?'

He took her muzzle in both hands, and she let him feel along her jaw until, when he reached the part right under her nose, he felt a trickle of something wet. She flinched, and in the torchlight he saw a smear of blood on his hand.

'You've cut yourself, Maschka. Be careful. There's something sharp.'

Carefully, he ran his hand along the edge of the casing where she'd been sniffing. There it was! A tiny hinge. It too was painted black, almost invisible to the naked eye. Its metal edge was sharp enough to cut.

If there was a hinge, then there must be an opening. He felt along the bottom edge, concealed from view – and his hand met something cold and firm. He ducked down and shone his torch on it. Yes, there it was! A padlock!

So whoever – or whatever – was inside the box… they were stuck in there. And it was tiny. About three feet across. Eighteen inches deep. Not big enough for an adult. Hardly big enough even for Maschka.

And yet the knocking had come from in there. No doubt about it.

'Hello,' he cried. 'Sit tight. I'll get you out as soon as I can.'

He waited for any reply. There was none.

He shone the torchlight around the lorry's interior again, in case he'd missed anything he could use to break the padlock open. There was nothing. And even if there'd been a handy crowbar, he wouldn't be able to use it in the tiny crevice where the padlock was hidden. Could he break the box open, perhaps? Not without harming whatever – or whoever – was inside. There had to be another way. He looked around, beginning to despair...

'Maschka! What are you doing?' She'd gone over to the other side of the lorry, and was sniffing at something on the wall, above the smaller wheel casing there. 'Careful, girl. You don't want to do yourself any more damage.' He went over to see what she was sniffing at. And there, taped to the wall, and painted over in black so it could hardly be seen... a key!

'Maschka, I knew it! I always knew you had a little of the bloodhound in you!'

He unpeeled the key and took it over to the padlock. His fingers were shaking as he slid it into the lock. It turned easily and the clasp fell open. The padlock clattered onto the floor.

Philipp took a deep breath and lifted the lid of the box.

What he saw inside, he knew he would never forget. It had the force of inevitability, and the shock of disbelief. There, crammed into that tiny space, was a human being. A boy, perhaps eight or ten years old. He was folded in on himself so that he could barely move, and was packed round with blankets and packing foam – whether to muffle any sounds or to provide some protection from the buffetings of the journey, Philipp didn't know. He'd clearly been cooped up in there for a long time. The stench rose from him like the blast of heat when you open a furnace door, and Philipp, clasping a sleeve over his mouth and nose, had to stop himself from reeling back.

Slowly, the boy raised his dusty head and blinked at Philipp in the torchlight. His eyes were wide and frightened, his face streaked with grime and tears. He tried to lift a hand, but the effort seemed too much. He began to tremble.

Clutched in that hand was a small plastic water bottle. It had been sucked dry.

SEVEN

A meagre haul

Leaving the bathroom door ajar, Philipp went quickly downstairs to the kitchen. He opened the fridge. There was a half-full two-litre bottle of Coca-Cola in there. That would do.

He got a dirty glass from the sink and gave it a good rinse under the tap. Clean enough. He poured Coke into it, right to the brim.

Food. He needed food. Was there anything in the house? Nothing that he could give the boy straight away. Wait, there was that packet of Pretzel Sticks he'd opened yesterday. Yes, there it was. He tipped the rest of the packet into a small silver bowl and went back upstairs with his meagre haul.

Steam, warm and fragrant, was billowing out through the bathroom door. He knocked gently and went in. The boy was sitting in the tub, a blanket of bubbles right up to his chest. Philipp turned off the taps and tested the water's temperature. It was a little on the warm side, but the boy didn't seem to mind. It would probably do his aching muscles some good. He put the glass of Coke and the bowl of Pretzels down on the side of the bath and stepped back. The boy looked up at him. His eyes, Philipp noticed now, were a piercing green. He seemed uncertain if the drink and the snack were for him.

'Please,' said Philipp, gesturing at him to help himself.

At once, the boy snatched up the Coke. He drank noisily with both hands on the glass. In a moment he had drained the lot. He put the glass down carefully on the side of the bath and reached for the Pretzels. He hesitated, seeing the foam dripping thickly from his hand. Philipp smiled and held out a towel. The boy wiped the foam off his hands, and then picked up a handful of Pretzels and piled them into his mouth. Philipp noticed there was a coffee-stain birthmark on one of his narrow shoulders. Other than that, the skin on his face and chest was a fine olive colour. He didn't seem to have any visible bruises or injuries. His eyes, with irises as green as freshly shelled pistachios, were bright and clear.

That was something, anyway. When Philipp had pulled him from his hiding space – no, his prison – in the lorry, the child had been so weak that he couldn't even support his own weight. His legs had buckled beneath him. Philipp had ended up carrying him down out of the lorry. And then, once they were out in the cold night air, in the harsh glare of the headlights flashing past, he made an instant decision to go on carrying him into the house. One thing had led to another, and before he could decide which of the authorities he ought to inform, he found himself running a bath and helping the boy out of his sodden, stinking clothes.

He picked up those clothes now, strewn about on the bathroom floor. Maschka came in and sat down on the bathmat with a stern expression. She had the look of an elderly matron who knew that, if she wasn't there to supervise, bathtime would be a debacle. Philipp gave her a pat on the head and left her to watch over their new friend while he took the dirty clothes downstairs and put them in the washing machine.

What was he to do? The boy was clearly traumatised. He'd clung to Philipp as he'd carried him into the house, his arms around Philipp's neck, his spindly legs dangling down like puppet limbs. He'd felt almost weightless, though that must have been the adrenaline in Philipp's system. He hadn't had to carry him far.

Maschka had gone ahead into the house, and then turned to watch as Philipp had carried him in and set him down in the corridor. He'd had to steady the boy on his feet, as he still didn't seem capable of standing without support. He'd thought about calling the police there and then, but they'd take an age to come, and he didn't want to leave the boy shivering in those soiled clothes. The bath had seemed the best place for him.

Carrying him up the stairs, he'd asked him if he was in any pain. The boy's eyes were closed, but there were no signs of discomfort in his face. 'Do you speak German?' There was no answer. 'English? You speak English?' Still nothing.

Running the bath, pouring in half a bottle of bubble bath, he'd turned to the boy and found that he'd opened his eyes.

'Hello,' he'd said to him. 'My name is Philipp.' Then, pointing at him in turn, 'Yours?'

The boy had shrugged his shoulders and closed his eyes again.

He set the washing machine now to a hot cycle and went back upstairs. There were soft, sloshing sounds coming from the bathroom. He went to the blue cupboard on the landing and took out a bag of clothes that had been in there for as long as he could remember, waiting to be taken to the recycling centre. He tipped them all out on the floor. Most of them were things that had belonged to his children when they were young and had been put to fresh use with his grandchildren. Some of them might even have been his when he'd been small. It was impossible to tell now who they belonged to, and anyway he'd always felt that clothes never really belonged to any one person. They were meant to be handed on.

He sifted through the pile on the floor. There must be something that would fit the boy. He pulled out a hoodie and T-shirt that were just about the right size. And there was a pair of jeans that might do, if he rolled up the legs.

He couldn't find any pants or socks though. Maybe there'd be some underwear in his son's old room. He hung the items he'd found over the radiator to warm them, and went to look.

When he returned to the bathroom – having located some boxer shorts and socks that were far too big, but better than nothing – he found the boy lying back in the water, soaking away. One hand was draped over the side of the bath, buried in the thick warm fur around Maschka's neck. Maschka herself had her eyes closed, with an expression of blissful contemplation on her face.

Ah well, he thought. Perhaps there wasn't such urgency after all. Maybe the boy just needed a good sleep, and something hot to eat. Or even the other way round?

'Hi Schlumpa, it's me.'

'Hi dad,' came his middle daughter's voice down the phoneline in the kitchen. 'How are the Christmas preparations going? We'll be seeing you very soon.'

'Oh, fine. Everything's fine. Listen, could you do me a favour?'

'Of course. As long as it's not driving around England again to fetch a spare part for your MG.'

'Nothing like that, no. I need you to look out some children's clothes for me. Nothing fancy, just anything you don't have any use for. Trousers, T-shirts, jumpers. Anything really.'

'Sure. For Emma, is it?'

'Slightly bigger, ideally.'

'Bigger? How big exactly?'

'For a nine-year-old, perhaps? Round about that age, anyway. A boy.'

There was a brief pause on the line. 'Which boy is this, dad?

'Look, whatever you can manage, okay? It doesn't have to be anything special.'

'I'm not sure I've got anything of that sort. I'll have a look though.'

'Great. Fantastic. Oh and Schlumpa, can you get it to me tomorrow?'

'Tomorrow? I doubt it. It's Christmas. Why do you need it tomorrow? Can't I just bring it when we come?'

'No, I need it tomorrow. Thanks, Schlumpa. Much appreciated.'

'I'll do my best, dad. No promises.'

Philipp hung up. He felt tired suddenly, immensely tired. The adrenaline had all ebbed away and he was starting to flag. He needed something to eat himself. But there was nothing in the house, and he didn't like the idea of leaving the boy alone while he went out shopping. Maybe now was the time to ring the authorities, let someone else take care of it…

He looked up. The boy was standing in the kitchen doorway, Maschka at his side. He was dressed in the clothes Philipp had left for him. They hung off his slender frame like he'd been raiding the dressing-up box indiscriminately.

'You look great,' he said with a smile.

The boy grinned back at him. His teeth were very white. He looked much cleaner, overall. He lifted his arms and held out the glass and bowl.

'Oh, you want some more, do you?' The boy's grin grew wider as Philipp took them from him. 'Well, I'm not sure if I should keep giving you Coke and Pretzels.'

The grin on the boy's face quickly faded. He pinched the fingers of his right hand together and put them to his mouth.

'I know, you're hungry. But I've got nothing in the house. You've eaten all the Pretzels. Sorry.'

The boy stared at him with incomprehension.

'I tell you what, do you like doner kebabs? There's a little place down the road. I bet they'll still be open.'

The boy looked at him blankly.

'Trust me, they're pretty good. Come on, let's see if we can find you a coat.'

EIGHT
Party season

It was just after nine in the evening when Nadja left the police station, and the temperature was dropping fast. It was a clear, cold night. She wrapped her scarf tight around her face and neck, and fastened her helmet under her chin as she went out through the front doors.

She was in a bitter mood. It had been a trying afternoon and, striding across the car park to her motorbike, she reflected on the serial idiocies and incompetence that had beset her.

The recovery team tasked with removing the lorry had failed to turn up. After being dismissed by Hannes Schnied in the morning (because the photographer had gone to Zeilsheim instead of the Zeilsheimer Road), they had disappeared off the map. They'd not responded to urgent enquiries. She'd rung them herself and received no reply. It was galling, and she had a fair idea of what was going on. It was Christmas party season. They must have knocked off early.

She had instructed Bremsberger to find an alternative recovery team, only to discover that there was not another outfit in the whole of Hofheim with the necessary towing equipment. Not one. It was, after all, a thirty-tonner, as Bremsberger explained to her with complacent assurance. A specialist job. There was a firm over in Frankfurt that could do it, but they couldn't come until the following day. It was their Christmas party, and half the team were already drunk.

She'd tried to console herself by digging up some dirt on the driver or on the haulage company. Or even on the haulage company's insurers. Anything, basically, that would look good in the report she had to present to Commissioner Rabbinger first thing tomorrow. But, to her intense annoyance, it turned out that Jürgen Fischer from Diedenbergen was entirely spotless. His licence was immaculate. He'd been delivering a consignment of medical aid to a charity in Turkey. That guy was a saint. Practically St Nicholas himself.

It had been an exceptionally long day, and she hadn't completed a single module for her police commissioner exams. Things were looking bleak. And she would even have to come in early tomorrow to write the report for Rabbinger. Still, if she was lucky, she might yet make her evening kickboxing class. That was some consolation – the thought of taking it out on somebody.

The Yamaha SR400 gave a throaty roar as she sped out through the gate and turned right along the Zeilsheimer Road.

Two hundred yards down the road, she had to slam on the brakes.

What the hell? There was the lorry on the side of the road, in its temporary traffic control zone, and one of its rear doors was hanging wide open! Unbelievable. Who'd left it like this? Couldn't they even get a single thing right?

She steered her motorbike up onto the pavement and kicked out its stand. Someone was going to get the chop for this, that much was certain. Hopefully it would be Schnied. She got out her phone and took a photo of the rear of the lorry. Then she took another one with the timestamp turned on. It was 21:07. She sent it to Schnied. *What does this look like to you?* read the accompanying message.

While she waited for a reply, she got off her bike and approached the lorry. She would have to secure the doors herself.

Wait, hadn't she better check inside the lorry first? There'd be no end of trouble if she locked someone in there. Or, God forbid, someone's cat. She flashed the torch on her phone around the inside of the lorry to make sure. Nothing. Except… what was that over there? It looked like an open box. It hadn't been there at five in the morning, when she'd inspected the interior herself.

Muttering bitterly, she climbed up into the lorry. Yes, part of the rear wheel casing was now lying open. And there was a cavity there, a crawlspace, lined with a blanket and some pieces of foam. There was a plastic water bottle too, its sides crushed together like it had been stamped on. And there was a powerful smell of urine and excrement that made her cover her nose. Christ! How had they missed this?

She took several more photos, and then climbed back out of the lorry, away from that awful stench.

She removed her helmet and put her phone to her ear. 'Bremsberger, do you know where Schnied is? He's not replying to my messages.'

'No idea, Sarge,' came Bremsberger's voice. 'He's probably at home.'

'And whereabouts are you?' She could hear sounds of merriment in the background. Tinny Christmas music and raucous shouts of 'Prost!'.

'Just out with some friends, Sarge. What's up?'

'We have a situation here, Bremsberger. I'm at the crash site right now. Looks like our lorry had some human cargo.'

'What's that, Sarge? Say that again, can you?'

The noise in the background had increased in volume. There were shouts of 'Prost! Prost! Prost!', and the clattering of tankards. Someone called out 'Matthias! Come back here!'. The voice sounded remarkably familiar.

'That's not Schnied there with you, is it?'

'Sorry, Sarge. I can barely hear you.' The sound of his footsteps, and then a door closing, muffling the music.

'Bremsberger, this is serious. There was someone else in the lorry when it crashed. You realise what that means? We've got a case of human trafficking here. And we didn't spot the secret compartment.'

'Impossible, Sarge. We looked all over.'

'You didn't look hard enough. There's a false casing over the wheel. Whoever was hidden in there, they're out now. We've let them go. Rabbinger's going to string us up for this!'

'I'm sorry, Sarge. I didn't hear you tell us to check the wheel casings.'

She gritted her teeth. 'We need to put an alert out now to all units. Maybe we can track this stowaway down before I meet with Rabbinger in the morning. I suggest you get out there now and start scouring the streets. Otherwise you can kiss goodbye to your Christmas leave.'

'What's that, Sarge? I can hardly hear you.' Bremsberger's voice came through loud and clear. 'It's a bad line, Sarge. You're breaking up.'

'You heard me fine, Bremsberger. Get out there now. Report to me in thirty minutes.'

There was a loud gushing sound on the line. It sounded exactly like a tap being turned on. 'No. Can't hear you, Sarge. Sorry!' There was a gurgling noise, like water going down the plughole. And the line went dead.

Nadja growled with frustration. It was insubordination, plain and simple. She would report him for this. And Schnied, both of them.

As she put the call through to the station to mobilise all available patrol cars, she cast her eye over the nearby houses. The one right next to the lorry was unoccupied, she knew that already. There was no sign of a break-in, the place looked secure. The next one along was Philipp von Werthern's house. No lights on there. She went over and looked down the alley at the side of his house. It was unlit. If the stowaway had escaped down there, they could be anywhere by now. She wasn't about to stroll down there without backup. They could be armed and dangerous. Besides, if it was her who was on the run, she'd want to put some distance between her and the lorry. Especially if she knew people were after her. She'd head towards town, where she could melt into the general population and disappear. That's what she would do. It's what anyone would do.

She went back to her bike. The best thing right now was

to drive around and keep a lookout for suspicious-looking persons. They might still be on the street. There was a window of opportunity here.

With the Yamaha rumbling beneath her, she began to feel a little better. At least she was doing something, unlike the rest of her useless team. The wind in her face. Lights flashing past. She kept her eyes on the pavements, looking for any solitary pedestrians... and had to screech to a halt at a red light.

There were people waiting to cross, wrapped up against the cold night air. Nobody who seemed to be on their own. She peered at their faces, lit up by the streetlamps and the bright lights of a nearby restaurant. A doner kebab place. Not the kind of joint she'd eat at herself, but suddenly – sitting out there in the cold, pursuing a hopeless case – she felt ravenous. Wait a minute, didn't she know that guy at the table in the window? Yes, it was whatshisname, she'd just been outside his house. Von Werthern. It was definitely him. Maybe she ought to go in and ask him if he'd seen anything? But wait, who was that with him? A small boy. Probably his grandson. Maybe not the best time to ask him then. Wasn't it rather late to be out with a kid? Perhaps there was something in what Schnied said about him. Eccentric. A timewaster. An amateur sleuth. She didn't want to get into a protracted conversation with someone like that, not right now. Every second she wasted...

A blast on a horn from the car behind her. The lights had gone green.

'All right,' she shouted through her visor. 'Keep your hair on!'

She revved furiously, and for rather longer than she needed to. Then, kicking the Yamaha forward, sped off towards town.

The boy had an appetite all right. He'd polished off a large doner kebab with all the trimmings. And then, after eyeing up Philipp's meal, he'd set about demolishing that one too.

They sat in the window of the restaurant, and Philipp watched him eat. The boy was still wearing the coat he'd found for him, a yellow one that had belonged to his son. It was far too big for him, but it was all he could find. He didn't mind the silence between them, but all the same he was glad the restaurant was busy, and there was a bit of a hubbub. It eased his mind. Even the cars flashing by outside seemed to have a soothing effect. Normality, or some semblance of it. Maschka sat obediently under the table, and Philipp pretended not to notice when the boy sneaked pieces of kebab-meat down to her in his fingers. The sound of her guzzling away caused a smile to spread across the boy's face, and it warmed Philipp's heart.

He wondered which part of the world he'd come from, this boy with the dark hair, green eyes and olive skin. He imagined it was somewhere with plenty of sun. He could picture him in some Mediterranean harbour, or perhaps a Middle Eastern souk, hanging out with kids his own age, kicking a ball about, laughing, having fun. A carefree existence. As a young man, Philipp had spent time on a Greek island, and that was where he pictured the boy, splashing in and out of the water, wearing one of those coloured plastic sunshields over his eyes, drinking a can of Fanta, calling out to his friends in whatever language he spoke.

What had brought him here, Philipp wondered, to this small, freezing-cold German town, bent double in the back of a lorry? What was there for him here? The boy couldn't even speak a word of the language. And what about his family? Were they here too, waiting for him? Or had they sent him on alone, to a foreign country where he knew no one, and there was no one to look after him? He couldn't imagine it. Maybe the family didn't know. Perhaps he'd been taken from them. Snatched. Kidnapped. Taken by force. The possibilities were all appalling.

Really, he was out of his depth with this. Probably he should have turned the boy over to the police right away. By keeping him, he was probably guilty of some obscure crime or other.

God knows, Hannes Schnied would love to pin something on him. Interfering with a crime scene. Removing a witness. Kidnapping. The list went on and on. He might even be putting himself in danger, if the people responsible for this were out there now, looking for the boy. A shiver went down his spine, and he snatched up his glass of water to conceal it.

The boy was still tucking in. Good. Let him eat. He needed time to recover from the ordeal of his journey, the crash, and then being stuck in that hellhole in the lorry for all those hours. If he took him to the police station now, handed him over to Hannes Schnied, the boy would probably end up in a cell overnight. It didn't bear thinking about. He would take him there first thing in the morning, after a good night's sleep. He'd ask to see Sergeant Bernstein. She'd know what to do. What had he been thinking, asking his daughter to send him some clothes? By the time the parcel arrived, the boy would be out of his hands.

He looked over at him again. The boy had stopped eating now. Full up, at last. He opened his mouth wide and gave an enormous yawn. Ready for sleep. When they got home, Philipp would make up the bed in Youssef's old room. Maschka could sleep in there too if the boy wanted, he'd make an exception to the usual rule about her not sleeping upstairs, just for one night.

And then tomorrow, he'd hand him over.

NINE

Ninety-nine per cent

Philipp woke early. He'd been woken by some horrible commotion. He blinked in the early morning light and realised it was his bedside alarm.

He'd had a fitful night. He had a dim recollection of a dream in which Maschka had suddenly started talking, but he couldn't make out what she was saying because there was a shattering crash, the exact same crash that had woken him the night before...

He groped for the alarm and turned it off. Why, he wondered, had he wanted to wake up so early? Oh yes, the boy! He needed to take him to the police station before ten, which was when he had to pick Emma up from Annelie's.

Stiff and aching, he parted the curtains and looked down at the street. The lorry was still there, occupying the pavement. He had the uncomfortable feeling that he'd become the main character in the film *Groundhog Day*. He closed the curtains again.

Looking in on the boy in Youssef's room, he found him tucked up, sleeping peacefully. He was lying on his back, his narrow ribcage rising and falling beneath the covers. He looked even younger than he had yesterday. One of his arms dangled down over the side of the mattress and his hand was resting on Maschka, who lay curled up on the floor next to the bed, her head on her paws. She opened her eyes to look at Philipp, gave a contented snuffle, and closed them again. It was going to be difficult parting the two of them, Philipp could see.

He padded downstairs to the kitchen, where he put some coffee on and inspected the contents of the fridge. It was woeful.

For some reason he'd put the Mettwurst packet back on the shelf, even though it was empty. There was a bowl of lamb's kidneys, which he'd been ignoring for a week or two. His housemate Michi must have left them there before he'd gone away to Lanzarote. Michi was a great advocate of nose-to-tail eating, the benefits of which he'd explained to Philipp on plenty of occasions, though Philipp was still unsure why exactly he ought to develop a taste for offal. The kidneys sat there in a pool of congealed blood. He certainly didn't want to eat them for breakfast.

Beyond that, there was only a carton of juice, past its sell-by date, and the remains of the bottle of Coca-Cola.

He sat and drank his coffee, brooding on the thought of the lorry driver's body lying flat on the coroner's slab. Dead meat. He wondered what new information had been discovered at the autopsy, if they'd found out the cause of death. A heart attack, or something else? A bullet, plucked from the body and placed in a bowl, swimming in a pool of blood. He shuddered. What had got into him? Such morbid thoughts.

What he really wanted for breakfast was some nice warm Brötchen, fresh from the bakery, slathered in butter and jam. He could pop out now, while the boy was still sleeping. Maschka was there to keep an eye on him, he'd be fine.

He pulled on his Nordic woollen jumper and grabbed his coat. Briefly he thought about changing from his clogs into winter boots, but dismissed the thought. His clogs were weatherproof enough. It was just after eight o'clock. There was still time for breakfast.

It was still not fully daylight outside. There was a frost on the ground. It glittered on the pavement and on the hard metal surfaces of the lorry. There wasn't much traffic yet. He liked mornings like this, though Maschka wasn't so keen on long walks over frosty fields. She preferred softer ground. He was glad he'd let her lie in with the boy.

The route to the bakery led past the lorry and, as he ducked under the cordon, his eye was caught by something on the road where the long dark tyre streaks were still visible on the tarmac. It was just inside the cordoned area. He went over to look.

It appeared to be a small disc of shiny black plastic. The frost hadn't settled on its glossy surface, and it sat like a dark chocolate button on a surface of white frosting.

He bent down and picked it up. Brushing away the dirt that had encrusted on its surface, he saw some lettering on it. *Skin cream*. The plastic was slightly buckled, but he could just about make out the words *anti-ageing* and *mature skin*. It was a screw-top lid, he realised, compacted into a disc. Perhaps it had been flattened under the lorry's tyres? It wasn't too much of a stretch to believe so. It was lying there, after all, right by the tyre marks in the road. Though it could equally have been some other vehicle. It might even have fallen out of a bin lorry.

He wondered at the combination of the words *anti-ageing* and *mature skin*, as if here in his hands lay some remnant of a miracle cure for ageing. Were people so easily taken in? Surely no cream could reverse the signs of ageing, and anyway why was it a good thing to go on looking young forever? What was this obsession with youth all about? The lines of ageing and experience could make a face so much more beautiful. It was all just a way to make money.

He was about to toss the disc back into the road when a fresh thought struck him. He really ought to put it in a bin. Or even better, recycle it. It was cold and wet in his hand. He felt in his coat pocket and hooked out one of the poop bags he kept for picking up after Maschka. They often came in handy for other purposes. He'd used them once or twice for collecting evidence, back when he was in the private detective business. You never knew what might turn out to be the very thing that cracked the case. Collecting evidence was ninety-nine per cent a waste of time, but once in a while you struck gold.

Anti-ageing cream! You might as well massage it into the tarmac, for all the good it did. And what was he thinking? It was just a piece of litter. He'd chuck it in the recycling bin as soon as he got home.

TEN

The facts

Nadja had come to work early. She'd been at her desk for nearly two hours, trying to assemble the facts into some kind of order that didn't reflect too badly on her. But whichever way she positioned them, they looked pretty bad.

Fact: A man had died on the Zeilsheimer Road, practically on their doorstep, a week before Christmas.

Fact: The lorry he crashed in was still sitting there on the side of the road, causing obstruction and delays.

Fact: The recovery team sent to remove it had been turned away by Officer Schnied, who was under her command. She hadn't been able to find any other suitable recovery firm who could do the job at short notice.

Fact: Commissioner Rabbinger usually travelled to and from work along the Zeilsheimer Road. He will have had to sit in traffic, waiting for the lights to change. Commissioner Rabbinger was not a man who enjoyed sitting at a red light. Not at any time of year, but least of all at Christmas.

Fact: In their search of the lorry, the officers under her command had failed to notice the concealed human cargo it was carrying. They had also failed to secure the doors of the lorry. Said human cargo was now at large, presenting a danger to members of the public, either in their homes or out doing their Christmas shopping.

Fact: Despite mobilising all available police units throughout the night, they had failed to track down said human cargo.

Clarification: There had been no police units available, apart from her. All other units had mysteriously become uncontactable. She had spent the entire night trawling the streets on her motorbike, alone, and without success.

Reasonable Supposition: The officers under her command had all been attending a Christmas party.

Cold Hard Fact: She had not been invited to this Christmas party, nor to any other Christmas party whatsoever.

She looked over what she'd written. She couldn't show this to Rabbinger. She took out everything he would find unacceptable, and was left with almost nothing.

Start again. Fail again. Fail better.

The problem was, the fact that they'd let a human trafficking case unfold right under their noses was guaranteed to render the Commissioner incandescent. He might even see this as a personal insult, a threat to his reputation and his chances of preferment. He was bound to see it in those terms. She knew he had ambitions. If a Commissioner's job came up in Frankfurt, or even Bonn, he'd be in pole position. He'd be out of here like a shot. Something like this might be enough to keep him in Hofheim until the day he retired.

What terrible timing for her. She needed to keep Rabbinger on her side, especially with that rabble beneath her. Once her exams were under her belt, she'd be out of here too. All she would need then was a decent reference. So it was imperative she didn't mess up. Why did this stupid thing have to happen right now? She should have known how useless they were, Schnied and Bremsberger. If only she'd taken a little more care, trusted them a little less. She even wondered if they might actually have seen the hiding place in the lorry and not reported it, to avoid the additional work it would involve. Or even, who knows, to make her look bad in front of Rabbinger? There was no telling what they were capable of.

At ten minutes to nine, on the brink of despair, she lifted the telephone and called the coroner's office. If he'd managed to complete the autopsy on Jürgen Fischer, the lorry driver, there might be some useful information she could drop into her report, if only to serve as a distraction. It was a long shot, but long shots were all she'd got.

The coroner's assistant politely informed her that the coroner had not yet arrived at work. He'd been at a Christmas party last night and was not coming in until later.

Nadja hung up and stared at her screen. That was it then. She had to work with what she'd got. She added a few inconsequential details, dropped in Schnied's name a few more times with negative insinuations, and put a handful of sentences into the passive to obscure the part she'd played herself. It would have to do. She sent it to print.

The worst of it was, nobody else in her team had turned up for work. Bremsberger, Schnied and all the rest were still absent, even now. No doubt they were tucked up in bed, sleeping off their hangovers.

On the other hand, this might work to her advantage. Rabbinger could hardly fail to notice their absence. Whereas she'd been up all night doing vital police work and had still come in at dawn to write her report. There was some hope for her yet.

Nine o'clock on the dot. She got up from her desk and went to collect the report from the printer's output tray. It was time to face the music.

ELEVEN

A busy morning

'Brötchen!' cried Philipp, placing the large brown paper bag full of still-warm bread rolls on the dining table in front of the boy, who had only just got out of bed.

'And tea!' he trumpeted, bringing in a freshly made pot. 'Butter! Jam!' The boy looked at it all with wide staring eyes. 'Go ahead. Dig in!'

The boy seemed to understand. He was a fast learner. Philipp sat back and watched from across the table. The lad tucked into the Brötchen but made a face at the tea.

'No? You don't like tea? What do you want then, coffee?'

He rose to fetch the coffee pot, but the boy was already out of his seat and halfway across the room. He let him go and, after a moment, heard the fridge door open in the kitchen. Soon the boy reappeared, carrying the bottle of Coca-Cola.

'What, for breakfast? I don't know about that.' The boy gave him an earnest look, but Philipp thought he could discern a hint of mischief too. He seemed to know he was pushing his luck. 'Okay, fine. Since this is our last meal together, we'll make an exception. But don't go expecting Coca-Cola for breakfast wherever you end up. It's a special treat. Very bad for your teeth.'

The boy unscrewed the top and lifted the bottle to his lips.

'Wait! Stop! No! We don't drink straight from the bottle. Not at all.'

He went to fetch a glass. Maschka was in the corridor, tucking into her breakfast. She wasn't going to find it easy, saying goodbye to her new friend. Best not to break it to her just yet.

As the boy helped himself to another bread roll, Philipp

wondered what he would be having for breakfast if he were in his own country. He didn't know the first thing about him, not even his name. Maybe it was time to find out.

'My name is Philipp,' he said. 'Philipp.' The boy looked up at him and stopped chewing for a moment. 'Can you say that? Philipp.'

'Fee… bip.'

'Very good. And again. *Philipp*.'

'Fee-lip.'

'Excellent!'

Maschka had come in and sat down on the floor next to the boy's chair.

'And this is Maschka. Masch-ka.'

'Mush-car.'

'Splendid.' Maschka gave him a slightly puzzled look. You could tell she'd never worked in a classroom before. 'Once again. *Maschka*.'

'Mash-ka.'

The dog thumped her tail on the floor, delighted.

'That's it,' said Philipp. 'Very good. At this rate we'll be old friends by the time you have to leave.'

The boy looked at him with a steady gaze. In the morning light, his green eyes had a touch of hazel in them, Philipp noticed.

'Now, what's *your* name?' Philipp pointed at him, smiled, and raised his eyebrows.

The boy said, 'Amin.'

'Ar-meen,' said Philipp.

The boy laughed and shook his head. He repeated the word. 'Amin.'

'Amin. Great. Now we know each other's names. Amin and Philipp. And Maschka, of course. Now we're getting somewhere.'

He took a Brötchen from the bag, broke it open, and spread it with butter and jam.

Just then the telephone rang. It was the landline. The cordless handset was usually lying around somewhere on the dining table, amongst all the crockery, paperwork and candlesticks. Yes, there it was, tucked under a car number plate. It was Sabine, his administrative assistant, who amongst many other tasks managed his appointments diary and looked after his daily schedule.

'Good morning, Sabine. I was just sitting down at my desk.' He gave Amin a conspiratorial wink.

'Morning, Philipp. You've got an appointment with Herr Schmitt-Dünkelmeyer at ten this morning, to go through that claim on his car…'

'At ten? Sorry. No can do.' Ten was when he had to be at Annelie's to pick up Emma.

'Oh dear. He'll be disappointed. He's going away for Christmas, and he needs it sorting out before then.'

'How about tomorrow? I'm free all day.'

'You have four appointments tomorrow, Philipp. I hope you haven't forgotten!'

He had forgotten. He'd no idea where his diary was, it must be here somewhere. He shovelled everything over to one side of the table with his outstretched arm, scattering Brötchen over the tabletop. Amin giggled at the mess he was making. There was still no sign of his diary.

'Of course I haven't forgotten. At eleven, I meant. I'm free at eleven, aren't I?' He tended to keep eleven o'clock free for his most important clients, the ones who liked to be served coffee and biscuits at the dining table.

'Yes,' said Sabine. 'I can slot him in at eleven, if he's free then.'

'Good,' said Philipp, making a mental note to stock up on biscuits. Herr Schmitt-Dünkelmeyer liked wafer rolls, he was fairly sure. Or was it Viennese whirls? He'd better get a selection box, just to make sure. 'If there's anything else, please call me after lunch today. I'm going to be out for the rest of the morning.'

He said goodbye to Sabine, poured the rest of the coffee into his mug, rescued a Brötchen from the floor where Maschka was sniffing at it, and settled down to finish his breakfast. Amin, watching everything with an eagle eye, helped himself to another roll.

'That's it. A good hearty German breakfast. Help yourself!'

The doorbell rang. 'I wonder who that can be. What time is it, anyway?' It was past nine o'clock. He was going to have to get his skates on, what with everything he had to do before picking Emma up at ten.

It was one of his clients, Frau Kaiser, an elderly lady who was forever getting him to tweak her insurance policy. She usually made an appointment, but Philipp was used to clients just dropping by. Today was going to be one of those days.

'Good morning, Philipp. I wonder if I might have a little word.' She patted her neatly coiffed white hair.

'Certainly, Frau Kaiser. Do come in.'

He showed her into the kitchen, where he could make her a fresh cup of coffee. 'Now, what can I do for you?'

'Well, I was just dropping some Christmas parcels round to the church – I do like the dear little ones to have something to open at Christmas. Some of them have nothing at all, you know… By the way, Philipp, is that your grandson I noticed in the other room? What a lovely-looking boy he is!'

'Thank you,' he said, glancing at the clock and deciding it would be wise not to go to the trouble of correcting her. 'Now, is there something I can help you with?'

'Oh, yes. Yes there is.'

As Philipp suspected, it entailed yet another amendment to her life insurance policy. Not to worry, he said, he could handle it for her, it would be done later in the week.

'I'm sorry to be such a fusspot,' she said, sipping delicately at her coffee. 'You just never know when something might carry you off, do you? It seems there's been another accident, right here outside your house.'

'Yes, I'm afraid there has.'

'I hope no one was hurt.'

'The driver was killed, I'm sorry to say.'

'Killed? How awful. What a dreadful thing to happen, and so close to Christmas. A tragedy. I'll make sure to pray for his family.'

Philipp stood up. 'Well, now, if that's all for now, I'll send the documents over to you for signature later this week.'

'Oh, don't worry about posting them,' she replied. 'I'll send my driver to pick them up.'

'You have a driver now, Frau Kaiser?' he said, ushering her out into the corridor.

'Yes, I'm not as nimble as I once was, Philipp,' she said, with what he thought was a wink. 'And it's so much more convenient than waiting around for taxis.'

'Indeed. Well, thank you for dropping in, Frau Kaiser.' He opened the front door.

'Oh, I nearly forgot.' She stopped on the doorstep to rummage in her bag, and finally brought out a small woollen jumper, knitted in vibrant red and blue stripes. 'For your little daughter. I hope it fits.'

Philipp thanked her very sincerely. 'She'll love it.'

'If I'd known about the other little one, I'd have brought something for him too.'

'You're very kind, Frau Kaiser. Goodbye!'

Before closing the front door, he had a glimpse of a large car, pulled over on the curb next to the lorry. A smartly dressed young man was waiting there, ready to help Frau Kaiser into her seat. Well, well, he thought, let her enjoy it all. She was a sweet old lady. She reminded him of his mother.

He went back in and found Amin and Maschka rolling around together on the dining room floor, having an absolute whale of a time. It was a shame it all had to end so soon.

TWELVE

The Commissioner sits in judgment

Nadja rapped twice on the door of the Commissioner's office. After a brief silence, she heard Rabbinger's voice telling her to enter. She squared her shoulders, took a deep breath and opened the door.

The Commissioner was sitting behind his desk, which was huge, spotless and clutter-free. He was looking at her with his usual severe expression, smoothing his moustache with his forefinger and thumb.

'Good morning, sir,' she said, attempting a smile as she crossed the wide expanse of carpet between the door and his desk.

His eyes flickered down to the report in her hand, and he tapped the desk in front of him with the tip of his finger.

'Of course, sir. It's all in there.' She took a step forward, placed the report on his desk, and stepped back.

He peered down at the report for a moment, then placed his finger on it and slid it aside.

'Just tell me, Sergeant. What went wrong?'

'Very good, sir.' She hesitated, wondering where to begin. 'Last night, after leaving the station at twenty-one hundred hours, I was driving along the Zeilsheimer Road when I observed that one of the lorry's doors had been opened...'

'No, no, no,' interrupted Rabbinger. 'I don't want the whole bedtime story. I want to know who's responsible.'

Nadja blinked a few times. 'Sir, it's likely the doors were opened from the inside by whoever was hiding in there.'

'Why were the doors not secured properly?'

She swallowed hard. 'That was something I left to Officer

Schnied, sir. The doors were certainly closed when I left the site. That's why I noticed they'd been opened again.'

'Officer Schnied, you say?'

'That's right. He was the duty officer at the site.'

'I see. Though of course he had to leave the site after being attacked by a lunatic on horseback.'

'I'm not sure I'd describe the man as a lunatic, sir...'

'Nevertheless, the doors were not secured. You say they were opened from the inside. You're confident that it's possible to open those doors from the inside, are you? You're familiar with that particular locking mechanism?'

Nadja tried to recall how the lorry doors had been fastened. She couldn't remember a single detail. 'No, sir. I'm not familiar with it.'

'Sergeant Bernstein, it's your job to be familiar with it. It has surely occurred to you that if this stowaway was sprung from the lorry by an accomplice, then we've got not just one but *two* illegals at large, threatening the good people of Hofheim over Christmas. It's really quite important to know.'

'Yes, sir.'

'But so far all we know is that you failed to secure the doors properly.'

'It was Officer Schnied, sir, as I said. But yes, sir, I do see your point. Obviously, we couldn't have known there was someone in the back of the lorry when it crashed...'

'Why not? You searched it, didn't you?' He was giving her a piercing look.

'Officer Schnied searched it, sir. But the hiding place was well concealed. It was difficult to see it in the dark.'

'You could have come back in the daylight, couldn't you? Your officers were stationed there throughout the day. You didn't think to have them conduct a fresh search?'

He certainly had a point. 'I was reassured by Officer Schnied that the vehicle had been properly searched. Our primary concern at the time was to have it safely removed.'

'Ah yes,' said Rabbinger, bristling his moustache. 'And even that you couldn't manage.'

'As you'll see in my report, sir, what happened was that Officer Schnied…'

'Sergeant Bernstein, did I appoint Officer Schnied to lead this investigation?'

'No, sir.'

'No, I did not. I appointed you. And you have failed to have the lorry removed. You failed to spot there was an illegal in the back. You even failed to secure the doors.' He was staring at her. She felt herself going red from the ground upwards. 'Tell me this. What happened after you discovered the stowaway had escaped?'

'I put out a call to mobilise all units, sir, to see if we could track him down.'

'Very good. But you couldn't locate him?'

'No, sir. I couldn't. There was no sign of him.' She paused. Should she risk it? She saw no other option. 'I think, sir, we might have had a greater chance of success had there been more of a response to my request. As it was, sir, I was left to conduct the search on my own.'

'Just you?'

'Yes, sir. I'm afraid so. I have reason to believe that several officers were out at a Christmas party. They chose not to respond.'

'A Christmas party, you say?'

'Yes, sir.'

There was a long pause. Finally, the Commissioner reached for the report she'd placed on his desk, folded it in two, and put it away in one of his desk drawers.

'Well, it's Christmas, isn't it? Who can blame them?' He smiled at her, closing the drawer.

Relief flooded through her. She broke into a smile.

'They do their best, sir. I'm sure they do.'

'But you, on the other hand, Sergeant Bernstein, have a responsibility here.' The smile had vanished from his face. 'A man has died. A fugitive is at large. People don't feel safe in their homes. The press are going to love this. It's their Christmas come early. And it's all because of you, Sergeant.'

'Sir, if I could just…'

He held up his hand. 'I don't want to hear any more. You've done nothing but blame your junior officers, and it won't wash. It simply won't wash.' He stood up suddenly and turned to look out of the window behind his desk. She waited, holding her breath. 'You'll hand in your badge and your firearm, and you'll remain suspended on half pay until the conclusion of an independent investigation. In the meantime, Officer Schnied will take charge of the case. Off you go.'

'Please, sir…'

'Off you go.'

She gulped. She was utterly stunned. How had it all come to this? She stared at Günther Rabbinger as he stood there with his back turned to her, looking out of the window as if he was wondering whether it might rain. Did he know that neither Schnied nor Bremsberger had reported for work this morning? Did he even care?

She turned and walked out of the door.

THIRTEEN
What child is this?

Nadja ran her fingers over the leaves of the aspidistra on her desk. A few of them were turning brittle, going brown at the tips. They rattled together like a quiver full of arrows. She hadn't watered it for a while. She'd always been useless with plants.

Why was it that her subordinate officers – all men – got away with negligence, unprofessionalism and an almost pathological disregard for the police rulebook, while she copped it as soon as she put a foot wrong? Was this what she'd worked so hard for, to be the scapegoat for a bunch of lazy, incompetent, bigoted blokes?

She gripped the stem of one of the sickliest leaves on the plant and squeezed it between her fingernails until she'd severed it completely. Then, rolling the leaf into a ball, she crushed it in her fist and dropped it into the wastepaper basket.

Opening the drawer of her desk, she took out the exam textbook she kept in there, away from prying eyes, and tucked it into her bag. She could at least do her exam preparation from home without fear of interruption. Though she was beginning to wonder if that, too, was a pointless enterprise.

The stapler and mousepad could stay there in the drawer, she had no need of them. She picked up the photograph of Sven. There he was, looking at her with those puppyish, lovelorn eyes. Don't give me that look, she thought. I'm absolutely fine. She tore it into tiny pieces and sprinkled them into the wastepaper basket, like pointless confetti.

What about the aspidistra? No, everything she took had to fit into her bag, since she'd be leaving on the bike. Sven's plant would just have to stay here. It almost certainly wouldn't get watered, but in that respect staying here was no worse than coming home with her. And she didn't want it in her flat anyway, reminding her of him.

Her desk was starting to look shipshape and orderly. Not unlike Rabbinger's, she thought, only in miniature. When she sat at it, all she could see were the panels forming the perimeter of her cubicle. She had the feeling they were pressing in on her, tighter and tighter. It was like being kettled in her own workplace.

All there remained to do was hand in her badge and firearm to the duty officer in reception on the way out.

The phone on her desk began to ring. She thought about leaving it. It would only be Schnied or Bremsberger, calling in sick. There was still no sign of them in the office. Or it might be Sven, in which case she'd have to tell him to stop calling her on her work phone. To never, ever call her here again.

'Sergeant Bernstein,' she said sharply into the phone.

'Sergeant, there's a gentleman here in reception, says he wants to speak to you.'

'Who is it?'

'Says his name is von Werthern.'

'Philipp von Werthern?' God almighty, this was all she needed. The amateur sleuth. 'Tell him I'm not here.'

'He knows you're here, Sarge. He's seen your bike outside.' Nadja cursed under her breath. 'He has some information, apparently. About the lorry. Oh, and there's a little kid here with him.'

'A kid?'

'That's right. Foreign-looking. Doesn't speak any German. And there's a dog.'

Nadja sat down in her chair. She opened her desk drawer, and then closed it again.

'Send them up.'

It had been a long while since Philipp had been upstairs at the police station. Normally Schnied made him wait downstairs. But when he told the officer in reception that he knew the way up, they were quickly waved through: him, Amin and Maschka. The whole place seemed to be rather short-staffed.

He spotted Sergeant Bernstein beckoning to him from inside a cubicle on the far side of the big open-plan office. They made their way over, past several other cubicles, some of which were decorated with sorry-looking pieces of tinsel. Amin steered Maschka along on her lead, which Philipp had insisted she keep wearing, though it was only for show.

'Herr von Werthern,' said the Sergeant when they arrived at her desk. She had the same brisk manner and directness of gaze that Philipp recalled from their previous meeting, on the street outside his house. And that remarkably thick, tumbling hair he remembered too.

'Sergeant Bernstein. Thank you for agreeing to see us. I'm sorry to come without an appointment.'

'Not at all,' she said, ushering them into the cubicle and towards two chairs that had been squeezed somewhat awkwardly into the corner. 'Sit down, sit down.'

Philipp lowered himself into one of the chairs, and the rest of the office instantly disappeared from view behind the cubicle screens. He signalled to Amin to sit down too, and Maschka joined in, sitting on the floor between the two of them.

'I've already met Maschka, of course,' said the Sergeant, reaching out and scratching the dog's head behind the ears. 'But now tell me, who is this?' She gave the boy a friendly smile, but Philipp could see she was burning to know.

'This is Amin,' he said.

'Hello, Amin.'

Amin gave a little smile, hearing his name, and bent down to give Maschka a cuddle.

'These two are the best of friends,' Philipp said. 'It's probably because Maschka's the one who found Amin hiding in the lorry.'

The smile dropped from the Sergeant's face. She sat back in her chair and stared at the boy in astonishment. She appeared to be lost for words.

'We heard knocking, you see,' Philipp went on. 'But only because Maschka knew there was someone in there. Didn't you, Maschka, old girl? Clever Maschka.'

Sergeant Bernstein stood up out of her chair, cast her eyes quickly around the office, and sat back down.

'Just to be clear,' she said in a hushed voice, leaning forward. 'This boy here was in the lorry? The one that crashed outside your house?'

'That's right. His name is Amin, by the way. He doesn't speak German, but he recognises his name.'

'Amin.' She nodded. 'And he was in the secret compartment, the one above the rear wheel?'

'That's right.' So she knows about that, thought Philipp. She was no slouch, this Sergeant. He was impressed. 'He wasn't in the best way after his journey. I took him into the house to get him cleaned up and, well, one thing led to another. I wasn't intending to keep hold of him. I realise it's a police matter. That's why we're here.'

'Quite so,' she said. 'A police matter. Yes it is. Exactly so.'

'He was ravenous of course. He hadn't eaten for some time.'

The Sergeant nodded. 'You took him down to that kebab place by the crossroads. I know.'

It was Philipp's turn to look at her with astonishment. He was discovering a new level of admiration for Sergeant Bernstein.

'Don't worry, Herr von Werthern. I'd have done exactly the same. It's good that you've brought him to me now though. There are procedures to follow.'

'I thought so,' Philipp said, shifting uneasily in his seat. 'Do you mind me asking, what procedures?'

'Well,' she said, 'There are forms to be filled in. All the necessary forms. And we'll have to get social services involved. The Youth Welfare Department. And the Immigration Office, of course, they'll need to be informed too. It's quite a lengthy procedure. And since he doesn't speak German – is that right?' Philipp nodded on Amin's behalf. 'Then we'll have to procure the services of a translator. Any idea what language he does speak?'

'I don't know, I'm afraid. Arabic, I expect.' Philipp looked over at Amin, who looked back at him with a grave expression.

'Then it looks like it's going to take a long while to sort this all out. Getting hold of anyone at short notice is tricky at this time of year. As I've been finding out myself recently.'

Philipp nodded. It was just as he thought. 'The problem is, Sergeant Bernstein, I have very little time. I have to be in Langenhain by ten o'clock. Would you mind telling me the time?'

She glanced at her watch. 'It's two minutes to ten.'

Philipp leapt to his feet. 'Already? Then I must go.'

The Sergeant ducked towards him, keeping her head low. Taking hold of his sleeve, she pulled him down into his chair. 'Please, stay down. Just a moment more. Please.'

As she turned her head to look nervously over the side of the cubicle, Philipp suddenly had the impression that she was hiding something. Or at least trying to stay out of sight. Who was she hiding from?

'I'm sorry, Herr von Werthern. This is a serious matter. I just need a few more details before I can report to the senior officer here.'

'But I thought you were the senior officer, Sergeant Bernstein.'

'I am. I was. No, I am.'

Oh dear, she seemed to be in a bit of a muddle. 'I'm afraid I have to go right away,' he said. 'It's absolutely critical, you see. I have to pick up my daughter.'

'Your daughter?' She looked like she didn't quite believe him.

'I have a daughter, yes. She's a year and a half old. Her mother lives in Langenhain. We're separated. If I'm not there by ten, it'll jeopardise the whole of Christmas.' He wondered if he'd gone too far, told her too much. It was generally his instinct to lay it all out there with complete honesty, and for some reason he trusted this woman. She was certainly behaving rather oddly, though.

'Look,' she said, 'You're not going be there by ten. It's fifteen minutes' drive at least…'

'Ten,' he interrupted. 'I know a shortcut.'

She seemed to be weighing up her options. 'I can maybe keep the boy here, out of sight, until you get back…'

'Why, Sergeant? Why do you need to keep him out of sight?'

She thumped her fist into the palm of her other hand. 'You don't understand. It's Rabbinger.' She was speaking through clenched teeth. 'I need to be sure about this, every last detail. I can't go to him until I know everything.'

He sat there, amazed. He knew of Police Commissioner Rabbinger by reputation. He'd heard plenty about him and had seen his picture in the newspaper. Schnied had mentioned his name a few times in some vague, threatening kind of way. The man was a tyrant, no doubt. But he couldn't understand why she was behaving this way. It seemed quite at odds with her earlier professionalism.

Still, there seemed to be one way to satisfy her. He was left with no choice.

'Very well,' he said. 'I'll come back here as soon as I've picked up my daughter.'

He stood up once again, and this time she didn't try to stop him. 'Goodbye for now, Amin. I'll come back later.'

The boy looked at him, and then suddenly lurched forward and clasped his arms tightly around Philipp's waist. 'Philipp!' he cried.

'Now look, Amin, I'll come straight back. We can continue our nice talk with Sergeant Bernstein then.'

Amin looked up at him doubtfully and shook his head.

'I thought you said he didn't understand German!' said the Sergeant.

'He doesn't. He just knows my name. And I think he can tell what's going on most of the time.'

'Come, Amin,' she said. 'You stay here with me. We'll play a few games. Would you like to see my police badge? Come, have a look.'

She tried to prise his arms off Philipp, but it only made the boy cling on more desperately. He started to cry. He sobbed and wailed, 'Philipp! Phiiilllippp!' And then for good measure he howled, 'Maschkaaaaa!'

Sergeant Bernstein tried to hush him, but it was no good, the boy was too agitated to take any notice. Maschka was up now too, making little yelping barks. Together they were creating quite a racket. One or two officers on the other side of the office were looking their way.

'Okay, okay,' said the Sergeant, holding up her hands in surrender. 'Let's try something else.'

Instantly, the boy began to calm down. He looked at her with wary eyes and kept holding onto Philipp. Maschka stopped yelping. The officers who'd taken an interest went back to their screens.

Philipp turned to the Sergeant. 'I think he's going to have to come with me.'

She nodded. She seemed to deflate a little. She looked away, then back at him. 'Okay, I'll come too,' she said. 'Langenhain, you say? Let's go.'

FOURTEEN

Hold on tight

Philipp pulled out onto the Zeilsheimer Road in his Opel Rekord – an eye-catching 1969 model in turquoise that had a tendency to conk out on long journeys but was perfectly sufficient for short ones – and put his foot to the floor.

On the back seat, Sergeant Bernstein, Amin and Maschka all scrabbled about for something to hold on to as the car shot over a roundabout. There was a child seat strapped into the front passenger seat, which meant they had to travel in the back as there wasn't time to rearrange the seating. It was already a quarter past ten.

'Sorry there aren't any seatbelts,' he called out to the passengers in the back. 'This thing was built long before all that.'

'If you could just watch your speed,' cried the Sergeant, clinging on to the seat in front of her.

He accelerated through the lights just as they were turning red.

The morning was bright and clear, and although it was still cold, the frost had lifted. Once they were out on the other side of town, the road curved gently up through the woods and the journey started to feel less like a helter-skelter ride. Up ahead, the foothills of the Taunus Mountains rose gracefully, dappled in winter sunlight. It was a pleasant route, and Philipp knew it well from countless trips between his house and Annelie's. He didn't think she'd be too cross. He was only twenty minutes late.

Annelie was waiting on the side of the road in front of her house, his daughter Emma perched on her hip, an overnight bag sitting beside her on the pavement. She always packed an overnight bag for Emma, even though there were plenty of toddler clothes at Philipp's house.

'You're late. We said ten o'clock,' she said as Philipp pulled up and got out of the car. 'I suppose it's better than the last three times.'

'Good morning!' he said with a broad smile, giving Emma's cheeks a gentle pinch. 'How's my little girl?'

Emma giggled and her dark eyes turned to see who it was in the back of the car.

'That's Amin,' said Philipp. 'He's a new friend. I think you'll get on very well.'

'What about the police officer?' said Annelie. 'Who's she?'

'That's Sergeant Bernstein. She's… well… it's complicated.'

'Philipp,' said Annelie, 'What's a police officer doing in the back of your car?'

'Don't worry, I can explain the whole thing – but it's rather a long story and I thought you had to be somewhere.'

'We're staying right here until you explain to me why there's a female police officer and a young boy riding in the back of your car.'

Philipp couldn't help himself. He smiled inwardly, mostly at the word 'female'. Annelie wasn't the jealous type, not in his experience. But maybe he just hadn't given her enough reason to show it?

'If you really must know,' he began, 'It all started with a lorry that crashed in the night…'

Nadja watched Philipp and this woman, his ex, from the back of the Opel. There was none of that stiffness and formality you normally get between separated couples at the handover of children. At least, there wasn't on his side. The woman did perhaps seem a little frosty. She kept glancing into the back of the car – whether at her or the boy, Nadja couldn't easily tell.

She was younger than Nadja had expected, younger even than she was. And attractive too, with her long blonde hair, almost Scandinavian, tied back in a ponytail.

Amin was busy stroking Maschka's head and chatting away to the dog in his own language. Nadja couldn't tell if it was Arabic, Persian or something else. Turkish perhaps. It was all the same to her. They would need to find a translator. If she could do that today, before returning to the police station, she could find out who he was before Rabbinger got wind of it. She could even break the case wide open. There was a chance then that he'd wipe the slate clean, maybe even reinstate her. It was her only chance.

It was a huge risk though. Rabbinger liked things done by the book. If he knew she'd left the station without handing in her police badge and firearm as instructed – that she'd disobeyed his orders and continued to work on the case – that she'd in fact gone off in the back of someone's car – a known lunatic, as Rabbinger called him – and in the company of a dangerous illegal who posed a threat to the good citizens of Hofheim… well, she could kiss goodbye to a career in the police force.

There was a noisy eruption on the seat next to her, and the car was instantly filled with a powerful stench. Amin looked at Maschka, and Maschka looked at Amin, and then the boy burst into an astonishingly loud peal of laughter. Nadja wasn't sure which of them was the culprit, but she wound the window down and hung her head out of it into the cold, clear air.

Philipp and his ex were there on the pavement, still in fervent discussion about something, and Nadja could hear him saying '… absolutely nothing to worry about…' before the two of them turned and saw her hanging out of the window.

The woman with the ponytail came over. 'Hello,' she said. 'I'm Annelie, Emma's mother.'

'Nadja Bernstein, Hofheim Police,' she replied. 'Pleased to meet you.' Nadja held her hand out through the open window and Annelie, who still had the little girl on her right hip, shook it awkwardly with her left hand.

The girl squirmed in her mother's grip and, looking past Nadja into the car, gave a little shriek of excitement at seeing Maschka – or possibly at the boy sitting alongside.

'I'm sorry I can't invite you in,' said Annelie. 'I'm late for an appointment.'

'Not at all,' said Nadja. 'You get going. Don't worry, your daughter's in good hands.'

Annelie looked doubtful. She kept hold of the girl while Philipp unstrapped the child seat from the front of the car. 'What are you doing now, Philipp?' she said.

'Just moving this to the back seat. She'll want to sit next to Maschka, I'm sure.'

'Doesn't the boy need a seat too?' said Annelie. 'How old is he?'

'We're not sure,' said Philipp. 'He doesn't speak German.'

Annelie blinked a few times.

'It'll be fine,' said Philipp. 'It's only a short journey. Sergeant Bernstein is here anyway.'

Nadja smiled with what she hoped looked like reassurance – she didn't feel the least bit reassured about it herself – and got out of the car so that Philipp could fix the car seat into the back. She went up to Emma to say hello, but the little girl shied away and buried her face in her mother's shoulder.

'Oh dear,' Nadja said. 'I seem to have that effect on children. It must be the uniform.'

Annelie said nothing. She stooped to pick up the overnight bag from the pavement and went to the back of the car. Seeing that she had both hands full, Nadja went to open the boot for her. Annelie looked down into the car and hesitated. Nadja's own bag was in there, full of the things she'd taken from the office. Thank goodness she hadn't taken the aspidistra too.

'All ready,' called Philipp. He came and took Emma from Annelie's arms and tucked her into the back seat. 'Right, all set.' He turned to Annelie. 'About Christmas,' he said. 'We'll be starting the festivities at about five on Christmas Eve, and we'll eat after that. Are you still okay to bring a dessert?'

'Yes, of course.'

'Great. Say goodbye to mama, Emma.'

But the little girl was too busy playing with Maschka, who was sitting in the middle, between her and the boy. Nadja climbed into the front of the car, wondering how Christmas was going to work out between these two, who didn't seem quite as cordial as they'd first appeared. It would be a long time before she'd even consider having Christmas with Sven. No, she didn't think she'd ever manage that, not in a million years. She'd have to break it to her mother soon.

Philipp drove at a more leisurely pace on the way back to Hofheim, and he could talk more easily to Sergeant Bernstein now that they were both sitting in the front.

'What will happen to Amin?' he said, 'Once all the forms have been completed.'

'He'll be in the hands of social services. The Youth Welfare team.'

'But what will that mean, exactly? Where will he stay?'

'They'll place him with foster parents in the community, while his circumstances are properly assessed.'

Philipp steered the car around a long bend in the road. He tried to imagine what it would be like for Amin, being shunted from pillar to post.

'Why can't I just keep him at mine? Wouldn't that be simplest?'

He saw Nadja glance at him. She didn't reply straight away. Eventually she said, 'I think the Youth Welfare Department would want a say in that.'

'And what if they didn't know about it?' Philipp said.

She didn't say anything. The road ahead of them went winding down towards Hofheim. There was chatter coming from the back seat, and shrieks of laughter.

'Listen to those three,' said Philipp. 'Good friends already.'

Nadja swivelled round to look at them, and in the rearview mirror Philipp saw Maschka lick Amin's face, and then turn to Emma and lick hers.

'It certainly would be a shame to split them up,' Nadja said.

'Let him stay at mine then. Nobody has to know.' He glanced at her. 'Apart from anyone who really has to know, of course.'

She nodded. 'I think it's best if we go straight to yours,' she said. 'Perhaps I can make some calls from there?'

'You can use my office, by all means.'

'It's just that if we can get hold of a translator straight away, we'll have a better chance of finding out where the boy comes from and how to return him to his own family. That's all.'

'Good plan. I've got a few work calls to make this afternoon, nothing much. I'm sure between us we can keep an eye on the two of them. Stay as long as you need to, Sergeant Bernstein.'

'That's very kind.'

Philipp smiled. The conversation had gone better than he'd expected. She was a sensible woman, this Sergeant Bernstein. He'd been right about her all along.

'Do you mind if we stop at the supermarket?' he said. 'I've got nothing in the house, and it's nearly time for lunch.'

'By all means,' she said. 'And do call me Nadja. At least while I'm in your home.'

After lunch, Philipp showed Nadja down the steps to his basement office so that she could use the landline. He had to explain to her that the car number plates propped on every step were there because he was helping to register them for clients, not because he ran some high-class getaway service for big-time bank robbers.

'That's good,' she said. 'Otherwise I'd have to arrest you.'

He went back upstairs to make some work calls on his

mobile, while the children played together in the living room. They were busy making a den and then serving a picnic tea, which was partly imaginary delicacies and partly supermarket Baumkuchen – neither of them the genuine article, in his view, but that didn't seem to matter to them. They chattered away in their own languages, as if having a perfectly normal conversation together. Not too different from the kind of conversation that took place in most families, thought Philipp.

When one of his calls was interrupted by a loud clanking sound from the street outside, he went to the window to see what was going on. The lorry's trailer had been detached from the cab at the front end and was being towed away slowly by a recovery vehicle, which was issuing shrill beeping noises as it did so. The two children came to the window to watch, and Philipp put his hand gently on Amin's shoulder, thinking the scene might trigger all sorts of traumatic memories. But the boy didn't seem too bothered. Perhaps he didn't realise it was the same lorry he'd come in. That all seemed so long ago, in any case.

With the trailer gone, the street was returned to a semblance of normality, though there was still the cab, lodged in the neighbours' fence. That would take them longer to remove. Philipp could see Hannes Schnied out there, waving his arms around as if he were in charge. What delusions of grandeur! Philipp felt sure that Nadja must have masterminded it all from down in his basement office.

Once he'd finished the call he was on, he went down the stairs to let Nadja know what was happening outside. She shrugged her shoulders, as if it was only to be expected: she gave the orders, and they were carried out – why all the fuss?

'The coroner's report has come through,' she said. She asked if she could use his computer to print it off.

They looked at it together. It came as a surprise to Philipp, who'd been expecting it to confirm that the lorry driver had died of a heart attack. He hadn't. But he hadn't been shot either. He'd died of sudden traumatic injuries to his head and body caused by the impact of the crash itself. The lorry had no airbags, and the driver's seatbelt was old and frayed, and had snapped through with the force of the collision. It was likely the man had died instantly.

'Strange, though,' said Philipp. 'What made him steer off the road?'

'Impossible to say,' Nadja replied. 'He probably fell asleep. It's quite common with long-distance lorry drivers. They work such long hours.'

'Yes. But you'd have thought if he was going to nod off, it would happen on the autobahn, not when he's just coming into a brightly lit town.'

'Who knows,' said Nadja, who clearly didn't think there was anything more to be said.

Philipp told her about the crack he'd noticed in the lorry's windscreen, and what he'd thought was maybe a bullet hole at the centre of it. 'What if someone was trying to stop that lorry? If they knew Amin was in there, and they wanted to get him out?'

Nadja was lost in thought for a while. 'I don't know,' she said eventually. 'If it had been a bullet hole, they'd have found a bullet.'

'Yes, but the coroner might not have. It could have missed the driver altogether, but still made him crash. It's possible, isn't it? Maybe it's there in the cabin somewhere.'

She nodded. 'But anything could have made that crack in the windscreen. The lamppost that got knocked down. The fence. It could have been made from the inside, the driver's skull smashing into it. Who knows?'

'Can't you get someone to check though?'

'I'll see what I can do.'

The landline started to ring, and they both reached for it at the same time.

'Sorry,' said Nadja. 'You answer it.'

'Go ahead. It might be for you.'

The two of them stood there, watching it ring. Eventually it was Nadja who answered it.

It was a translator she'd phoned earlier, now ringing her back. She spoke to him for a moment and then turned to Philipp. 'Can he speak to Amin? He says he'll be able to tell pretty quickly.'

Philipp nodded and went upstairs to fetch Amin.

When they returned, Nadja gave the phone to the boy. He listened intently for a moment, then looked up at Philipp and handed him the phone.

'Keep listening,' said Philipp, indicating what he meant.

Amin put the phone to his ear again and went on listening. Eventually he said something in his own language. It was one brief sentence, and then he fell silent again. His eyes kept flickering over to Philipp. Then he passed the phone to him once again.

Philipp gave the phone back to Nadja.

'It's Sergeant Bernstein again. Well? Did you get what you needed?'

She listened. Philipp patted the boy on the back and told him he'd done well.

Nadja hung up and looked dejectedly at them both. 'No good,' she said. 'He's speaking Kurmanji. A kind of Kurdish, apparently. Spoken quite widely in parts of Turkey, Iran and Syria. The translator can recognise it, but he doesn't speak it. We'll have to find someone else.'

'That's okay,' said Philipp. 'At least we know now. One step closer.'

He went upstairs to make the children's tea – spaghetti bolognese – and when Nadja came up to join them, he asked if she wanted to stay for a bite to eat. He would put Emma to bed, and Amin too if he was ready, and then they could have dinner, just the two of them.

'I probably shouldn't,' she said.

He noticed the slight hesitation. 'It's too late to go back to the police station now, surely?'

'Well, no. It's open all hours. But I was thinking I should go home.'

'I'll run you back, if you like. It's already dark.'

'It's fine,' she said. 'I've got my motorbike.'

Yes, he'd forgotten about that. She'd left it in the police station car park.

'And anyway,' she went on, 'You mustn't leave Amin on his own. And there's your daughter too.'

She was right, he would have had to bundle them into the back of the car. He wouldn't have thought twice about doing that, but he wasn't going to argue with her. He didn't want to pressure her into staying if she didn't want to.

'Well, I really appreciate everything you've done,' he said. 'And for letting Amin stay here.'

'It's just for now. We'll have it all sorted out tomorrow. I've arranged for another translator to come tomorrow afternoon. He'll be here at about two, if that's OK? I can be here then too, so it's not a problem if you're busy.'

Philipp was dimly aware that he had several pressing appointments. 'That's fine,' he said. 'Tomorrow at two.'

'And whatever you do, don't let the boy out of your sight. I'll give you my mobile number. Call me on that if you need me. Don't call the police station, I might not be there.'

He went to show her out at the front door, and then, seeing his coat hanging there in the hallway, remembered something.

'Look at this,' he said, taking out the disc of crushed plastic he'd found in the street. It was still in the 'evidence bag' in his coat pocket.

'What is it?' she said, holding it up to the light. 'Looks like the lid off a pot of skin cream.'

'Exactly,' he said. 'It was lying in the street, just alongside the tyre tracks left by the lorry.'

She examined it closely. 'Anti-ageing cream,' she nodded, and then looked up at him. 'I've been using this stuff for years. It's as good as useless.'

He laughed. 'I know. But what if this had something to do with the lorry crashing?'

'What, you think it might have skidded on a pot of skin cream?' She smiled and handed him the evidence bag. 'Sorry, Philipp. There are probably hundreds of bits of rubbish lying out there on the road. Police work is ninety-nine per cent a waste of time. It's only amateurs who think they'll find the crucial clue at the first attempt.'

He nodded and went to open the front door for her. She was probably right. But even so, what she'd said had stung him. Did she see him as an amateur, meddling in her case? A nuisance? An irritant? He had a sudden bitter feeling of disappointment – and it wasn't because she was leaving.

'See you tomorrow,' she said.

'Indeed. In the morning.'

'In the afternoon,' she said, correcting him. She smiled and put her hand on his arm for a moment, giving it a squeeze. And he watched her go down the steps and turn right towards the police station.

FIFTEEN

It's cold outside

He woke early again. He always woke early when Emma was sleeping over at his. She liked to get the day started long before any reasonable hour.

At the first sign of daylight, he looked out of the window at the street. There wasn't much traffic going by yet, but he could see that the road was open in both directions now that the lorry had been removed. All that remained was the hole in the neighbours' fence and the broken stump of the lamppost. He checked in on Amin to make sure he was still there, and that it hadn't all been some strange and elaborate dream. The boy was fast asleep.

He brewed a big pot of coffee and put some toast on for Emma. She munched away happily, wearing the knitted jumper that Frau Kaiser had brought for her. It was slightly too big for her, but the red and blue stripes suited her very well, and she'd grow it into before long. Maschka drummed her tail on the kitchen floor, and Philipp filled up her bowl before realising he'd already given her her breakfast. She'd wolfed down the lot. She really was getting more and more greedy, though with two youngsters in the house it was hardly surprising. She was having to work extra hard to keep them both entertained.

At eight he went in to wake Amin. He'd have liked to let him lie in, but they all had a busy day ahead of them. With the translator coming in the afternoon, Philipp would have to squeeze all his jobs into the morning. And since Herr Schmitt-Dünkelmeyer was also coming at eleven, they needed to get out early so he could run some errands at the Vehicle Registration Office.

While Amin was eating his breakfast, Philipp got Emma

ready, zipping her into her snowsuit. She toddled up and down the corridor in it, looking very much like a snowman that had just discovered its legs. 'We go shops?' she asked, beaming. She loved going to the shops, it was one of her favourite activities at any time of the year, and she'd become even more enthusiastic now that they were full of toys and shiny Christmas tat. He wondered if she had any idea what lay ahead over the next few days. Probably not. She was too young to remember the last Christmas, or to have any fixed concept of what it should be like. For her, it would simply be a time full of wonder and family, and he couldn't wait to see it through her eyes.

What about Amin? Did they celebrate Christmas where he came from? He didn't expect they did. And in any case, he was unlikely to be with his family this year. Who knew where he'd be?

Philipp pulled on his Nordic woollen jumper and slipped his feet into his clogs. Maschka was ready by the front door, the lead dangling from her chops. There was no way she was staying in the house, not if the other two amigos were going out.

'Right, Amin. Time to put your coat on. That's it, your coat. It's cold outside. Very cold. Brrrr!' Philipp crossed his arms and rubbed his hands up and down to show just how cold it was going to be. He was acting things out, he realised, just as he did for Emma.

'Cold,' said Amin, imitating him. 'Brrrr!'

He was sharp, this boy. Definitely a fast learner. If he kept this up there'd be no need for a translator. Philipp helped him do up the zip on the big yellow coat he'd borrowed from his son, then went to select the number plates he needed from the steps leading down to his office.

'Car number plates,' he said to Amin. 'Vroom vroom!'

'Vrum vrum!' echoed Amin, and then Emma joined in the chorus, 'Vrum vrum!', and they all laughed.

They went out through the front door making 'Vroom vroom!' noises, and Emma reached out for Philipp's hand as they went down the stone steps together to the car.

From the car park at the front of the Vehicle Registration Office, where Philipp parked the Opel, he could see that it was busy inside. He'd hoped to beat the crowd, but queues had already formed at each of the service desks. It was going to take a few minutes. He'd better take the boy in with him.

Emma could go in the baby carrier, he decided. She was too big for it really, but after the short journey in the car, her eyelids were looking heavy – it wouldn't take much for her to drop off. It would be so much easier if she had a little nap while he dealt with the paperwork.

Taking Maschka with him was out of the question. It was far too busy in there. She'd have to stay in the car.

But Amin had other ideas. As soon as he twigged that Maschka was staying put, he held on to the Opel's door handle and refused to let go. Philipp tried to be firm, but it quickly became apparent that he was risking a scene. He didn't know how he'd explain to anyone who asked what he was doing, grappling with a foreign-looking boy who didn't speak German.

He looked uncertainly at the Registration Office. Someone else was just going in through the door. The more he delayed, the longer it was all going to take. It was already half past nine, and there was so much else to do this morning. He'd be able to keep an eye on the car from in there anyway, through the big windows at the front.

'Okay, okay,' he said. 'Stay in the car with Maschka.'

'Okay!' said Amin. 'Maschka!'

'Don't go anywhere. I can see you from inside. I won't be long.'

'Anywhere! Long!' Amin was already cuddling up to Maschka, playing with her ears. She seemed more than happy to put up with it.

As soon as he went in through the door, he noticed that

Jennifer, the woman who normally served him at the Registration Office and who was especially helpful, was sitting behind a different desk today. If he stood in that queue, he wouldn't be able to see the car through the front window. Perhaps he should try one of her colleagues?

Jennifer looked up, saw him, and gave him a little wave. He smiled back at her and went to join her queue. It couldn't be helped. It had to be her anyway since one of his clients had requested a number plate with his own initials, and it was best to go to Jennifer for that kind of thing as she tended to waive the additional fee.

Emma still hadn't dropped off in the baby carrier, and in fact she was starting to grizzle a bit. He swayed gently from side to side, and then, when that didn't work, tried rocking his hips and gyrating like he was getting down to some old-school disco. People in the next queue looked at him oddly, but he didn't mind. They'd like it even less if Emma started wailing.

The woman in front of him was taking ages, asking all sorts of questions, and Philipp began tapping his foot on the floor, then drumming the number plates he was carrying against the side of his leg. He was just about to break out into a full Donna Summer routine when, mercifully, the woman collected up all her documents and, giving him a cold stare, walked out of the office.

'Good morning, Philipp,' said Jennifer. 'I see you've brought the little one with you today.'

He looked down at Emma and saw that she was asleep at long last.

'What a beauty she is. She looks just like you, Philipp.'

'Do you think so?' He gave her a dimply smile.

'Oh, absolutely! All that dark hair. Unmistakeably a Werthern. She'll steal some hearts when she's older, I bet.' Jennifer sighed and looked at him with shining eyes.

Philipp steered the conversation round to business, and soon she was organising all the stamps and signatures he needed with great efficiency. She even handled his special request. 'For you, Philipp, no problem at all.' Clearly, it had been worth the wait, though he wasn't able to get away before she'd told him all about some new ten-pin bowling place in Frankfurt where you could also do karaoke. It was great fun, apparently.

'You should come along some time. They have singles events.'

'Me? I can't sing for toffee.'

'Oh, that doesn't matter. Nobody cares what you sound like. They have a Happy Hour!'

He glanced at the clock. It had been twenty minutes since he'd got out of the car. He thanked Jennifer profusely, said his goodbyes, gave an apologetic nod to the man in the queue behind him, and rushed out of the door.

Outside, he stopped. It felt like an iron hand had reached in through his rib cage and taken hold of his heart. The car was empty.

Amin? Maschka?

He looked round the car park. Had they got out of the car for some reason? Had they gone to find him? Maybe Amin hadn't understood. Or he'd panicked. No, surely he'd have seen Philipp going into the Registration Office. Perhaps he'd needed to pee?

He walked along the row of parked cars, hoping to see a mop of dark hair, a wagging tail. Nothing. Were they hiding from him?

'Amin! Where are you?' There was no reply.

'Maschka! Here, girl!' The boy might not come when he was called, but Maschka certainly would.

There was nothing. Not even a bark.

Panicking now, he ran to the edge of the car park and started searching through the sparse undergrowth there. He wasn't even sure what he was looking for. They couldn't be hiding here.

Think, Philipp. Think.

He pushed aside the terrifying thoughts that were crowding into his head and told himself that he needed to think calmly and logically. Panic would get him nowhere. He'd already looked between all the cars and behind all the bushes. It was clear they weren't in the car park.

He set off at a jog, turning right along In Den Nassen towards the Nordring. The road was busy with traffic but there were hardly any pedestrians. A woman with a pushchair. A boy on a bike. Nothing that could be the two of them.

He needed a plan. Looking around aimlessly was a waste of time. What he needed to do was search in a systematic way. He'd start with the streets that were closest to the parked car, going more or less in a circle until he'd gone all the way round. And if he hadn't found them by then, he'd start again, do another circuit, only wider. Concentric circles, covering every possible place they could be. He'd find them somehow.

He turned right onto the Nordring, towards the large Baumarkt store. Parked cars on the side of the road. Metal fences. Big, faceless buildings. He ran along the pavement, Emma's head thumping against his chest. She was heavy and cumbersome. She was sure to wake up at any moment. What then?

Keep going. Got to find them.

He turned right again by a big car showroom. More parked cars. Dead end.

He doubled back. Emma was awake now and starting to grizzle. He had a terrible stitch. He couldn't go on like this. He stopped to catch his breath, and leaned against a wall, shifting Emma's weight to ease the pain in his shoulder. One of the straps on the baby carrier was coming loose. It was no good, he needed another plan.

Maybe he should go back to the car? He could use it to continue the search. Better than doing it on foot, he could cover more ground.

He started walking back towards the car. But what if they'd only gone for walk? What if they went back to the car and found it gone? No, he couldn't risk that. What should he do?

He felt wretched. It was all his fault. He shouldn't have let them out of his sight. Nadja had told him to keep a close eye on the boy. He only had himself to blame.

Maybe they'd be there by the car when he got there. He began to picture it in his mind, the boy beaming at him, Maschka dancing about with her tail wagging away. 'Where were you? We were here all the time.'

But he'd told them not to get out of the car. Hadn't he told them that? He felt sure he had. What was Amin thinking? Couldn't that boy just sit still for a few minutes? Maybe he was playing a trick on him, hiding somewhere, laughing to himself. And he'd taken Maschka too. That was unforgiveable.

Philipp knew it wasn't possible. Amin would never do that. If they'd got out of the car, it was to go and find him. At least they'd be together. Wherever Amin was, he was with Maschka. They were having an adventure. They'd be fine.

He turned into the car park, and there was the car.

No Amin. No Maschka.

He was exhausted and out of breath. Emma was bawling. His clogs were chafing. He could hardly go on. He had to go on.

But first, think. He couldn't do this all on his own. He needed back-up. He could call Annelie, but it would take too long to explain. She'd want all the details. He'd only got halfway through telling her everything yesterday, and he could see she didn't approve.

The only other person he could think of was Nadja. She would crucify him for letting Amin out of his sight.

He took out his phone and called her mobile.

SIXTEEN

Though the frost was cruel

Within ten minutes, Nadja pulled up outside the Registration Office on her Yamaha.

Philipp had been sitting in his car, catching his breath after his strenuous exertions. Emma had fallen asleep again in her baby carrier, strapped to his chest. He'd been planning to give her a couple of minutes' respite before continuing the search, but the time had gone by very quickly.

He got out of the car and went over to Nadja. She wasn't in uniform this time. She was wearing leggings, trainers and a leather jacket. When she took off her helmet, her hair tumbled down in two stiff, slightly frozen plaits. It had clearly been wet when she'd set out.

'Thank you for coming,' he said, glumly.

'Don't be silly. Right. Where shall we start?'

He explained where he'd searched so far, and that his plan was to go on looking in concentric circles around the parked car where he'd left Amin and Maschka forty minutes before.

Nadja suggested they split up. She'd go down Niederhofheimer Street on the bike, and then do a big loop around the Nordring. He could retrace his steps but turn left on the Nordring instead of right, and they'd meet there at the crossroads where it joined the main road.

He nodded, hardly able to take in what she was saying.

'I'll keep checking my phone if you need to ring me again.' She put her helmet back on, gave him a quick thumbs up, and drove off down the road.

He'd been amazed at how calmly she'd taken the news, how

little resentment she seemed to have towards him. But maybe that was only her police training. Perhaps inside she was fuming.

He set off again wearily, determined to keep going. With every minute that passed, their chances of finding Amin and Maschka diminished. If they hadn't found them within the hour, it would be very bleak indeed.

He walked as fast as his sore feet would allow, and this time when he reached the Nordring he turned left. It looked pretty much the same in this direction, more metal fences on the side of the road and, behind them, more big faceless buildings. One of them was the SPD political party headquarters for the Main-Taunus district. He hurried on.

He'd given up thinking that Amin had gone looking for him. Maschka wouldn't have let him go far. She wouldn't even cross a road without Philipp's permission. And if the boy had gone off on his own, he felt sure she'd have returned to the car. No, something must have happened.

Maybe Amin had seen someone he knew? Was that possible?

Or someone had taken him. That was the explanation he didn't want to consider. What if he'd been bundled into a car and was being driven away to God-knows-where? He might even have been abducted by the same people who'd brought him here, the trafficking gang. They might have tracked him down, waited for their opportunity, and then snatched him while Philipp's back was turned. The thought was too terrible to contemplate.

But then why would they snatch Maschka too? Surely they'd leave the dog? Unless they'd had to do something to keep her quiet. The last thing they'd want was to be chased through the streets of Hofheim by a noisy Golden Retriever. Easier to silence her altogether…

Philipp thought sadly of the day, six years ago, when he'd brought Maschka home as a puppy. How her paws had been way too big for her, like she was wearing snow boots, and she'd skittered about on the wooden floors of his house, dashing from room to room, full of excitement and trepidation. He remembered that day like it was yesterday. The two of them had been inseparable ever since. What would he do without her?

The road turned to the left, heading back towards the main road – was that where he was supposed to meet Nadja? His mind was a muddle. Never mind. Keep turning left, always in the same direction. Isn't that how you get out of a fix?

He stopped. There on the ground about twenty yards away, in front of a row of lock-up garages, was a bundle of golden fur.

He rushed over. There she was, Maschka, half on the pavement and half in the gutter. From her mouth hung a trail of saliva, pooling on the tarmac.

His first thought was that she'd been hit by a car. He got down on his knees beside her and looked for signs of injury. There didn't seem to be any blood. He felt her flanks and along her spine. There was no obvious wound. He wasn't sure if she was still breathing. With Emma in the carrier strapped to his chest, it was impossible to get down and listen properly. The body was still warm at least. That was a good sign, wasn't it?

What was this, though? Where was this fluid coming from? It took him a moment to realise it was coming from him. The tears were pouring down his face.

'Maschka! Poor Maschka. Please don't go!'

He was sobbing uncontrollably. He hadn't even noticed that Nadja had pulled up beside him on her bike. The first he knew of it was when she put her hand on his shoulder, and he looked round at her with grateful, tear-filled eyes.

She bent over Maschka and gently pulled open her eyelids. Then she felt for a pulse.

'It's not too late,' she said. 'We'd better get her to the hospital as quickly as possible.'

Philipp nodded. He didn't understand a word she was saying, but he thought there might be some reason for hope.

He was sitting on one of those blue plastic chairs in the waiting room at the veterinary hospital, just down the road from his house on the Zeilsheimer Road. Nadja was there in the chair on his right. He couldn't recall very clearly how they'd got there.

On his left, Emma was sitting in her car seat, wide awake and looking about at the others in the room. Especially at the large, bearded man with a sickly-looking gerbil in a cage on his lap.

There was a tense silence. Philipp was beginning to find it unnerving. It felt as if everyone was under strict instructions to keep noise to a minimum, as if any noise at all might induce pandemonium. Even Emma seemed to understand this and was sitting there in silence for once.

Nadja was fiddling with an empty plastic cup from the vending machine in the corner. From time to time, it made an alarming crackling noise in her hands, amplified in the hushed atmosphere of the room.

Then the silence was broken by someone's mobile phone ringing. Everyone turned to look. Even the gerbil was startled. Philipp realised it was his.

He answered it as quietly as he could. 'Hello?'

'Philipp, it's Sabine.'

Her voice sounded very loud in his ear. He stood up and went over to the window. In the distance the Taunus hills lay under a thick blanket of cloud.

'Herr Schmitt-Dünkelmeyer just called. He says you're not at home.'

Philipp looked at the clock on the wall. It was just after eleven.

'I'm sorry, Sabine. I can't meet with him today. Could you tell him there's been an emergency? I'll need to rearrange.'

There was an awkward pause.

'What about your other appointments?'

'Could you rearrange those too? I'm so sorry.'

'I'm not sure we'll be able to fit them all in before Christmas. I'll do my best.'

'Just do what you can. Any day, apart from today.'

There was another pause.

'Is everything okay, Philipp?'

'I don't know, Sabine. I really don't know.'

A door opened and a man in a white coat stepped out into the waiting room. 'Herr von Werthern?'

'I have to go,' he said quietly, and hung up.

The man in the white coat had a sombre expression. Philipp gulped. He felt Nadja get up and come to his side.

'Would you like to come through?' said the vet to them both.

Philipp nodded. He looked at Nadja, who bent to pick up Emma in her car seat. They all followed the man out of the waiting room, down a corridor and into a consulting room.

The vet gestured to them to take a seat. 'I can bring in a seat for your daughter, if you'd like?' he said to Nadja.

She glanced at Philipp, and then turned back to the man. 'It's okay, she'll be fine in the car seat.'

'Good. Well, let me just say right away, Maschka is doing pretty well, considering.'

Philipp felt himself trembling. A painful lump had formed inside his throat, and he found it hard to swallow. 'Considering?' he managed to say.

'Well,' said the vet, scratching an eyebrow. 'She's been through a lot. It looks like she's swallowed a powerful sedative. She'll be out of it for a while.'

'A sedative?' said Philipp, aware that he was simply parroting whatever the vet said.

'A narcotic, I should think. We'll know exactly what it was when the results come back from the lab. For the time being, we've pumped her stomach and put her on a drip. She's out of the woods. I expect her to make a full recovery.'

Philipp felt a wave a relief wash over him.

'Needless to say,' he went on, 'Whatever it is she's taken, it's extremely dangerous to leave it lying around the house. Especially with little ones in the family.'

Philipp couldn't help it. A sudden nervous burst of laughter broke out of him. The vet looked startled. 'Don't worry, Doctor, it was nothing like that. My daughter's not in any danger, I promise you.'

The man gave him a stern look, and Philipp thought of telling him that the woman he'd taken for Emma's mother was in fact Sergeant Bernstein of the Hofheim Police Force. But on reflection, he thought it might be wise not to go into it.

'But Maschka will make a full recovery, you say? No lasting damage?'

'I expect so. It looks like we got to it before it took full effect. It's always more complicated with dogs in her condition, of course. We'll need to keep an eye on her overnight.'

Philipp blushed a little. 'If you're talking about her weight, doctor, this is something I've been meaning to ask about. She's had a big appetite recently and…'

'Her weight is absolutely fine. Nothing to worry about. It's perfectly normal for dogs in her state to eat a lot more than usual.'

'I don't follow you. Her state?'

The vet gave him a puzzled look. 'You do know she's carrying, don't you?'

'Carrying?' said Philipp, turning to Nadja.

She smiled at him. 'I think he means that she's carrying pups,' she said.

'I do indeed. Nine of them, to be precise.'

'Nine pups?' Philipp said, taken aback.

'You didn't know? She's due in about two weeks' time. It all looks fine, though it was touch and go with everything she's been through.'

'Nine?' said Philipp, unable to take it all in. 'Nine pups?'

Emma, sitting in her car seat, gave a raucous chuckle.

'You hear that, Emma? Maschka's going to have babies! Just in time for Christmas!'

'Well, not quite,' said the vet. 'In two weeks. Should be in time for the New Year.'

'Puppies!' cried Philipp, taking Nadja's hands in his. 'We're going to have puppies!'

Once the news had sunk in a little, the vet said they could all go through and take a peek at Maschka.

She was fast asleep, lying on a padded bench in the recovery room. Philipp could see now that the extra weight she'd put on was all around her middle. The softness made her look maternal, that was all. He wondered who the father might be, and what her puppies would look like. They'd be beautiful anyway, he was sure. They were bound to be, having Maschka for a mother.

There would have to be celebrations of course. Nine mini-Maschkas! Who'd have thought it?

Nadja leaned over and whispered in his ear: 'What on earth are you going to do with nine little puppies?'

But Philipp was suddenly feeling solemn. He was thinking about something else, about someone who ought to be there with them, sharing the news. Amin was out there somewhere, and now he didn't even have Maschka by his side.

They simply had to find him.

SEVENTEEN

Oh, bring us some figgy pudding

It was nearly midday by the time they left the hospital. Emma would be needing her lunch soon, Philipp knew, but they still had a little time. They drove back to the Nordring where they'd found Maschka.

It was one of those roads where the traffic was almost constant, but there was hardly anyone going about on foot. No one to ask about a missing boy or a sedated Golden Retriever. Nadja tried the doors of the lock-up garages, but they were all firmly secured. When a courier van pulled up looking for a residential address, they asked the driver if he'd seen anything suspicious there, about an hour earlier – but he'd only just come from the depot. It turned out the address he was looking for was at the other end of the Nordring.

Philipp concluded bitterly that, if what you wanted to do was sedate a dog or bundle a boy into the back of a van, it was more or less the ideal spot. There was nobody around to care what you did.

Nadja said she would run a check on CCTV footage throughout the area, just as soon as she got back to the police station. But first they ought to return to the Vehicle Registration Office to ask if anyone had seen anything there.

They hadn't. Nobody had noticed a boy in an oversized yellow jacket get out of a turquoise Opel with a Golden Retriever. He'd vanished into thin air, it seemed.

By now it was almost one o'clock, and Philipp could tell that Emma's mood had gone past the point of lively curiosity and was bordering on a murderous tantrum. She needed lunch, fast.

The easiest thing, since he wasn't sure he had anything left in the fridge, was to head for a café in town. He was surprised when Nadja said she'd come too.

'We need to make a plan,' she said. 'It'll be a working lunch, okay?'

Philipp readily agreed.

Venezia, the ice cream parlour in the centre of Hofheim, was doing a brisk trade even though it seemed rather cold outside to be eating ice cream. Still, they did a very acceptable ham and cheese croissant, and the coffee was good and strong.

As the three of them made their way past the ice cream counter towards the tables at the back, Philipp heard a shrill 'You-hoo!' assailing him from one of the larger tables. There, in the midst of a group of elderly ladies, all busily knitting away, was an unmistakeable bob of bright white hair.

'Philipp! Over here, dear.'

'Frau Kaiser!' he called out. 'How nice to see you!' He was always bumping into clients like this, and generally he rather enjoyed it, though today he was in no mood for idle chatter.

'Fancy seeing you here,' she said, directing the comment not so much at him as towards the company she was with. 'And your dear little daughter too. I see she's wearing the jumper I knitted for her.'

'Oh yes. It suits her very well, don't you think?'

'I knew it would. I chose the colours specially. She has such beautiful dark eyes, like yours.'

Philipp thanked her. He ought to be more attentive to Frau Kaiser, he felt. He hadn't yet made those amendments to her insurance policy that she'd requested. She was a bit of a busybody, for sure, but there was something about her that was quite striking. While all the other ladies dyed their hair all manner of outlandish hues and tints, Frau Kaiser left hers a natural white. He hoped he was going to age even half as gracefully as her.

There was a strong smell of something wafting about – he thought at first it was hashish, but no, it couldn't be that. He looked down at the little bunches spread out all over the table in front of the old ladies. Some kind of craft project was in full swing.

'We're making lavender parcels for Christmas,' Frau Kaiser chirruped. 'Let me introduce you. This is my little knitting circle. We meet every week for a natter. I call it my "Stitch and Bitch" Club.'

Philipp chuckled. He'd never heard it called that before. Frau Kaiser had used the English words, and he wondered if she knew exactly what they meant.

She was busy scrutinising Nadja. 'And who is this charming lady you're with?'

'I'm sorry, yes, this is... Nadja Bernstein.' He'd wondered whether to say 'Sergeant Bernstein', and then decided against it since she wasn't in uniform. 'A friend of mine.'

'How lovely,' said Frau Kaiser with what he thought was a wink. Had he given her the wrong idea?

'Well,' he said, 'We'd better let you get on with your lavender parcels.'

'Yes, I'm afraid now you know what you'll be getting for Christmas!'

'Oh no, Frau Kaiser, you've been too generous already.'

'Don't be silly,' she said. 'You've been so helpful. I'm always telling my ladies, if you ever need any little thing insuring, Philipp's your man!'

Philipp thanked her. Perhaps, he thought, this was her way of reminding him about those revisions to her policy. He promised to have the document ready for her the following day, and took his leave.

'Did you smell that?' he said to Nadja as they sat down at a table at the back, half-obscured behind a coat stand. 'I thought it was something else at first. All that lavender, it was quite overpowering!'

'I didn't smell a thing,' she said. 'It's one of my principal failings as a police officer, I have an appalling sense of smell.'

They ordered lunch – a ham and cheese croissant for Philipp, cheese on toast for Emma, and a salade niçoise for Nadja – and got down to business while Emma chewed on a cardboard coaster.

'Whoever it was, they must have planned it,' said Nadja. 'They knew how they were going to deal with Maschka. They had a sedative ready prepared.'

Philipp let the thought sink in for a moment. 'You think they've been watching my house?'

'Most likely. They probably followed you this morning, saw you park up outside the Registration Office and drove round the corner to park out of sight. Then they came back and took their chance, while you were inside.'

Philipp nodded. This all made sense. She was sharp, this Sergeant Bernstein. She had a nose for it, all right.

'But why would Amin get out of the car?' he said. 'Why didn't he put up a fight?'

'We don't know that he didn't.'

'If there'd been a struggle, surely someone would have intervened? Besides, if there'd been a lot of shouting, I'd have heard it myself from inside the building.'

It occurred to him then just how easily Amin had come with him into his house that day he'd found him. Was he simply too trusting, that boy? No, that couldn't be it. Amin had been so confused and out of it that day, he'd have gone along with anybody. It had been completely different this morning, outside the Registration Office. Trusting or not, he wouldn't have gone off with a complete stranger, Philipp felt sure of it.

'You think he knew whoever it was?' said Nadja. It was as if she were reading his thoughts.

'I think so. Or he had a reason to trust them. He went willingly, in any case. I'm sure of it.'

A waitress brought over their orders, and for a while they fell silent, picking at their food. Even Emma seemed to have lost her appetite, pushing segments of cheese on toast around her plate.

'What I don't understand,' Philipp said, 'Is why they didn't just come and knock on my door? I mean, if it was someone Amin knows, and they knew he was there at my house, why couldn't they just say so? We could have straightened it all out.'

'I think we have to accept, since he came here hidden in the back of a lorry, that these people – whoever they are – aren't strictly legitimate.' Nadja stopped picking at her salad and put her fork down on the side of her plate. 'For whatever reason, they're trying to stay hidden.'

Philipp shuddered. The thought that these people had been watching his house, waiting for an opportunity to snatch the boy, filled him with horror.

'It seems to me,' she went on, 'We're dealing with dangerous people here. They're organised. They're unscrupulous. They're prepared to drug a harmless animal if it'll get them what they want. They might even be armed.' She paused and looked up at him. 'We could be getting ourselves into deep water.'

'But don't forget, we've got the whole of Hofheim Police Force on our side. That's something to be reckoned with.' He smiled at her with a confidence he didn't altogether feel. She poked at a piece of lettuce on her plate.

Emma wasn't making any inroads into her lunch either. He pronged a piece of her cheese on toast with his fork and held it up to her lips, but she made a face and pushed it away.

'What's the matter, you don't like it?'

'Want ice cream.'

'You're not having ice cream, no.' Philipp had laid down the law on this. She wasn't to have anything sugary until she turned three, it would rot her teeth.

'Ice cream!' shouted Emma, petulantly. She picked up a piece of the cheese on toast and flung it across the table. It landed on the floor.

Philipp had seen this kind of behaviour before and knew how to deal with it. What she needed was not ice cream, but milk. Milk from her bottle. She was overtired after all the stimulation of the morning, and her gums were probably hurting from the teething. She just needed to curl up in his lap with a bottle of milk.

But he hadn't brought any milk with him. He'd even forgotten her bottle.

When he asked the waitress, she said she'd go and see what she could do – and very shortly afterwards she came back with a bottle they kept behind the counter. It was full of warm, frothy milk. He thanked her and tested the temperature of the milk on his wrist. It was perfect.

A minute later, Emma was nestling into his arm, one hand on the bottle, happily sucking away while the other hand stroked at Philipp's knitted jumper. Her eyelids drooped, and slowly she closed her eyes.

Philipp glanced over at Nadja. She was watching Emma intently. 'I know,' he said. 'You don't have to tell me. She's too old for this.'

'I wasn't thinking that.'

'You weren't? Then what were you thinking?'

Her phone began to ring. She checked the caller ID.

'Sorry, I'd better take this outside.'

He watched as she made her way through the café to the door.

It was a bad habit, this milk business, he knew. He and Annelie would have to wean her off it soon. Not today though. He'd do it another day.

He thought of Amin, going to fetch the bottle of Coke from the fridge. Poor Amin. He should never have left him like that in the car.

Emma was asleep in the crook of his arm. Good. He gently removed the bottle from her grasp and put it on the table. Then he reached for the sugar bowl, took three sachets from it, ripped the tops off them all in one go with his teeth, and tipped the contents into his cup. It formed a heap on the surface of the coffee. The grains darkened one by one, and then all of a sudden sank out of sight.

'Sven, what, you called me at the station? I told you not to call me there.'

'I know you did, Nadja. I'm sorry. It slipped my mind.'

Nadja crossed the street outside the café and went over to the public bench by the bank.

'Is everything okay, Nadja? They said you were on long-term leave and wouldn't be at work for some time. I didn't know what that meant.'

'It means I'm taking some time off work, that's all.'

'You're not ill or anything?'

'I'm fine, Sven. I couldn't be better. I just wish you wouldn't keep ringing me at work.'

'I know, you told me not to. It's really unforgiveable, Nadja, I know it is.'

Nadja gritted her teeth. 'What did you want to speak to me about anyway?'

'I was just wondering if a parcel had arrived for me at the flat? Quite a large one. I stupidly forgot to change the delivery address.'

'Not that I know of. Is it anything urgent?'

'No, not urgent, no.' There was a pause. 'It's a Christmas present, that's all. I sort of really need it today or tomorrow.'

'Well, it hasn't arrived, so there's nothing I can do.'

'No, of course not. That's absolutely fine.'

'I'll ring you if it does turn up.'

'Fine, fine.' Another pause. 'If it does, would you mind not looking at the label on the box? I was hoping to keep it a surprise.'

'Sven, if it's for me, I'll be sending it back. We agreed we weren't giving each other presents this year. Or in fact ever again.'

'I know we did. I wanted you to have something though. It's only small.'

'That's not what you said just now. Quite a large parcel, you said.'

'Okay, yes, well… hands up. You got me there.'

'Sven, I'm going to be sending it back.'

'Okay, Nadja. Whatever you think best.'

'And please don't ring me at work.'

'I won't. I'm sorry.'

She hung up. When would he learn? When was he going to accept it was over? This was torture. It was as bad as having him mope about the house.

No, it probably wasn't that bad.

Embarrassing, though. She wondered who he'd spoken to at the office. She could imagine Hannes Schnied gloating about it. Smirking at Bremsberger. 'You'll never guess who that was on the phone…'

She was sitting on the bench in front of the bank, her back towards the café where Philipp might be watching her right now through the window. Quickly she put the phone to her ear again. She needed a moment to think things through.

The situation was getting worse all the time. She'd had a chance to redeem herself with Rabbinger, and she'd let it slip through her fingers. If it came out that she'd had the stowaway in her grasp – inside the police station even – and that she hadn't acted on it, she'd be facing a far more serious disciplinary procedure. Everything she'd done since being suspended had been unauthorised, illegitimate, illegal even. She could be prosecuted for this. Her career would never survive it. Goodbye, Nadja. *Adiós*.

The only solution was to find him again. And fast. Without Rabbinger or anyone else knowing about it.

Which meant she couldn't rely on any of the usual backup. She couldn't put out a search for the boy. She couldn't force entry into those lock-ups on the Nordring. She couldn't even request access to the CCTV recordings that might show who'd abducted him, and where they'd taken him.

She'd have to do everything with one hand tied behind her back.

Should she tell Philipp? There was a danger that if she didn't, if she kept him in the dark, he might mistakenly give her away. He could call up the police station and end up talking to Schnied, or Rabbinger even. It was a possibility. Maybe she should make a clean breast of it? He seemed trustworthy. They could work on it together. Two were better than one.

But wouldn't he be furious with her? She'd been deceiving him all along, ever since he'd turned up with Amin at the station. He was obviously devoted to the boy, and she'd made everything worse. Perhaps he'd decide his best chance of recovering the boy lay in turning her in, joining forces with Schnied and Rabbinger? She wouldn't even blame him if he did.

Was it worth taking the risk? She didn't know how far she could trust him. She'd have to decide soon.

A pigeon landed at her feet, a sorry-looking, half-feathered sort of thing. It tilted its head and looked up at her, as if it knew she wasn't really on the phone to anyone.

She stood up, put the phone away, and headed back towards the café.

'I've been thinking,' Philipp said, watching Nadja as she sat down again opposite him. 'Why did the lorry crash right there outside my house? Where was it even going?'

'It was returning to the haulage depot in Frankfurt, as far as we can tell from the manifest.'

'But it was going in the other direction, wasn't it? It was heading towards town, *away* from Frankfurt.'

'Right,' she said. 'So the driver must have had some other destination in mind. And the lorry was empty, so the only thing he could be delivering was…'

'The boy,' Philipp said. 'He must have known Amin was in the back of his lorry. It doesn't make sense that he was driving it around empty, just for fun. He was going somewhere to drop Amin off.'

Nadja got her notebook out and flicked through it.

'The driver's name was Jürgen Fischer. He lived in Diedenbergen, right over the other side of town. Maybe he was taking him there?'

'And perhaps this somebody, whoever it was, wanted to stop him before he got there?'

'Or, you know, maybe he just crashed. People do.'

'That's what we've got to find out. I think we should start there, with the neighbours. Somebody must have seen something.'

'Philipp,' she said, putting her notebook down on the table. 'Can I be straight with you?'

'Please do,' he said, shifting Emma's weight in his lap as she began to stir.

Nadja seemed to be weighing her words. 'We don't know who we're dealing with. These people could be dangerous. They might not want someone snooping around. Also, they already know where you live. Are you sure you want to do this?'

He looked down at Emma. She was rubbing her eyes with two little, balled fists, just like she'd done as a baby.

'They've got Amin,' he said. 'I don't think we've got any choice.'

They split the bill between them and thanked the waitress for the bottle of milk. On the way out, Philipp waved at Frau Kaiser and all the ladies in her 'Stitch and Bitch' Club. They were hard at it still.

EIGHTEEN

In the bleak midwinter

When Philipp pulled up outside his house in the turquoise Opel – with Nadja on her motorbike just behind – he was surprised to see a stranger standing on his doorstep.

He was instantly on the alert. The man was wearing a hat and had the collar of his coat turned up, so you couldn't see any part of his face. It was probably because of the cold, but even so the hairs on the back of Philipp's neck began to prickle.

He left Emma in the back of the car and went to see who it was.

'Herr von Werthern?' said the man in a clipped voice as Philipp went up the steps to his own front door.

'Yes? How can I help?'

'I was told you would be here at two o'clock. This is what I was told by Sergeant Bernstein.'

Nadja was coming up the steps now too. 'You must be the translator,' she said. 'I'm sorry, we won't be needing your services any longer.'

'I see,' said the man. He spoke German with an indefinable foreign accent. 'This is actually quite inconvenient…'

'Perhaps this will be acceptable,' said Nadja, folding a banknote into his hand.

The man glanced down at it, then slipped it into his pocket. 'Very well. If you should happen to change your mind…'

'Then we'll certainly be in touch,' she said. The man, taking his dismissal rather badly, trudged down the steps and crossed the road to his car.

'He's been waiting here nearly an hour,' Philipp said, feeling sorry for the poor man.

'He'll doubtless survive.'

Philipp was about to open his front door to let Maschka out when he remembered she was still sleeping it off in the animal hospital up the road.

'Let's take a walk up the street now, shall we? Before it gets dark.'

He went to get Emma out of the car and persuaded her that they were all going for a nice little stroll. Sometimes she noticed things he'd never notice himself, although mostly she just liked to wave at the garden gnomes.

They went along the pavement, past the gaping hole in the neighbours' fence, and followed the tyre tracks that were still visible in the road. They extended on and on past several houses.

'Here,' said Philipp, coming to the place where the tracks began. 'The lorry started skidding right here. So whatever caused the accident, it must have been somewhere around this point.'

'Do you know who lives in this house?' said Nadja.

'Not this one. The one next door belongs to Beatrix and Klaus. Clients of mine. I know them a little.'

'In that case, why don't we start with them?'

Philipp went in through the gate and up to the door. He was about to knock when Nadja called out, 'Wait. Have a look at this.'

She was just inside the gate, by the bins. She'd opened the yellow recycling sack and was peering into it.

Philipp went over. The sack was half full of glass bottles and jars. Nothing much of interest.

And then he saw it. A tub of moisturiser. *For mature skin.*

He scrabbled in his pocket for the evidence bag containing the lid from the pot of skin cream. Yes, it was the very same brand. He looked at Nadja. 'Do you think…?'

'Who knows,' she said. 'Let's not jump to conclusions. Ninety-nine per cent of police work is…'

'A total waste of time!' Philipp smiled grimly, and then went again to knock on the door. But before doing so he turned back once more.

'You know, it doesn't mean she's got anything to do with this,' he said. 'The person who did it could have been looking for something to throw at the lorry, and found what he needed in her recycling sack.'

'You're right. Perfectly right. Well, there's only one way to find out.'

Philipp nodded. He went and knocked on the door.

It was answered by a rather gaunt-looking woman in her fifties with mousy brown hair wearing a dressing gown and slippers.

'Philipp?' she said. 'Oh goodness, have I forgotten an appointment?'

'Not at all, Beatrix. We were just passing. I wondered if we could pop in for a chat?'

She peered past him at Nadja.

'This is Nadja, a friend of mine. We're asking people on the street if they know anything about the accident the other night.'

'I don't think so,' said Beatrix, keeping her hand on the door.

'What about Klaus? Is he in?'

She shook her head. 'He's away visiting his sister.'

'Do you mind if we come in? We won't keep you long.'

Beatrix looked very uncertain about it, but Emma had already walked in right past her and was heading straight across the hallway towards the living room.

'I'm afraid the place is in a bit of a mess,' Beatrix said, standing aside to let Philipp and Nadja through.

It was indeed. Philipp wasn't normally one to judge, since his own house was always in a fine state of disarray, but he was taken aback at the sight that greeted him in Beatrix's living room. There were clothes heaped on every available surface, piles of books in the middle of the floor, Christmas decorations that seemed to have been abandoned halfway through being put up, and a tree that tilted so far over in its pot that more than half of the baubles had fallen off. Emma was going round delightedly, collecting them all up.

'Oh dear,' said Beatrix. 'Sorry about this.'

'That's quite all right,' said Philipp. 'There's never enough time at Christmas.'

Beatrix offered to make them both a cup of tea, but Philipp politely declined. 'We won't be here five minutes. We just thought if you had any information about the other night – anything at all – it might be helpful to the police.'

He glanced quickly at Nadja, who nodded and said nothing.

'What night did it happen again?' said Beatrix.

'Monday night,' said Philipp. 'Or in fact early Tuesday morning.'

'That's right. We were out that night, staying over at my mum's. We weren't even here.'

'You weren't? Oh. Okay. And Klaus? He wasn't here either?'

'No, we were both out.'

'Well, I imagine you got a better night's sleep than I did. It was quite a commotion.'

'I know,' she said. 'I mean, I could tell. The lorry was still there when we got back. Truly dreadful. I hope nobody was hurt.'

'I'm afraid someone *was* hurt,' Philipp said. 'Rather badly.'

'Really?' said Beatrix, putting her hand to her mouth.

'The driver was killed,' said Nadja.

Beatrix gasped. She looked stricken.

'Perhaps you'd like to sit down,' said Philipp, taking her gently by the arm and steering her over to the sofa, where she collapsed on top of a heap of ironing. 'Shall we make you a cup of tea? It looks like you could do with one.'

'I had no idea someone had actually died!' she said.

Philipp glanced at Nadja again.

'I'll go and make tea,' she said, and slipped out of the room.

Emma had found a box of plastic animals, the Schleich variety that she loved playing with. She tipped the whole box out onto the floor.

Philipp sat down carefully next to Beatrix.

'Tell me, Beatrix, has something happened?'

She turned to him with tears in her eyes. 'It's Klaus,' she said.

'He's left me.'

'Left you? I thought he was just visiting his sister?'

'He's gone off with some floozy of his. I'm such a bloody fool!' She wiped her eyes. 'I'm sorry. What an embarrassment.'

'Not at all. How dreadful! I'm so sorry, Beatrix.'

'She's only twenty-five, can you imagine it? Twenty-five! Not much older than our own daughter. He makes me sick!'

She was shaking now. Philipp wasn't sure if she was in shock or just absolutely furious – and either way, he didn't know what to do about it. Down on the carpet, Emma was making crude animal noises and chuckling in delight. He hoped Nadja would come back in soon with that tea.

'It's unforgiveable,' he said. 'And at Christmas time too!'

Now Emma had got hold of a hippopotamus and was busy making it bite a poor innocent giraffe on the backside. Each time the hippo took a bite, the giraffe spun round to see who'd attacked it.

Beatrix looked over at her and smiled. 'Those animals belonged to our daughter, Silke. She's at university now, would you believe.'

Nadja appeared in the doorway with a cup of tea. She caught Philipp's eye and, when he nodded, she came in and handed it to Beatrix. 'There you go.'

'Thank you!' Beatrix took the cup and sat nursing it for a moment. 'Silke used to love playing with those animals. Her favourites were the farmyard ones. The pig, especially. She always loved little Piggy Wiggy.'

'Beatrix,' Philipp said, 'There's something we ought to mention. Nadja here is a sergeant in the Hofheim Police Force. She's investigating the death of the lorry driver.'

Nadja got out her police ID and showed it to Beatrix. 'If there's anything you haven't told us,' she said, 'It would be a good idea to do so now.'

Beatrix looked from Nadja to Philipp in confusion.

'It's okay,' he said. 'There's no need to worry. You can tell us anything at all.'

'We already know about the pot of skin cream,' said Nadja.

Beatrix's jaw dropped. 'You know about that?'

'We'd like to hear your side of the story, of course.'

Philipp flashed Nadja a look. She was taking this too fast. Beatrix had the look of a woman whose whole world had been turned inside out, along with her living room.

'What Sergeant Bernstein means is, this is your chance to get everything straight. In case anything's got a little muddled. And if it has, it would be perfectly understandable. Given the circumstances.'

Beatrix nodded. She lifted the cup of tea to her lips, and then lowered it again without taking a sip. 'He's dead, you say? The lorry driver?'

'Yes, he is.'

'I didn't know that.' She looked imploringly at Philipp. 'You do believe me, don't you?'

He reached out and took hold of her hand. 'Of course.'

'It was all my fault. We were upstairs in the bedroom, Klaus and me. We didn't go to bed all night. He said he was leaving me for that piece of… .' She put her hand to her mouth. 'I was so angry with him and so… I just couldn't believe it. I started pulling all his things out of the drawers, throwing it everywhere. I just went completely crazy.'

Philipp sensed Nadja fidgeting at the edge of the sofa. He urged her silently to let Beatrix continue.

'And do you know the worst thing? He kept saying how much he *appreciated* me. How much he *liked* me. How much he *respected* me. Well, I wasn't having *that*. I wanted to hurt him. Really *hurt* him. I picked up the nearest thing and I… and I…'

'What happened then, Beatrix?'

'Well, I threw that tub of skin cream at him.' She laughed momentarily, and then the smile fell from her face. 'I missed, of course. It went right out through the window.'

They waited for her to say more, but nothing came.

'Okay, Beatrix,' said Nadja. 'And the window was open?'

'Of course.' Beatrix turned to Philipp. 'You know what Klaus is like. Such a fresh air fanatic. The window always has to be open, whatever the weather. I don't think he cares if I'm lying there freezing my face off. I don't know why I've put up with him for so long. These last few nights since he left, I've had the best sleep of my whole life!'

She was looking at them both now with triumph in her eyes. It lasted a moment, and then puzzlement broke through.

'Wait. What was I saying?'

'You were saying you threw the tub of skin cream,' said Philipp. 'What happened then, Beatrix?'

'That's right. It went out through the window.' Beatrix nodded gravely. 'Oh, there was a terrible sound. It went *skreeeeee*, and then there was a great big crash. It shook the whole house. I thought the world must have come to an end.'

'Did you go outside to see what had happened?'

'I wanted to, believe me. But Klaus wouldn't let me. He said, "What's happened has happened". He locked the door, you see, and went to bed. Straight to sleep like always. He's a good sleeper. Not like me. I sat up the rest of the night. I thought, if he's decided to stay the night, maybe he's changed his mind. Maybe he's going to stay.' She smiled, fleetingly. 'But then, in the morning, he packed his bags and left.'

'Do you know where he is now?'

'Of course. He's with her.' She pulled a tissue from the pocket of her dressing gown and blew her nose. 'I really believed he'd changed his mind. But of course he just wanted to make sure I didn't go and turn myself in to the police.' She looked at Nadja. 'There, I've told you everything anyway.'

Beatrix began to cry, softly, terribly. There was nothing Philipp could think of to do.

In the end, Emma came over and pressed something into Beatrix's hand. 'Piggy Wiggy,' she said. 'For you.'

Beatrix put the pig to her lips and kissed it.

NINETEEN

Behold, the moon has risen

Philipp and Nadja made their way back to his house in silence, with Emma riding on Philipp's back. Darkness had fallen. Their breath rose like plumes in the cold air.

Philipp felt utterly dejected. He'd tried to console Beatrix as best he could, but his heart wasn't in it. All he could think about was the windscreen of the lorry shattering in front of the driver's face, and then what must have been his terrifying final moments before the vehicle ploughed into the neighbours' fence. All because of a pot of skin cream hurled at a cheating husband…

The moon was in the sky, like one last bauble left on the tree.

'What's going to happen now?' he said to Nadja.

'Well, at least we know it wasn't a bullet.'

'I mean what's going to happen to Beatrix? Is she going to be charged with something?'

'Oh, I should think so. But don't worry, she won't get much of a sentence. She was aiming for her husband, not the lorry. And there are mitigating circumstances. She was provoked, to say the least. She'll probably get away with a hefty fine.'

'Poor Beatrix.' It was all so unfortunate, Klaus leaving her, and now this. He wondered how the woman was going to cope.

They were standing at his front door now, and he looked around for Maschka before remembering again that she was in the hospital.

'Will you come in for a bit?' he said. Nadja was fiddling with the straps of her motorbike helmet. Perhaps she needed to go straight to the police station and report everything they'd discovered?

She hesitated. He could see she was undecided.

'Let me just get Emma inside,' he said. 'It's freezing out here.' He entered the code into the keypad beside his front door and it unlocked itself with a click. 'I'm just going to be out here for a moment, Emma,' he said. 'You go inside and get warm.'

Emma toddled into the house in her snowsuit, and he turned back to Nadja, pulling the door to so that it was almost closed.

'Is it really necessary to drag her through it all? The poor woman doesn't seem well at all.'

'Philipp, what are you saying? You think I should *cover it up*?'

'No,' said Philipp, looking down at his clogs. 'I'm not saying that. It's just that it was a freak accident, wasn't it? But the court won't see it like that. They always find someone to blame, don't they?'

'There's a process, Philipp. It has to be followed.'

'I suppose it does.'

'The best thing is if she goes to the police station first thing tomorrow and makes a full statement.'

'Who does she need to speak to? You?'

'Not me, no.' Nadja looked away. 'She'll need to speak to the duty officer.'

'Who will that be? Hannes Schnied?'

'It might be, I'm not sure.'

'God help her if it's Schnied!'

They both looked out at the street where Nadja's Yamaha was propped on its stand, just behind his turquoise Opel.

'Philipp, there's something else I need to tell you.'

He looked at her in surprise. She seemed to be waiting for some kind of response.

'Of course, go ahead.'

She spoke in a trembling voice. 'I've been suspended. My badge has been revoked. I'm on unpaid leave pending an investigation into my handling of the case.'

'What?'

'I should have told you before. Sorry.'

'Since when?'

'Since yesterday morning, just before you came to the station with Amin. I had no right to even speak to you about the case. They've put Hannes Schnied in charge. If they find out I've been actively investigating, that we had the boy in our hands and we lost him, it'll be the end of my career.'

Philipp stared at her. 'What did you do to get suspended?'

'I missed the boy in the back of the lorry.'

'That's all?'

'It's enough. Once the story gets out about a stowaway, and that we let him go, there'll be no end of trouble. There has to be a fall guy.' She smiled bitterly. 'And that's me. I'm the fall guy.'

Philipp nodded. He thought about all that time over the last two days that she'd spent not going to the police station, not reporting her findings, not doing what needed to be done. They'd been working alone all this time. And they'd got nowhere. 'Why didn't you tell me before, Nadja? I don't understand.'

She glanced at him quickly and looked away down the street. 'I thought we could do this ourselves. Put everything right. I thought if we did that, it would all go back to normal, and I might even get promoted. Sounds silly, I know, but that's what I thought.'

They stood there in silence, watching the evening traffic go by.

'If you want to go to the station right now, report everything to Schnied, that's fine by me. You've every right. And who knows, maybe that's the best way to find Amin now. The *only* way.'

She might be right. Every lead had come to nothing. And without the authority of the police behind them, what could they hope to do? But… Hannes Schnied? In many ways Philipp would rather go it alone.

'If I do go to Schnied,' he said, 'They'll know everything you've done.'

'Can't be helped. You decide.' She lifted her helmet, placed it on her head, and went down the steps to her bike.

'Wait,' he said. 'What about Beatrix? If she goes to the station and gives a statement, like you said she should, then she's bound to mention you. You still think she should do that?'

Nadja climbed onto the bike, put the key in the ignition, and started the engine with a roar.

'It's all about the boy now,' she called out. 'That's all that matters.'

She pushed the bike out into the road and accelerated away towards town, the sound of the engine dwindling in the cold night air.

Philipp was shivering, he noticed. He wasn't sure how long he'd been standing there. He'd better go inside.

Emma was sitting on the kitchen floor, struggling to take off her snowsuit. 'Let me help,' he said, pulling it up again so he could get her legs out of it.

'Where Maschka?' she said.

'Maschka's in the animal hospital, remember? We saw her there today, didn't we?'

Emma nodded thoughtfully. 'Maschka poorly?'

'She was, but they're taking good care of her. She has nine little puppies in her tummy too, don't forget.'

'Nine?'

'That's right. Nine of them!'

Emma put her hand on her tummy. 'In here?'

'Yes, that's where babies are before they're born. You were in your mummy's tummy too.'

Emma giggled.

'I think it's time for your tea, isn't it?'

He went to the fridge. As usual, there was very little in there. The empty Mettwurst packet. A jar of jam and some butter. Those kidneys that Michi had left. He'd have to do a big Christmas shop tomorrow – but for now, perhaps there'd be something in the freezer down in the cellar?

It was hard not to feel gloomy, going down there into the darkness at the bottom of the steps. He flicked on the light and rummaged around in the gigantic chest freezer. Mostly it contained packets of filleted venison – the bounty he'd brought back from a hunting party he'd been on in the autumn with his cousins. There were about twenty portions of it, all neatly labelled *Philipp's Venison*. Anything in the freezer had to be labelled to avoid confusion. He'd once defrosted and cooked something that turned out to be Michi's sister's wedding cake, and he didn't want to repeat the mistake.

He was beginning to think that a trip to the shops was on the cards after all, when he spotted a portion of fish pie. It had only been in there a month or two. Perfectly edible.

Climbing the stairs again, he thought about that day with his cousins, riding out across their estate in the glorious sunshine. He was unfamiliar with hunting etiquette, and felt it was all rather fusty and eccentric, but he never turned down an opportunity to go out riding. And the countryside was spectacular. He'd not actually succeeded in shooting anything, thankfully – but even so, his cousins wouldn't let him go home without taking a side of venison in the back of the car. He'd probably never get around to eating it.

His mind was wandering, dwelling on days out hunting in the sunshine – anything to distract him from the situation with Amin. But now, as the fish pie was defrosting, he had time to think.

He'd intended to ask Nadja into the house so that they could talk about their next steps, but now that seemed so utterly hopeless. He was as far as he'd ever been from knowing what to do.

Should he go straight to the police station and speak to Hannes Schnied? That man was totally useless, but at least he might be able to organise some kind of search. Philipp could even suggest to him that he might like to check any CCTV footage around the

Nordring area. If they had a visual on who'd abducted the boy, or even a vehicle number plate, that would at least be something. Nadja's obstinacy had meant they'd lost a great deal of time – Amin could be hundreds of miles away by now. But something told him that wasn't the case. They'd brought him all the way here to Hofheim. Chances were, he was still somewhere nearby.

The microwave pinged. It was time for dinner. Nothing could be done just yet. He could go with Emma to the station as soon as they'd had their tea.

But once tea was over, Philipp found that the prospect of reporting everything to Schnied had lost its appeal. He'd never got anywhere with the police, and in fact they'd spent more time and effort putting obstacles in his way than they'd ever spent on solving a case. The man was a fool, and a vindictive one at that. He'd only sneer at Philipp's idiocy at leaving the boy in the car, as if that was the most serious consideration at this precise moment.

And if he told everything to Hannes Schnied, then Nadja's career was over. He'd have that on his conscience too.

Besides, Emma had got a boardgame out on the living room floor and was insisting that he come and play it with her. It was a vintage one called Fang Den Hut or 'Capture the Hat', the object of which was to move your pieces around the board, capturing your opponent's pieces by landing on top of them, and then carrying them back to your base where you could imprison them. Emma was still a bit young for it and didn't quite grasp all the rules, but she liked moving the multicoloured conical pieces around the board and yelled in triumph whenever she landed on one of Philipp's pieces. The game could go on for hours, the two of them lying side-by-side on their bellies, and there was hardly ever a clear winner. So it wasn't a great surprise when Philipp looked at the clock and realised that it was well after bedtime.

It was in any case too late now for them to go to the police station. He went upstairs with Emma and helped her brush her teeth, then sat by her bed and sang an old lullaby, 'Der Mond *ist aufgegangen*' or 'The moon has risen'. The song had been passed down from generation to generation in his family, and its mournful description of the moon rising over a dark wood always made him feel both lonely and safe. It had worked its magic on him ever since he was a boy. He felt the sadness of the song seep down into him now, singing it to Emma as she drifted off to sleep. He switched off the light, leaving the little nightlight on, and tip-toed out of the room.

Plodding down the steps to the kitchen, he couldn't help thinking again of that little boy he'd let down so badly, and whether anyone was tucking him into bed or singing him a lullaby. His heart contracted painfully. Would there be anyone in the police station now? He felt sure there would be. He'd have to take Emma with him, of course. It couldn't be helped. It was the only thing to do. He'd better do it right away.

TWENTY

Bring me food and bring me wine

As Philipp turned back towards the stairs, resolved now to wake Emma and bring her along with him to the police station to report everything that had happened, he passed the wall calendar hanging in the corridor. His eyes happened to glance at tomorrow's entry…

The gallery opening! The one at the Museum of Modern Art in Frankfurt, where he was supposed to be doing the catering. It was tomorrow at five, and he'd completely forgotten!

What a fool he was. How was he going to supply drinks and canapés for two hundred guests, as well as securing the services of the necessary serving staff, at less than a day's notice? Though of course he'd had plenty of notice. The event had been marked on his calendar for months. And the Museum's Director was a close personal friend, someone he'd known since their school days, and who always trusted him with jobs like this. He couldn't quite remember all the details – hadn't his friend mentioned some dignitary who was going to be speaking at the event? Philipp had a vague idea that it was going to be quite a special occasion, not just some everyday *vernissage*. If he let his friend down now, he'd never land another catering job with him.

But how could he possibly manage it? He hadn't prepared a thing. And there was nothing in the house that he could throw together overnight.

Unless… the venison in the freezer! There was certainly enough of it. But what could he do with venison? It wasn't your standard canapé ingredient. This wasn't necessarily an issue – he'd always made a virtue of necessity in the kitchen. His avocado sherry soup had been widely admired, and that time he prepared a Kartoffelsalat using parsnips simmered in pilsner would live long in the memory. But venison? It needed something light and crisp as a contrast. A vol-au-vent pastry casing, perhaps? Now that was an idea. Yes, something might yet be done!

He rushed down to the chest freezer in the cellar and fetched up all the packets of venison into the kitchen, where he laid them out on the worktop and popped them one by one into the microwave to defrost. It was an agonisingly slow business, but at least it gave him time to make the necessary arrangements.

First, he rang Annelie to see if she could have Emma for the day. It was more than a little tricky, she said, as she was going to be at work. He could practically hear the eyeroll. Still, there was a nursery next to her workplace, and they'd probably have space for her there. She'd give them a call in the morning, and all being well she'd collect Emma by eight on her way to work. Philipp had to admit, she was really very decent about it.

He kept the phone jammed between shoulder and ear as he began to fry up the onions in a large pan on the hob. It was already nearly ten o'clock at night and he had to ring round all his contacts before he found two – Annette and Magda – who were willing and able to come along and be his serving staff. That made three of them altogether, just about enough to get by.

Once the meat had finished defrosting, he browned it nicely in batches before stirring in the onions, some bay leaves, and plenty of good red wine. It smelled delicious, but it still needed a little something to bind it all together. Something sweet, perhaps? There was that big jar of plum jam sitting on the shelf – would that do? He tipped it all in and gave it a stir, then left it to bubble away while he got on with the ironing: two frilly white aprons for Annette and Magda, and a larger chef's apron for himself.

When that was done, he took a big wooden spoon and tasted the ragout. Ah, delicious! Yes, this was fit to be eaten. It was certainly no disgrace. He was even beginning to think it might have a touch of class about it. He popped the lid on, turned off the heat, and went upstairs to collapse into bed.

He woke to the sound of the doorbell. It was ten to eight. That must be Annelie at the door!

'Were you still in bed?' she said as he let her in. 'Incredible!'

Emma was already up. In fact, now that he was almost fully awake, he remembered getting up hours before to give her some breakfast and get her dressed. Somehow he must have gone back to bed.

He waved them off. Right, first things first. Coffee.

After that, he jumped in the car and drove to the supermarket, where he bought up all the packets of puff pastry that were on the shelf. He threw a ham-and-salad roll into the trolley too, and ate it on the way to the wine wholesalers. What would go well with his venison vol-au-vents? He decided on a nice Spätburgunder, six cases of it, and four cases of a decent Sekt, plus the requisite soft drinks. Luckily the Museum always provided glasses and tableware, so he needn't worry about that.

The rest of the morning disappeared in a flurry of pastry-cutting, hand-crimping, case-filling, egg-brushing, sweat-mopping and crisping up under the grill. It was a delicate operation, and more than once he cursed himself for not having the sense to buy readymade vol-au-vent cases. He groaned under the task and kept throwing glances at the kitchen clock, which ticked ever closer towards the time he would have to leave if he was going to get to the Museum before the guests arrived.

But finally it was done. Three huge crates packed with crispy vol-au-vents, each finished with a star of pastry he'd cut out using a Christmas cookie cutter which he'd last put to use on a batch of Zimtsterne biscuits he'd baked with Emma. He had to admit, the vol-au-vents looked fantastic. He was in business. And there was just enough time to get changed.

As he dashed up the stairs, he nearly tripped over Maschka's lead. He'd forgotten about her, too. He'd have to give the animal hospital a ring from the Museum, there was no time to do it before.

It wasn't the only thing he'd pushed to one side. He was well aware of that. He just couldn't bring himself to face it.

TWENTY-ONE

An unlikely Santa

When he pulled in at the service entrance around the back of the Museum of Modern Art, he was stopped by two armed guards. They weren't local police. The Museum had certainly stepped up its security since the last time he'd catered for an event here.

After checking his ID against the details on their docket, they waved him through. There were further security measures in place as he carried the first of the three large crates of vol-au-vents into the building. A guard approached him with an electronic wand and proceeded to wave it over the contents of the crate.

'Don't worry, it's nothing volatile,' he said. 'Just vol-au-vents.' The guard didn't seem to appreciate the joke, but he let him through anyway.

Philipp went on up the steps to the first floor, where the event was to be held in the large, wedge-shaped exhibition hall. It had high ceilings and stark white walls, which were hung with eclectic works of art, some painted, some woven, some constructed out of bits of straw and broken pottery. Several large banners proclaimed a Middle Eastern theme, and it seemed that the work in the exhibition was the result of a series of collaborations between German and Middle Eastern artists. He'd probably been told this at some stage. Was venison halal, he wondered? He thought it probably was.

The service area had been set up already, with all the glasses and plates set out. There were ice buckets for the sparkling wine and serving platters for the canapés. Good. Everything there. A sound engineer was doing checks on a microphone, which had been set up on a small stage opposite. There were more security guards positioned at the doors. They'd really gone to town with the security.

Annette and Magda arrived just as he was bringing in the last case of wine. He handed them each an apron, and they got going with pouring out the drinks so that they'd be ready when guests started to arrive. He spotted his friend, the Museum's Director, talking to security and they exchanged a friendly wave. Philipp gave him a thumbs up for good measure.

'Make sure the Director gets a glass of the Sekt, won't you?' he told Magda, and started plating up the vol-au-vents.

Everything was ready, he saw to his satisfaction, and right then the first guests started filtering through the doors. Soon there was a buzz about the place, and Annette and Magda were busy circulating with drinks and canapés. They knew exactly what to do, had precisely the right combination of discretion and charm, and he began to relax now, seeing that the vol-au-vents were being snatched up and noisily appreciated. He stationed himself behind the serving stand where he had a good view of proceedings, and busied himself pouring out more drinks. Guests kept arriving through the big doors at the far end of the room, rosy-cheeked from the cold and glad to be offered something to eat. Some of them, he noticed, had Christmassy Lebkuchen hanging on red ribbons around their necks. They must have got them from the biscuit stall at the Gallusmarkt, the annual Christmas Fair that took place just round the corner. There were some families with young children too, he spotted. He probably should have made something more suitable for the little ones. He'd missed an opportunity there, but you can't think of everything.

Amidst all the hustle and bustle, the refilling of drinks and the replenishing of canapé platters, Philipp spotted a young boy holding what looked like a large teddy bear. He was over the other side of the room, and something about his dark hair and olive complexion made Philipp take a second glance, but by then he'd disappeared behind a group of guests who were looking at one of the paintings. It was quite natural there'd be guests here that looked like Amin, he told himself. He mustn't dwell on it.

An elderly man in bifocal glasses came up to ask about the vol-au-vents. He'd been having a debate with some others about whether it was beef or lamb in them – could Philipp settle the question? Philipp smiled and told him it was venison. He was able to give the gentleman a full account of the provenance of it, where the deer had been raised and the precise place on his cousin's estate in Castell where it had been shot. The man went away satisfied, helping himself to another vol-au-vent as he did so.

Just then, three people mounted the stage. One, Philipp saw, was his friend the Museum Director. Alongside him, facing away from the crowd, was a strangely familiar, slightly stooped figure all in red – and for a moment Philipp wondered if it was some rather elegantly attired Santa Claus, here to entertain the youngsters.

Then the figure in red turned to face the crowd, and with something of a shock he realised it was Angela Merkel, the Chancellor. He'd only ever seen her on television, and beholding her up close like this gave him that peculiar, uncanny feeling that he was watching a meticulous impersonation rather than the person herself. It was very convincing. She had exactly the same round-shouldered stance and slightly weary, good-humoured demeanour. No, there was no doubting it now, it really was the Chancellor.

The third person up there – a towering, dark-suited man with an earpiece and a menacing expression – now retreated a few steps, and a hush promptly fell over the audience.

Well, this was an unexpected turn of events. Listening to his friend introducing the Chancellor, Philipp wondered whether she might perhaps have eaten one of his vol-au-vents. And if so, could he somehow use this to his advantage? He imagined a photo in tomorrow's Frankfurter Allgemeine Zeitung:

'Chancellor Merkel was delighted to taste one of Philipp von Werthern's homemade canapés!'. He ought to take a picture right now on his phone, or would that look unprofessional? The massive bodyguard was scanning the crowd from the back of the stage, and Philipp thought he'd better leave his phone in his pocket. It was a shame though. 'The Chancellor couldn't resist trying another one of Philipp's famous venison vol-au-vents'.

Applause broke out as the Chancellor stepped up to the microphone. She was about to speak. Out of the corner of his eye, Philipp noticed a huge teddy bear pushing its way towards the front, above the heads of the crowd. It was the same one he'd spotted earlier. He couldn't see the person holding it.

People were still clapping, and the Chancellor was waiting politely – if ever so slightly impatiently – for the applause to die down. Flashbulbs were going off just in front of her. Perhaps he could take a quick snap of her himself without anyone noticing? 'Chancellor Merkel declared Philipp's vol-au-vents truly irresistible!'

He was reaching for his phone when he caught a glimpse, through a gap in the crowd, of the boy who was carrying the teddy bear. He gasped. It really was Amin!

The gap closed and his view was lost, but he was sure of it now. For that instant, he'd had a clear view of his face. The dark hair. The olive skin. And most clearly of all, the eyes – those green eyes that could only belong to Amin.

He'd had the impression that those eyes were haunted by something, flicking nervously about the crowd, and he thought he'd seen Amin turn back, as if reluctant, or perhaps looking for reassurance. The crowd was blocking Philipp's view now, but as he turned his gaze in the direction that Amin had been looking, he saw a broad-shouldered man with a black beard standing at the back of the room, apart from the crowd. The man was nodding urgently and doing little 'keep going' gestures with his hands. And then the teddy bear began to move forwards again, edging towards the stage.

The Chancellor had started talking, saying something about cultural exchange and art transcending borders, but Philipp wasn't really listening. He was watching the teddy bear as it made its way nearer and nearer the foot of the stage. He still couldn't see Amin underneath it, but that look in the boy's eyes was something he couldn't forget. It was a look of pure terror.

The teddy was climbing the steps at the side of the stage. He could see Amin holding it now. He looked pale and fragile. He was dressed in a thick green woollen jumper, much too big for him. He could barely hold the teddy in his arms. Why was the teddy so heavy? Was there something hidden inside? The boy was clearly terrified.

Philipp glanced back at the man with the beard. He seemed to be reaching for something in his pocket.

A cold sweat broke out across Philipp's forehead. Time thickened like jelly. Amin stumbled in slow motion onto the stage. The Chancellor had seen him now. She stuttered, and then stopped. The bodyguard was stepping forward, hand raised. The Chancellor smiled. She waved the bodyguard away. The press cameras were clicking like crazy. Didn't they realise something was wrong? The Chancellor was beckoning Amin forward. All Philipp could hear was the blood pounding in his brain.

'Stop!' he tried to shout, but the word got stuck in his throat and he was left gasping. Why wasn't anyone doing anything? Couldn't they see what was happening?

Time seemed to come to a halt, and Philipp saw with horror a vision of the teddy bear, blackened and horribly dismembered, lying on the floor in the aftermath of a terrific explosion.

The man with the beard had something in his hands. A device. He was pressing a button...

There was no time for anything else. Philipp reached out, took hold of one the last remaining vol-au-vents, and flung it as hard as he could at the stage.

The Chancellor was bending down to take the teddy bear from Amin when Philipp's flying canapé struck her on the side of the face. It exploded on impact. The pastry disintegrated, leaving her cheek splattered with a thick, dark, meaty ragout.

At once, all hell broke loose. Someone in the crowd screamed. The bodyguard threw himself at the Chancellor, knocking her to the floor. Security guards came sprinting from all directions, colliding with guests who were running for the doors. The Museum Director was shouting instructions, inaudible in the cacophony. The last thing Philipp saw before powerful arms took hold of him and bundled him away was Amin standing there on the stage, terrified and alone, the still point of the turning world, clutching the as-yet-unexploded teddy in his arms.

TWENTY-TWO

Under interrogation

Darkness. Moaning. A slammed door. Footsteps echoing down a corridor.

It took Philipp a while to realise that the moaning was coming from him. 'Let me go. You don't understand. They're trying to kill the Chancellor!'

'Shut it, will you!' came a voice from outside the room. It wasn't a room, it was a cell. There was a grille in the door, and through it you could hear everything that was going on in the other cells. He wasn't going to get a wink of sleep tonight.

They'd brought him to the Sachsenhausen police station in Frankfurt, he remembered now. He'd been questioned by two police officers, one male and one female, both of them burly, neither of them possessing any airs or graces.

He'd told them everything he knew. Or nearly everything. He held back only the bits they didn't need to know. The bits about the lorry, and Nadja being suspended, and how she'd carried on investigating anyway. They didn't need to know any of that.

They kept wanting him to go over and over it, about what happened at the Museum. He had the impression they didn't believe a word of it.

'I keep telling you,' he said. 'The kid had a teddy bear full of explosives. There was a guy at the back with a beard, he was about to set the thing off. We were all going to be blown to smithereens. I keep telling you.'

'And this guy with the beard, you remember anything else about him?'

'Not really. I only saw him for an instant.'

'What about the boy? You say his name was Amin. You don't happen to know if he has any other names?'

'I told you, no. He comes from the Middle East somewhere. He doesn't speak any German.'

'What's his relation to this guy with the beard?'

'I've no idea.'

'You ever seen him with this teddy before?'

'No.'

'How d'you know it was full of explosives?'

'The guy had a detonator. What else would it be for?'

'So naturally you thought, I'll chuck this canapé, start a good old food fight, that'll do the trick. Be a hero for the day. That your thinking?'

Round and round again in his head, over and over, ceaselessly. It didn't help that the bunk was so narrow and uncomfortable. That alone would keep him awake.

Gradually his mental soundtrack of the interview began to fade, only to be replaced by a jagged score of other worries. What had happened to Amin? Had they arrested him too, or had he got away? What was the man with the beard planning to do next? Would he strike again? And if so, what would his next target be?

What haunted Philipp was the look he'd seen in Amin's eyes. A look of pure terror. How much did the boy know about what he was being made to do? Had he seen through the lies he'd been told?

At the back of it all lay the sickening thought that the child had been brought all this way, stowed in the back of a lorry, with only one purpose in mind: to carry out this mindless atrocity. One man had already died in the process. Collateral damage. How many more did they intend to slaughter?

The cops thought he was insane, of course. A lunatic. In their wisdom, they'd gone and locked up the whistleblower. He began to appreciate what someone feels when they've been put away for a crime they didn't commit. It made him want to shout and scream, to rattle the bars of his cage.

But that would only be playing to their expectations.

Best just to wait until morning. And keep playing that tape, over and over again.

Then, in the morning, the same questions, only different people asking them.

'What made you think the teddy bear contained explosives? Can you explain this to me?'

'The guy had a detonator. I saw him pull it out. He was about to use it.'

'What did it look like, this detonator?'

Philipp thought about it for a moment. His mind was bleary. He hadn't had his coffee yet. 'It was black. Rectangular. About the size of a mobile phone.'

The officer smiled. 'So, pretty much exactly like a phone, would you say?'

'I couldn't see it clearly. It looked like a detonator.'

'Herr von Werthern, it looked like a phone. Those were your very words.' The two of them locked eyes. 'The way I see it, this guy was getting his phone out to take a picture of his kid standing up there with the Chancellor. Who wouldn't want a picture like that?' The officer left what he must have thought was a meaningful pause. 'Let's face it, Herr von Werthern, you made an error of judgment here.'

Philipp looked down at his hands resting on the interview table. He could see the point the officer was trying to make. He did have a point. He wasn't entirely stupid. He was no Hannes Schnied, this one. But still, he wasn't in possession of all of the facts. If he knew what Philipp knew...

'Either this was a serious misjudgement of the situation, or you went there with a plan to assault the Chancellor. Which is it? What protest group do you belong to?'

'I don't belong to any protest group. I'm telling you what I saw.'

He rocked back in his chair and looked up at the ceiling. 'Maybe it *was* a phone. So what? You can use a phone as a detonator. I'm sure you can.'

The officer stood up and exchanged places with the other officer. There was a long pause as the second officer shuffled some papers on the table. Then she looked up at Philipp.

'It's your lucky day, Herr von Werthern. The Chancellor has decided she doesn't want to press charges. I've no idea why. Maybe she likes a good vol-au-vent in the face.'

There was a chuckle from the first officer at the back of the room.

'As it is, you're free to go.'

Philipp stepped out through the glass doors of the police station, into the bright morning sunlight. It was cold. He was wearing his catering clothes. No coat or woolly jumper. The apron and his phone were in a tatty plastic bag at his side. His first thought was, coffee.

His second thought was, what are all those journalists doing here?

There was a sudden scuffle on the pavement as they grappled for the best position. The flash of a dozen different cameras.

'Herr von Werthern, look this way! Give us a smile!'

'What made you do it, Philipp?'

'Do you have a personal grievance?'

'Was it an anti-immigration protest?'

'Do you have any political allegiances?'

'Can you tell us, what was in that vol-au-vent?'

Microphones were being thrust into his face. A barrage of requests from all directions. Philipp put his arm up to shield himself and stumbled backwards on the steps.

'Back off! All of you! Get back down those steps!'

The voice came from just behind him. He felt a firm hand on

his shoulder, stopping him from falling over.

'No further questions today. Off you go, all of you.'

The pack retreated down the steps, allowing Philipp to regain his balance. He turned to see who'd come to his rescue. It was a uniformed police officer. A woman.

He blinked in disbelief.

'Nadja? What are you…'

'Get moving,' she hissed. 'That way. Left, then left again. My bike is parked round the back.'

Philipp put his head down and did as he was told. As he hurried round the corner of the building, he heard her issuing more threats, telling them she'd have their press passes torn up unless they dispersed at once.

The Yamaha was there, just as she'd said.

A moment later she was there too, getting helmets and jackets out of the tail box.

'How did you…?'

'Shut up,' she said. 'Put these on. We'll talk later.'

Philipp nodded. The jacket was too tight, but it didn't matter a bit. He climbed on behind her and they swept out into the traffic along Kennedyallee, leaving bewildered journalists in their wake.

They pulled in at a petrol station on the edge of town so that Nadja could refuel, and Philipp went in to buy coffees.

He watched her through the window, standing there with the pump in her hand. You could hardly tell she was a police officer. She'd taken off her helmet, and her long dark hair fluttered in the breeze. Sitting behind her, racing through the streets of Frankfurt, his arms thrown around her, he'd had the same feeling as when he'd first ridden pillion on a motorcycle, back when he was a boy. The wind in his face, the thrill of moving at speed over the cold hard tarmac. The scent of Nadja's shampoo lingered in his nostrils, along with the reek of petrol and leather.

She joined him inside so they could drink their coffees in the warm.

'Just so I know, Philipp,' she said, 'Do you have a thing about throwing food at famous people? Or is it at the Chancellor in particular?'

Was she joking? He couldn't tell. 'First time,' he said. 'Never chucked a vol-au-vent at anyone before.'

'I did wonder.'

'How did you know about it, anyway?'

'Philipp, everyone knows.' She laughed and got her phone out to show him. She scrolled through her newsfeed: picture after picture of the Chancellor raising her hands to her face, her mouth wide open in shock, her cheek splattered with sticky ragout. One or two were of him, taken in the immediate aftermath, though he was barely recognisable. His name was in some of the headlines. The police must have released his details.

'People are cruel,' she said, showing him one image of Angela Merkel that had been photoshopped into a near replica of Edvard Munch's *The Scream*.

He asked her how she'd come to be there when he'd been released. It turned out she had a contact at the Sachsenhausen police station, someone she'd worked with at the Downtown Station over the river before she'd got her transfer to the Hofheim Police Force. It was easy enough to get the information she needed. They didn't know she'd been suspended.

'You don't have to tell me if you don't want to,' she said.

'Tell you what?'

'Well… why?'

Philipp looked at her, confused. 'You don't know? It wasn't in the news?'

Nadja shrugged. 'They said you were a loony. An opportunist. That you were acting alone.'

'Acting alone!' So that was the line they were spinning. A blatant lie. 'Nadja, he was there!'

She looked blankly at him. 'Who was?'

'Amin. The boy. He was there in the Museum.' She was gaping at him. 'He was going to assassinate the Chancellor.'

Nadja dropped her coffee. It exploded on the floor.

TWENTY-THREE

In the picture

'Are you sure it was him?'

'Yes. Absolutely. I saw him clear as day. It was definitely Amin.'

'Then he must be in one of these photos somewhere.'

They'd driven back to Philipp's house. He and Nadja had gone straight down to the basement office to look at the newsfeeds on his computer. There were plenty of close-ups of the Chancellor's stricken face, and one or two blurry shots of Philipp in his catering apron. But nothing much of anyone else.

'He was standing just there, to the left of the Chancellor. Look, that's a bit of the teddy bear, see? They must have cropped him out.'

He flicked through dozens more, without luck. There just wasn't enough interest in the boy with the teddy, it seemed. He'd vanished from the record.

'Wait,' said Nadja. 'Go back. Wasn't that a wide shot of the stage?'

It was a photograph taken just before the canapé incident, the first in a series of images showing the action unfolding, and the only one that wasn't a close-up of the Chancellor.

'Yes, there he is, look,' Philipp said, pointing to a slender figure, out of focus at the edge of the shot. 'That's him.'

Amin's face in the picture was hidden behind the huge teddy bear he was holding, but it was definitely him. He was wearing that baggy green knitted jumper and was climbing the steps up to the stage.

'It could be him,' said Nadja, sounding rather too doubtful for Philipp's liking.

'Trust me, that's him. Now what we need is a photo of the other guy, the one with the beard. He was standing at the back with the detonator.'

They flicked through more and more images, until they came to the end.

'No such luck,' said Nadja. 'Seems like nobody was interested in taking shots of the back of the crowd.'

'Is there any video footage, maybe?'

There wasn't. Only a few gifs of the Chancellor in shock, with mindless captions such as *Not another four years!* and *Leader of the Pie World*.

'You'll just have to trust me,' Philipp said. 'It was him alright, and the teddy was obviously packed with explosives.'

He reached across his desk for the tin of Haribo Colafläschchen that he kept for emergencies. He was suddenly feeling immensely tired, and the small, chewy Cola-bottle sweets were exactly what he needed. Suspense always lowered his blood sugar levels. He offered them to Nadja. 'They're for the kids really, you know, but…'

Nadja took a handful of the Cola bottles and tossed two of them at once into her mouth. Philipp liked to 'open' them first by biting off the bottleneck, and only then putting the rest of the bottle onto his tongue.

'How do you think they got a bomb inside the building?' said Nadja, chewing away. 'You said there was heavy security.'

'Yes, but I don't expect they'd check inside a teddy bear. That's probably why they brought Amin all the way here in the first place. They needed someone beyond suspicion. All part of the plan.'

Nadja knocked back another couple of Cola bottles. 'If you're right, then we're dealing with a fully-fledged terrorist cell. One with the capacity to plan and carry out an attack like this.'

'Also, they still have that teddy bear,' Philipp said. 'Do you think they'll go to ground and wait for this all to blow over? Or do they go and use it somewhere else, now that it's primed and ready?'

'What would you do?'

Philipp didn't have to think about it. 'I'd use it straight away. The first opportunity. They can't be sure that the police aren't onto them. For all they know, the cops are out there, searching high and low. They're likely to move fast.'

'Right. And you wouldn't want a load of homemade explosives lying around the place, would you? They could go off by accident.'

'Also, they've got to use Amin now. They can't keep him waiting forever. Not now that he knows what's going on.'

'Why do you think he knows?'

'I could see it in his eyes. He was terrified.'

Nadja stopped chewing for a moment. She swallowed.

'Then it looks like we'd better get out there and find him,' she said. 'And we can't count on any help from our friends in Frankfurt. Not from what you're saying.'

Philipp shook his head. 'They're convinced it was a political stunt. Or else that I'm just a nutter. They couldn't be less interested in a plot to assassinate the Chancellor. They weren't even willing to consider it.'

'So we're on our own. Unless…' She hesitated. There was a moment of awkwardness. She reached for another Cola bottle, and then stopped herself.

'Help yourself,' said Philipp, pushing the tin over to her. 'And no, I didn't go to the police station, if that's what you're thinking.' He glanced at her. 'I was going to, but the thought of Hannes Schnied… I just couldn't do it.'

He saw a smile break out on her face. She grabbed another handful of Cola bottles.

An hour later they were leaving the house, heading into town to meet a man named Jens Martler.

Jens was a police sketch artist, a good one according to Nadja. They'd get him to do a sketch of Amin, and then put posters up all over town. They would offer a reward for information, any information at all. Someone must have seen him somewhere.

Jens had agreed to meet them at the Galileo, a restaurant in the centre of town. They had to eat, they couldn't survive on Cola bottles alone. And there was no time to waste. They could get the sketch done and eat ravioli at the same time.

Describing Amin was harder than Philipp had expected it to be. The image he had in his head kept morphing and transforming, until he wondered if he was making it up from scratch. Nadja had her own impressions of Amin too, and they seemed to differ from Philipp's in important respects.

'The chin was narrower, I think,' she said.

'Rounder,' said Philipp. 'With dimples when he smiled.'

'His eyes were a little further apart, maybe.'

'They were closer together. And green. Pistachio green.'

'Were they? I thought they were blue.'

They showed Jens the photograph of Amin climbing onto the stage at the Museum, but since his face was obscured, it was very little help. All it gave them was the green woolly jumper.

Tactfully and with great skill, Jens steered a path between their differing accounts, and something very like Amin began to appear – as if by magic – on the page before them. Philipp, tucking into his ravioli, was startled by the likeness, and had to put his fork down for a moment.

'Are you okay?' asked Nadja, putting a hand on his arm.

Philipp nodded. He couldn't speak.

As soon as they'd finished their lunch, they took the sketch back to Philipp's office and used it to put together a missing person poster.

'What shall we put as the reward?' asked Philipp.

'Just leave it unspecified,' Nadja said. 'We can bung them a twenty euro note, maybe fifty if it leads to something. And put your phone number on it, we can't use mine.'

They printed out two hundred copies, and then set out once again. This time they went in Philipp's MG, a low-slung, sporty convertible that he'd brought back from one of his trips to the UK. It was his pride and joy, a dashing little motor in British racing green with only minor defects. He enjoyed driving it, particularly as the steering wheel was on the other side of the vehicle, and it made people stop and look. As soon as he started the engine, there was an almighty rattling sound that didn't bode well. Nadja looked at him in alarm.

'Don't worry,' he shouted over the noise. 'It drives like a dream.'

Their first stop was the animal hospital to pick up Maschka.

As soon as he set eyes on her, he realised how much he'd been missing her. She wagged her tail at him and snuffled at his hand. She'd made a full recovery, the vet said, and the pups inside her were doing well. A good sleep and some hearty meals were really all she'd needed.

She did seem slightly more rounded than before, Philipp thought, and she moved about in a more tentative, considered way. It gave her a distinctly regal air, as if she knew she was the focus of everyone's attention, and for good reason. She seemed pleased to see Nadja too, and when they went back to the car, she jumped in and settled herself in the footwell between Nadja's feet.

Before they set off again, Philipp unclipped the MG's hood and folded it back behind the seats.

'What on earth are you doing?' said Nadja. 'It's December! Are you trying to freeze us to death?'

'It's only a short drive,' said Philipp. 'You'll see.'

This time when Philipp started the car up, the engine's unholy racket was almost unbearable. Driving down the Zeilsheimer Road, the wind made Nadja's eyes stream, and her hair flew out behind her like a thick black cape. The noise made it impossible to talk, which was probably just as well.

They were heading for the newer estates on the outskirts of Hofheim, which was where they'd decided to start their postering campaign. In Nadja's view, if you wanted to keep a foreign boy hidden for a period of time, this was probably where you'd do it, in one of the high-rises where there were lots of immigrant families and short-term tenants. Philipp agreed, it made sense.

As they pulled up, the MG issued another series of cacophonous bangs and wallops, followed by some rattling hiccups, which immediately attracted the attention of several groups of children and teenagers who were out cycling the pavements or leaning against the concrete bollards.

Soon the car was surrounded by a dozen or more curious youngsters, eager to know what was wrong with the engine, and why the steering wheel was on the wrong side, and what they were doing driving around without a roof on. They were delighted when they saw there was also a dog!

Philipp fished out the posters and showed them all the picture of Amin. Nobody seemed to recognise him, but they did say they'd be happy to put the posters up. Quickly, he organised them into groups of two or three, and gave each group a handful of posters and a small roll of sticky tape. Soon they'd dispersed around the area and were busy sticking the posters to every available surface. Only one little girl remained behind, besotted with Maschka and tenderly stroking her head.

Nadja turned to Philipp. 'I suppose that's one way to get the job done. You think they'll do it properly?'

'Of course they will,' said Philipp. 'Kids love to help. Take a look.'

Already the neighbourhood looked like it had been freshly wallpapered. There wasn't a single lamppost or road sign that didn't have a poster stuck to it.

'We'd never have done it so quickly on our own,' he said.

He started the engine again and they drove on, leaving the little girl standing on the kerb, waving at Maschka.

TWENTY-FOUR

Waiting for a call

Once the posters had all been distributed, they went back to Philipp's house to consider their next move.

'There's no use us going out looking for him,' Nadja said. 'They'll have gone to ground for the time being. Especially if they think we're after them.'

'And now they know we are,' said Philipp. 'Those posters are everywhere.'

There wasn't much more they could do, not until someone rang with information. They'd have to sit and wait, or come up with another plan.

Maschka was just settling down for a nice afternoon nap on the sofa when Philipp sprang to his feet.

'What day is it?' he cried.

'It's Saturday. Why?'

'Saturday! Good heavens!' Maschka looked up at him with a weary expression. 'That means they're all arriving tomorrow!'

He explained to Nadja that his entire extended family was coming to celebrate Heiligabend. As well as the traditional festivities on Christmas Eve, they would all be staying on for a few nights. This year, in addition to his four adult children and their partners, six grandchildren and two ex-wives, there would be Annelie and Emma too. And of course his housemate Michi, back from Lanzarote. That made twenty altogether. And they couldn't be expected to go without eating, not at Christmas!

'Metro is closed on Sundays. I'm sorry, Nadja, I'll have to go and do the food shopping right away.'

Metro was the big out-of-town wholesalers where Philipp did all his bulk food shopping. It was considerably cheaper than the supermarkets, and you could also get some unusual items there that he liked to have tucked away for special occasions. It was just annoying that, like most other shops, it wasn't open on Sundays.

'Would it help if I came too?' said Nadja. 'That way, if we do get a call about Amin, we can react straight away.'

'Excellent idea,' said Philipp, secretly pleased that she'd suggested it.

They decided to go in his VW Transporter, which was the most spacious vehicle in his fleet – except for his removals lorry, which just wasn't practical for a trip to the shops. The T4 Transporter had originally served as an ambulance in Wolfsburg back in the 1990s, and it still drew admiring glances from passers-by. It also had the capacity for this kind of all-in shopping trip.

They decided to leave Nadja's motorbike behind so that they could discuss plans side by side in the van while en route. Maschka settled herself once again in front of the passenger seat at Nadja's feet.

'By the way,' he said as they pulled out onto the A66 towards Mainz, 'You haven't told me, what are your plans for Christmas?'

'Oh,' she said airily, 'I haven't really decided yet.'

He glanced at her. 'You don't have family?' He realised he didn't actually know the first thing about her private life. He didn't even know where she lived.

'I might spend it with my mum, I don't know. She and I aren't getting on well at the moment. It's been difficult since I left my partner recently. I think she saw him as the son she always wanted.'

Philipp nodded. So, she'd split up from her partner. That made sense. It was probably why she'd had a spare motorcycle helmet and jacket lying around. 'I'm sorry to hear that,' he said.

'I haven't been a great daughter to her anyway. I don't know, maybe it's best if she and I have our own Christmases this year. Go our separate ways. She can invite Sven round and have the

Christmas she always wanted.'

Philipp laughed. 'I'm sure she wants to spend it with you really. It's family time, isn't it, Christmas?'

Nadja shrugged and said nothing.

'Well, if you really don't have anywhere to go, you're welcome to come to mine.'

'Philipp, you already have twenty people coming!'

'Exactly. What does it matter if there's one more?' He smiled at her. 'No really, you'd be very welcome.'

There was a pause as Philipp negotiated a roundabout.

'I think I'll have a nice quiet time on my own,' she said.

'Of course. If that's what you want.'

The shop was busy, everyone making their last-minute purchases, stocking up on Lebkuchen, Glühwein, beer and chocolate treats.

Nadja steered the massive, sprung-platform trolley up and down the aisles in her police uniform with her leather jacket over the top, trying to avoid smashing into anyone's ankles or toppling the Christmas displays, while Philipp lugged heavy items into it. Crates of mineral water, Fanta and Coca-Cola. Gallons of milk. Huge rounds of cheese. Cold meats. Fish. Frozen peas. A twenty-kilo sack of rice and several enormous bags of pasta.

'Are you sure this will get you through?' she said with a smile.

'I don't want to run short. You just never know who might drop by.'

He placed a small bag of Brussels sprouts on the very top.

'If you're thinking of me, I'm not so keen on sprouts.'

'Nor me! But one of my daughters loves them, so we have to get them or she'll feel Christmas isn't being done properly.'

The sweets aisle was last, and Philipp somehow found room in the creaking trolley for some large tins of Saure Zungen, Fruchtgummi and Haribo Frogs. Nadja chucked in another tin of Colafläschchen to round things off.

The queues at the checkout were predictably long and slow-moving.

'Have we had any responses to the poster yet?' Nadja asked.

Philipp checked his phone. His heart sank. 'None at all.'

They waited in the queue, feeling dejected.

'Do you think we've been targeting the wrong areas?' he said. 'Maybe we need to look further afield.'

'I don't know how we'd do that,' she said. 'Unless we go through the usual police channels. If we did, we could maybe get something out on local news. But with it being so close to Christmas, they're unlikely to give a story like this much exposure.'

They shuffled forward with the trolley. The checkout was still a considerable distance away.

'I've been thinking,' Philipp said. 'If you were going to make a bomb, how would you go about it?'

'I'd look it up on the internet, like anything else. Making bombs is easy these days. Practically child's play. You can order everything you need from an online chemist, no ID needed.'

'Okay. But say you wanted to do a trial run, test out a small bit of explosive – you wouldn't do that in a built-up area, would you? Not in a high-rise anyway. You'd want somewhere isolated, where it would go unnoticed.'

'Uh-huh. Where are you thinking?'

'I don't know. Somewhere like the old Krebsmühle building. Do you know it? The derelict mill out towards Lorsbach. I often pass there and think what a great place it is. I could store all my cars in there under one roof. It's enormous. And nobody ever goes near it since it's way out of town.'

'I know the place you mean. But it's not somewhere you'd want to stay in for long, is it? It's cold and draughty. It'll be freezing this time of year.'

'Yes, but it would be fine if you just wanted to do a few tests without anyone noticing.'

'There must be hundreds of places like that though. I wouldn't know where to start.'

'We could start with the Krebsmühle.'

Nadja was silent for a moment. 'I don't know, Philipp. It's all the way over the other side of town.'

'We could drive there in twenty minutes, no problem.'

'Fine. But we don't have any backup. It's just you and me. I don't even have my firearm.'

'You don't?'

'It's in my desk drawer, back in the police station.'

They fell silent and shuffled forward a little more. At this rate, they might not even reach the checkout before Christmas.

Philipp's phone rang as they were loading the shopping into the back of the Transporter.

'Aren't you going to answer it?' said Nadja.

It was an unknown caller. He put the phone to his ear.

'Hello?'

A man's voice came over the crackly line. 'Hello? Is that Herr von Werthern?' The voice was weak and uncertain. He sounded elderly. 'I'm ringing about the poster.'

Philipp signalled to Nadja and switched the call to speaker. 'Go on,' he said.

'Yes. It looks like that boy you're after is foreign, am I right? From the Middle East or somewhere like that?'

Philipp didn't like his tone at all, but he urged him to continue.

'Well, I haven't seen him. But I thought you might be interested to know...' The line went crackly for a moment.

'Yes?' said Philipp.

'I thought you might like to know, there's a lot of that sort around here, where I live. You know the sort I mean? Dark skin. Funny beards. Women all wearing headscarves. That's the sort I mean.'

Philipp was losing his patience. 'Have you noticed anything unusual in the last day or so? Any comings and goings, say, from one particular location?'

'Not really, no. I just thought I ought to let you know. We never used to get that sort round Hofheim, but now they're almost everywhere. Here in the Kapellenberg, even. And the shops are full of foreign things too. It's not right, if you ask me.'

Philipp rolled his eyes. The Kapellenberg! No wonder. That was one of the poshest parts of Hofheim. It must be a shock to them up there, to see someone who didn't fit in. 'Well, thank you for letting me know. You've been most helpful.'

He shook his head as he hung up. 'Some old chap from the Kapellenberg. Very concerned about all the foreigners.'

'I'm afraid that's what you always get. At least he didn't ask for the reward.'

'I hung up before he could.'

'What now? Shall we go back and unload the shopping?'

Philipp felt crestfallen. All that hard work with the posters, only for this.

'Yes. And let's check out the Krebsmühle on the way,' he said. 'At least we'll be doing something.'

TWENTY-FIVE

The darkness deepens

Dusk was beginning to set in as they took the road out through the woods towards Lorsbach. It was already dark under the bare boughs of the trees on either side of them.

Philipp pulled in at the rusting Krebsmühle sign. The track dipped through an archway under the railway line and then opened out into a large, gravelled area, long since colonised by weeds. The dilapidated mill buildings lay scattered about like they were waiting for some final, irrevocable collapse.

'Have you actually been inside any of these buildings?' asked Nadja.

'No. But I've always wanted to.'

'Maybe we should come back when it's light,' she said, looking around apprehensively. 'This place gives me the creeps.'

'We're here now,' Philipp said. 'And I've got a torch, look.'

He waggled a mini flashlight attached to his keyring. It was about the size of his little finger.

'I just have a feeling we shouldn't do this without backup,' she said.

'I could give Hannes Schnied a call, if you think he'll be any help?'

She gave him a stern look.

'No, I didn't think so,' he said. 'Look, you can see there's no one else here. And anyway, we've got Maschka to protect us if somebody comes.' He looked down at Maschka, sitting in the footwell at Nadja's feet. 'You'll chase them off, won't you, girl?' Maschka thumped her tail a couple of times.

'I doubt it,' said Nadja. 'Not with nine pups in her.'

'What's the nasty police lady saying, Maschka!' He gave the dog's head a good scratch. 'Come on. Let's take a look around, before it gets any darker.'

They left Maschka in the van and went over towards the biggest of the buildings. It looked like it must have been the warehouse. From where they were standing, the roof seemed to be intact, though there was no obvious way in, not from this side. The windows high above them were all boarded up. They walked to the end of the building, towards a row of pine trees that stood like sentinels in the gloom.

'There's a door here, look,' Philipp said, pointing to a darker rectangle in the wall.

It was made of heavy-duty metal, but it was unlocked and gave way reluctantly on rusty hinges. Philipp pushed it open as far as it would go and squeezed his way through.

He found himself in a narrow, windowless corridor that led to another door at the far end, right at the limit of his torchlight. He turned to help Nadja through the doorway.

Once they were both inside, she got out her phone and used the torch function for some additional light. There was dust and debris all over the floor. On the wall hung a noticeboard with a single, curling poster: *Safety Procedures*. The rest of it was blotched with damp and completely illegible.

'That's a pity,' chuckled Philipp. 'How are we supposed to stay safe now?'

Nadja turned away and he saw her put her hand to the empty holster on her belt.

'We'll be fine,' he said, giving her shoulder a gentle squeeze. He could feel the tension in her.

They crept down the corridor, shining their lights on the uneven floor. They had to step over some boxes and an overturned chair.

'What are we even looking for?' Nadja whispered.

'I just want to see what's on the other side of that door.' Philipp was whispering now too, though he didn't know why. They were free to make as much noise as they liked.

They reached the door at the end of the passageway, and Philipp tried the handle. It was locked.

'Oh well,' said Nadja.

'Wait. Let me try this.' Philipp reached into his pocket and took out a set of spindly keys on a chain, holding them up to the light.

'What are those? Skeleton keys?'

'You could call them that, I suppose.' He tried them in the door, one after another, feeling carefully for the point of contact. 'When I worked in the hotel business, we called them "master keys". They'd get you into any of the rooms. I held on to them after the hotel switched to electronic keycards. They come in useful sometimes, just so long as the lock's old and not too rusty.'

There was a click. Philipp withdrew the key and opened the door a crack.

'Philipp,' said Nadja, 'You really are quite something.'

'Just lucky, really. Come on, let's take a look.'

He pushed open the door and they went through into a large, hangar-like space, far bigger than their torches could illuminate. A pale grey light filtered through some holes in the roof high above, but it didn't seem to reach all the way down to ground level. As they walked out across the dusty floor, he felt like they were deep-sea divers walking on the seabed, looking up at the light on the surface of the sea.

'Amazing,' said Philipp. 'Just think how many cars you could store in here.'

'Yes, just think,' said Nadja, without much enthusiasm.

They flashed their lights around the space. There was a rickety metal staircase over to one side that must have served some purpose, but now just stopped in mid-air about twenty feet off the ground. The shadow it cast on the wall looked just like a hangman's gibbet.

As they made their way forward, stepping cautiously around

piles of rubble and rusty lengths of pipe, their shoes crunched on a thick carpet of pigeon droppings. There was a smell of dampness and decay, and something else… disappointment?

'Doesn't look like anyone's been here in a while,' said Nadja. 'Apart from the pigeons. And they're busy dropping bombs, but not the ones we're after.'

Philipp went on ahead and shone his torch up against a set of huge metal doors at the far end of the building.

'If these open up, this is where you'd get in and out,' he said. 'Must be where they reversed the lorries up.'

The doors were mounted on enormous iron hinges. They seemed to be rust-free, but there was no obvious latch or lever. He gave the doors a tentative push. No, they were firmly secured on the outside.

He turned back. Nadja was over by the side wall, casting her light over the ground.

'Have you found something?'

'I don't know,' she said. 'Come and look.'

As he made his way over, Philipp's torch began to flicker. He knocked it against his palm, and it went out. 'Batteries gone.' He took out his phone and used that instead.

Nadja was crouching on the floor, looking at some tracks in the dust. 'It does look like someone was here. There are several sets of footprints, coming and going.'

'Where do they lead to?'

'The storage bins there, look.'

Fastened to the wall was a row of large metal containers, big enough for the two of them to hide in, and each with a lid that could be secured with a latch. Most of the latches were broken off. One of them was still there, and it was fastened with a shiny new padlock.

'That's odd,' said Philipp. 'Why use a padlock in a place like this? It's a bit of a giveaway.'

'It's probably to keep out any nosy kids who hang out in here.'

'Well, it's not even doing that,' said Philipp, giving the padlock a tug. It fell open. 'It wasn't locked.'

'Sloppy.'

'Yes, or they left in a hurry.'

'Well, aren't you going to have a look inside?'

Philipp put his hand on the latch. Something was holding him back. The last time he'd opened a locked container, he'd got more than he'd bargained for. He shuddered. The metal was cold in his hand. He flipped it up and raised the lid.

The container was empty. Or nearly so. The bottom was lined with a sheet of plastic, presumably to keep the contents dry and clean. But whatever had been in there, it was gone now.

Nadja shone the light from her phone down inside the container. There was something caught on a ridge in the plastic sheet. A light dusting of something like flour, which gleamed in the light. She licked her finger and dipped it in the powder, then put it to her nostrils.

'What do you think it is?' said Philipp.

Nadja rubbed the tip of her finger against her gums. She grimaced.

'Yep. Cocaine.'

They looked at each other in the light from their phones.

'So, what do we do now?' said Philipp.

'Well, I suppose we should take some photos for the Feds. And maybe they'd appreciate it if we took a sample too.'

'In this, maybe?' Philipp took a doggie poop bag from his pocket and handed it to Nadja.

'Perfect.'

While she transferred some of the white powder to the evidence bag, he had a quick look in the other containers, just in case. There was a dead pigeon inside one. How on earth had it had got in there? He closed the lid again.

'Can we get out of here now?' said Nadja. 'I don't think there's anything left to see.'

'Of course.'

Philipp felt dejected again. They'd come here looking for

Amin and found only cocaine. The whole thing was a waste of time.

Since they couldn't get out through the big metal doors, they went back to the one they'd opened earlier with the skeleton key. It had closed behind them.

'Did you lock this after we came through?' Nadja asked, trying the handle.

'No. Won't it open?'

Philipp got out his set of keys again. He knew which one should open the lock, but this time it didn't.

'It's not locked,' he said. 'The handle's stuck, that's all. It won't budge. There's something blocking it on the other side.'

'Blocking it? How could there be?'

Philipp stepped back from the door. He turned to Nadja. Was she thinking the same thing? She must be. *Someone had blocked the door.*

As quietly as he could, he put his ear to the door and listened. There was nothing. No sound at all from the other side.

Turning to Nadja, he signalled that they should cross quietly to the other door, and as quickly as they could. If someone was trying to trap them inside, they had to find another way out, fast.

It was perilous, running through the darkness, trying to avoid the scattered debris, skidding on the pigeon mess. Nadja, who was much fitter than he was, reached the other side first. She put her hands against the great metal doors and shoved hard. They creaked but held fast.

'Let's do this together,' she said.

They both took a run at the door, timing it as best they could in the darkness. Philipp hit the metal hard with his shoulder. He felt a crack, and then a shattering pain that shot through his shoulder and neck, and right down his back. He shouted out in pain and collapsed onto his knees on the hard ground.

'Philipp! What's happened?'

He grimaced. There was a searing, white-hot pain in his left shoulder, and his arm was hanging limp at his side. He tried to cradle it with his other one. The pain was getting worse. He was worried he might even black out. He'd dropped his phone on the floor. The light was still on, piercing the darkness in front of him.

'You've put your shoulder out. I can see what you've done.'

Philipp whimpered. It was impossible to speak with the pain shooting through him.

'Lie down,' said Nadja. 'Lie down on the floor.'

'Nnngghhhh!'

'You've dislocated it. Do what I say.'

He flopped over onto his right side, protecting his left arm, and managed to roll onto his back. He could feel his mobile phone underneath him now, in the small of his back. How had he managed that?

'We've got to do this quickly, and the pain will stop. Are you ready?'

'NNNGHHHHHYYYESSS!!'

She took hold of his injured arm and, with her foot braced against the side of his body, gave it a savage downward tug.

Something shifted inside of him. There was a dull, gristly pop, and the pain leapt in intensity.

Then everything went from dark to absolute black.

TWENTY-SIX

Caught in a trap

The next thing Philipp knew, a bright light was shining down into his eyes.

He screwed them shut. There was a nagging pain in his left shoulder, and something digging into his back. He was lying on the cold ground. Where was he?

He opened his eyes again. There was a shape hanging over him. A face. He couldn't see who it was.

'Can you hear me?'

That voice. Nadja's. Oh no, he was back at the Krebsmühle. He hadn't gone anywhere.

'Nnngghhhh!'

'Come on now, don't make such a fuss. You'll be fine. I've popped your shoulder back in. If we'd waited any longer, it would have been even more painful.'

'Mmmmmaarggghhh!'

'I've no idea what you're saying. Come on, why don't you try to sit up?'

She helped him into a sitting position, using his good arm. It was his phone he'd been lying on, he realised. The light from it, uncovered now, gave the scene an eerie glow.

'That's better. We'll get you up in a moment, and then we'll find a way out of here.'

He blinked. His head was groggy. He wanted to lie down again.

'Oh no you don't,' she said. 'Come on, up on your feet.'

As she helped him slowly up, the world began to spin and he had to reach out and put his hand on the metal door for support.

'That's it. Now. We're going to try walking.'

He shuffled forward, one step, two… and then she put a hand on his chest and shushed him.

They listened.

From the other side of the door came the sound of shoes treading on gravel. Someone had approached the door. They waited, holding their breath, hoping their lights couldn't be seen under the door. Philipp didn't think they could, but silently he turned his off, and Nadja did the same.

It must be dark out there now, he thought. He thought about Maschka, waiting in the van. Waiting there in the dark. Would she remember what had happened the last time she'd got out of a car with a stranger? Poor Maschka. He hoped she was okay. He hoped she'd stayed in the van.

The footsteps had come to a halt on the other side of the door. Whoever it was, they were only a step away, separated by a few millimetres of bare steel. Were they going to unlock the door and come in? Or were they standing guard, waiting for others to arrive? The possibilities all flickered through his mind. Why had he been so foolish, insisting they come in here to investigate? Now they'd got themselves caught up with a drug gang as well as a trafficking one! They were making enemies on every side, and they couldn't even count on the police to protect them.

They waited in the darkness, listening for any further sound. For a long while there was nothing. Philipp thought he heard the rasp of a lighter. He thought he heard an intake of breath, like someone taking a drag on a cigarette. He might have imagined it. It might only be the echo of something he'd seen in a movie.

He felt Nadja reach out and take his hand. He felt the squeeze of her fingers, the pinch of her fingernails in his palm. He gave her hand a squeeze in return, hoping she'd understand. He was sorry. He'd got her into this. It was all his fault.

Just then there was the sound of footsteps again. Going away this time. Quieter and quieter on the gravel, until they were gone.

Had they gone for good, he wondered, or were they circling

the building, keeping watch? Philipp turned his phone light on again. He met Nadja's darting eyes.

'We can't just wait here for them to go,' he said, keeping his voice as low as he could. 'There must be another way out.'

'Where? We've tried both doors.'

He shone his phone up at the windows, twenty feet above their heads. If they could move that metal staircase over to the wall, maybe they could climb up? But what then? The windows were all boarded up. Even if they could remove the boards, there was a drop of twenty feet on the other side. And he was in no shape for climbing.

He turned to Nadja. 'As far as we know, there's only one of them out there. For now, at least. If we act fast, we can get someone here before more of them arrive.'

'Who though?'

His mind raced through the options. There were the lads in his removals team, they would probably come out without asking too many questions. But it was the weekend before Christmas, they were most likely just sitting down to dinner with their families. And none of them lived nearby.

There was Annelie. She was only round the corner in Langenhain. But he couldn't ask her, it was out of the question. He just couldn't get her involved in a situation like this.

What about Nadja's ex? He probably wasn't an option. It sounded like they weren't even on speaking terms anymore.

They could simply make an emergency call to the police, perhaps. It's what any normal person would do if they found themself in danger. It was bound to get back to Schnied in the end, but what did that matter now?

'Nadja, we have to call the police. It's the only thing we can do.'

'No. Absolutely not. Anything but that.'

'I don't see any other possibility.'

'But don't you see? We've come so close. If we call them now, I lose my job, and we still haven't got Amin.'

He was about to say that, in his view, they were further than they'd ever been from finding Amin… when his phone began to ring. The sound of it was clamorous in the silent building. Panicking that it could be heard outside, he answered it.

'Philipp?' It was Annelie's voice. 'Are you at home? I'll drop Emma over in a few minutes. Is that alright?'

'Annelie? Can you hear me?' Philipp tried to keep his voice as low as possible.

'Yes. Where are you?'

'I'm out. I'm not at home. Sorry.'

'Well, when will you be back?' He winced at the impatience in her voice.

'Difficult to say.'

'What do you mean? Are you in Hofheim at least? I need you to have Emma, like we agreed.'

Philipp glanced at Nadja. She didn't react.

'We've got a bit of a situation here, I'm afraid,' he said into the phone.

He'd never been able to keep anything from Annelie. Quickly, he told her where he was, and that he was stuck there for the time being.

'You're at the Krebsmühle? I'll be there in five minutes.'

'No, Annelie. Absolutely not.'

'I'm on my way.'

'Wait. There's something else I need to tell you…'

But his phone had gone dead. Had she hung up? No, it was his battery. It had gone now on his phone too.

They listened for any sounds outside. It was silent. Was there someone out there, waiting? Impossible to tell.

What would Annelie do when she arrived? She'd see the van. She might even see Maschka inside. Perhaps she'd let her out – he'd left it unlocked, as he always did. Would Maschka find her way into the building?

The thing that worried Philipp most of all was the thought that Annelie was bringing Emma with her. Bringing her into danger.

'Give me your phone,' he said to Nadja.

'Why?'

'I'm calling the police.'

'No.'

'I'm calling them, Nadja. We have to.'

'There's no point. They won't get here in time. She'll be here well before them.'

'What if someone's out there?'

'There's no one out there. They're long gone.'

'You don't know that. They could be lying in wait.'

'Why would they do that, Philipp? If they wanted to shoot us, they'd just come in here and do it.'

Philipp fell silent. There was no budging her, it seemed. It was her career above everything else. How did she know there wasn't someone out there, waiting for reinforcements?

He couldn't go on just standing there. He'd go and wait by the other door – the one they'd come through earlier. He started shuffling forward in the dark, feeling his way carefully with his feet, nursing his sore left arm as he went. It was painfully slow without the light from his phone. Nadja stayed where she was, at the other end of the building. From time to time a pigeon flapped its wings in the rafters overhead.

He groped for the door handle and eventually his fingers found it. It still wouldn't turn. He listened. Silence. If someone came, how would he know if it was Annelie, and not a man with a gun?

Another minute passed. He thought he heard tyres crunching on the gravel. Nothing happened. He'd probably imagined it. The pain in his shoulder was growing worse again.

Suddenly, from the end of the corridor on the other side of the door, there was the sound of a bark.

'Maschka!' he called. 'Here girl!' He knocked on the door, then listened again.

'Philipp?' Annelie's voice, through the door.

'In here!' he called.

There were footsteps down the corridor.

'Someone's jammed a chair under the door handle,' said Annelie, much nearer now.

'Can you unjam it?'

There was a scraping sound, and then the handle moved – and the door opened.

'Papa!' came Emma's voice, jubilantly. She was bouncing on Annelie's hip.

Philipp threw himself on them both, and put his good arm round Annelie, and gave them both a kiss. Maschka jumped up, whipping her tail, and making little joyful whimpering noises.

'What are you doing in there in the dark, all on your own?' Annelie said.

'I'm not on my own. Nadja's here too.'

They turned and looked into the cavernous interior. A solitary light was picking its way through the darkness towards them.

'Nadja? Who's Nadja?'

The light had almost reached them now. Nadja's face appeared out of the shadows, eyes downcast.

'The police sergeant?' said Annelie. She looked from Nadja to Philipp, astonished.

'Can we just get in the car?' he said. 'I'll tell you everything then.'

TWENTY-SEVEN

What kind of world?

'And this person outside,' said Annelie, 'You didn't get a look at them?'

'Not a peep,' said Nadja. 'Worse luck.'

They were all back at Philipp's house now, sitting around his kitchen table, drinking cups of tea and eating Butterkringel biscuits while Emma played with Maschka in the dog basket in the corridor. Philipp had insisted that Nadja come in for tea since she'd driven the van back for him, his arm not being up to the job. Annelie had found a pot of Ringelblumensalbe in Philipp's bathroom cabinet and had made him strip off his jumper and shirt, right there in front of Nadja, so that she could rub it into his sore shoulder. 'It'll do you good,' she promised, making no concession for how painful it was, nor how embarrassing he found it to be tended to like this, half-naked in his own kitchen. 'Be brave now, Philipp,' she said as he yelped in pain. 'It won't take long, and it'll ease the swelling.'

'Whoever it was out there,' Nadja went on, 'They must have been there at the Krebsmühle already, or we'd have heard them arrive.'

'But there were no other vehicles outside when we got there,' said Philipp.

'They could have parked out of sight,' said Nadja. 'I'm guessing they heard us turn up and had to leave in a hurry. It would explain why they left the padlock undone. They must have gone out through the doors at the front just as we were coming in at the other end. Then they went round the outside and blocked the door behind us.'

'Why would they do that?' said Annelie.

'They didn't want us running out and catching them red-handed,' said Nadja. 'And they probably needed to buy themselves some time while they loaded the stash into their vehicle.'

Philipp shuddered at the thought of how close they'd come to an even worse confrontation.

Annelie must have felt the shiver go down his spine, because she stopped rubbing his shoulder. 'I think you're crazy going in there, just the two of you. Why didn't you wait for backup?'

Philipp looked over at Nadja. She said nothing, just took a long drink from her mug.

'We didn't know about the drugs,' he said. 'We just went there looking for Amin.'

'You've got your own children to look after, Philipp. Before you go rescuing other people's.'

'But Amin doesn't have anyone looking out for him,' he said, reaching for his shirt. 'And what kind of world would this be if we stood by and did nothing while kids are being trafficked and made to blow themselves up?' He winced as he pushed his arm through his sleeve.

'I'm not saying you should do nothing,' Annelie said. 'But why can't you just let the police handle this? Look at you. That shoulder will be black and blue in the morning. Nadja could have gone in there with one of her colleagues, surely?'

'She couldn't,' Philipp said. 'She's been suspended. We're doing this all on our own.'

Annelie stared at them both from the other side of the table. 'You mean the police don't even know?'

Philipp shook his head. 'We didn't have a choice, Annelie. We're the only ones who know about Amin. It's down to us.'

'You're going to get yourself killed one day, Philipp. Yourself and probably others too.' She sat down and put her head in her hands. 'I should've known. It's always the same with you. One day you'll go too far, and then Emma's going to be left growing up without a father.'

Philipp went to try and comfort her, but she pushed him away. He glanced at Nadja, but she was stony-faced, staring at the floor. He had the feeling she was annoyed with him too.

Just then there was a noise from the corridor, and Maschka put her head around the kitchen door. She had a weary expression on her face, and from each of her ears dangled one of Emma's bright red socks.

A helpless smile spread across Philipp's face. 'Maschka, my girl, what's she done to you?'

There was a mischievous giggle from the corridor, and then in romped Emma, resplendent in her pyjamas with Frau Kaiser's knitted jumper over the top. She seemed delighted with Maschka's new headwear.

'Poor Maschka!' said Philipp. 'Did she have cold ears?'

'Yes! Told ears!' Emma beamed.

She ran over to Philipp and pulled at his shirt until he reached down and lifted her onto his lap with his right arm.

'Biscuit!' she cried, catching sight of the Butterkringel on the table. And before Philipp could do anything about it, she'd helped herself to two of them, straight from the packet.

'Now wait a second,' he said. 'You know the rules, no sugar until you're three years old!' But she'd already managed to shove a significant part of both of them into her mouth, and since he had only one good arm, he was helpless to intervene. 'Oh, go on then!' he said, giving in and taking another biscuit for himself.

Annelie, who was smiling herself now, stood up from the table. 'I suppose I'd better make something proper to eat,' she said.

'If you don't mind,' said Philipp. 'And I'll get the shopping out of the van.'

'Oh no you don't. You'll sit there and rest that arm.'

'I'll bring the shopping in, if you like,' said Nadja, putting her mug down and getting to her feet. 'I might as well.'

'Okay,' said Philipp. 'But then you must stay and eat with us.'

Nadja shrugged. She looked at Annelie.

'Of course,' said Annelie. 'You must.'

So Nadja went out to get the shopping while Annelie put a saucepan of water on the hob to boil. Philipp sat there with Emma on his lap, watching the hustle and bustle going on around him. 'Bravo, Emma,' he whispered in her ear. 'You and Maschka saved the day again. It was getting quite bad-tempered in here.'

Her bare little feet felt cold to the touch, and he rubbed them with his one good hand.

As they were finishing dinner, Emma began to look sleepy. She wriggled in her high-chair and pushed the last few bits of her pasta around in her bowl.

'I'd better get her back home,' said Annelie.

'I thought she was staying with me tonight?'

'She might as well come back with me. You're no good with only one arm, you'll barely be able to get her undressed.'

'I'm sure we'll manage,' he said.

'Let me take her. I'm coming back tomorrow anyway.'

Philipp thanked her. That was fine. Privately he thought it was because she hadn't had time to pack Emma's overnight bag. It didn't matter, he had plenty to do in any case. There were still all the beds to prepare in readiness for the family's arrival tomorrow. How was he going to manage that with his bad arm? He had no idea.

Emma was already asleep as Annelie strapped her into the car seat in the corridor.

'See you tomorrow,' he said, giving them both a kiss.

'Get some rest,' said Annelie. 'I don't want to be doing all the cooking over Christmas!'

'You won't be. I've got plenty of helpers.'

'Yes, well. Just make sure you don't make your injury worse and end up in the hospital!'

He waved her off. As he went back down the corridor, he

suddenly felt very tired. She was right, he needed to rest.

In the kitchen, Nadja had started doing the washing up. He grabbed a tea towel. Clearing up after a meal wasn't always his strictest priority, but it seemed like the right thing to do. Besides, it was an opportunity to address any grievances without having to look at each other at the same time.

'I probably shouldn't have told Annelie about your suspension. I'm sorry.'

'I thought we were keeping it between ourselves.'

'Yes.'

'Philipp, if all this gets out, I'm done for.'

'I know.'

'And I don't fancy your chances of finding Amin with Hannes Schnied on your back. He'll do everything he can to stop you, you know he will.' She handed him a dripping colander.

'I suppose he will, yes.'

'I didn't think you'd blurt it out like that.'

'Nadja, you don't have to worry about Annelie. She won't tell a soul. She knows how it is with Schnied and that lot, believe me. She lost a toe due to them.'

'I thought that was due to you.'

'There are differences of opinion about it.' He smiled ruefully, and tried to turn the colander over to dry the inside of it. It was proving tricky to hold it and dry it at the same time.

Nadja stacked the last saucepan on the drying rack and drained the sink.

'She's family to me,' he said. 'I can't not tell her things. That's how it is in my family.'

'Really? It's not like that in mine. We don't tell each other anything.'

'That must be difficult for you.'

'Not at all. It works just fine.' She watched him struggling with the colander. 'Why don't you let me do that? Go and sit down.'

He gave in and did as he was told.

'I feel useless,' he said. 'And I've still got all the beds to make up before tomorrow.'

'I'll give you a hand. Where does this thing live?' She waved the colander at him.

Philipp looked at her with gratitude, and not inconsiderable affection. They were like a couple who'd skipped the first flush of love and gone straight to the bickering. Right now, they were at the point where they had a decision to make: they could kiss and make up, or sue for divorce. Metaphorically speaking, of course.

Philipp led the way up the creaking staircase to the first floor. The bed linen was all in the blue cupboard on the landing, and he even needed her help to get it down off the shelf. There were some old mattresses up in the attic, and she managed to lug them down without any assistance from him.

'They just go on the floor in here,' he said, showing her into Youssef's old room.

Very soon they'd created a nice-looking camp on the floor, big enough for four people to sleep on. Philipp shook the feathers out of some old pillowcases and Nadja buttoned the duvet covers. They repeated the trick in two other rooms, and then Philipp went round all the beds, placing little chocolates on each of the pillows.

'There. We're all set.'

'I don't know how you do it, your whole family under one roof,' Nadja said. 'I've only got my mum, and that's difficult enough.'

'I couldn't imagine Christmas without them all,' he said.

'Seriously? Your ex-wives? Annelie? Everyone's children? Doesn't it get a little… awkward?'

'Not in the slightest,' he laughed. 'With a bit more room, we'd have the grandparents too.'

She smiled at him and shook her head.

He went over to close the shutters. He stood there for a moment, looking out at the Zeilsheimer Road. 'Nadja, do you think it might be time to talk to Rabbinger now? It's all become too big for us to handle, hasn't it?'

There was no sound from behind him. He turned to check if she'd left the room. She hadn't. She was standing there, looking at the wall.

'We're no closer to finding Amin,' he said. 'And now there's drugs involved too. I just don't think we can keep going with this on our own.'

Nadja turned to face him. She looked shattered.

'If we'd found him, Philipp... If we'd found Amin. If we'd been able to hand him over and say, "Look! We've solved this! We've made everything okay!" Then I could have done it. Then I could have gone to Rabbinger and said, "Give me my job back".' She looked at him. There were tears in her eyes. 'Now? We have nothing. Nothing at all.'

As she began to cry, he went across the room to her and put his good arm around her shoulders. She rested her head against him and sobbed.

It was a long time before either of them could say anything.

'Why don't we sleep on it,' he said, once the tears had dried up. 'We'll decide what to do in the morning.'

'What time are your family coming?'

'Oh, they'll be arriving all through the day. But don't worry, they'll understand if I have one or two little things to do. They're used to that.'

He offered her one of the beds if she wanted to sleep over, but she said she needed to get home. She was still in the uniform she'd put on to collect him that morning from the police station in Frankfurt.

'Was that this morning?' he said. 'It doesn't seem possible.'

'We still had some hope then, didn't we?'

He went with her to the front door. As she went down the front steps to the roadside, he thought she seemed smaller somehow. Not quite so solid. Even with her helmet and leather jacket on, she looked unprotected. Vulnerable. He wanted to call her back into the house.

She got on the bike and drove away. He closed the door.

TWENTY-EIGHT
Missing at Christmas

Philipp was restless. He paced the living room, turning things over in his head. Nadja. Amin. Annelie. Emma. All of them going round and round like some demented Christmas carousel. An hour ago he'd felt exhausted and ready to drop, but now sleep was a distant hope, an impossible dream. He was full of an anxious, irritable energy that wouldn't let him rest.

Maschka was watching him with a wary expression, resting her muzzle on her paws.

His thoughts kept coming back to Nadja, and the aspects of her that didn't quite fit together. Her single-mindedness about her job, and yet her reckless disregard for following orders. How capable she'd been when he'd dislocated his shoulder, and yet how fearful when she took hold of his hand in the darkness of the Krebsmühle. And then the look in her eyes when he'd been talking about his Christmas plans – how lonely she'd seemed, and forlorn. It must be a difficult time for her, spending Christmas all by herself after her recent break-up. But then, would she be any happier at his house, amongst all of his family? The thought seemed to terrify her. He didn't want to press her on it, she might get the wrong idea.

He felt relieved that they hadn't parted on bad terms after all. But he also had a nagging sense that the biggest obstacle in their search for Amin was her refusal to involve the police. He was feeling more strongly than ever that they'd have made better progress were it not for her stubbornness about telling her superiors. Why could she not accept that at some point she'd have to come clean? If they had all the resources of the Police

Force at their disposal, there was no telling what might happen. Maybe she'd have a change of heart in the morning? And if not, he could take things into his own hands and go to the police station himself.

Nadja was a brilliant police officer, no doubt about it. But she was blind to anybody's interests except her own. She would only do things her own way, whatever the cost to everyone else. A little voice in his head told him that, in this respect, she wasn't so very different from him...

Come on, Philipp, when have you ever done anything except exactly what you wanted? Let's face it, all those cars, all those children... all those women!

But I've loved them all! Every single one of them!

The cars, yes, you've certainly loved all the cars.

No, I mean the children. And yes, the women!

But most of all, yourself.

That was unfair. He *had* always loved them, all of them. Still did. And he loved Amin too. He'd loved him from the moment he'd found him out there in the lorry. He loved him now, wherever he was. He couldn't rest until he was found.

Yes, tomorrow he was going to have to bury the hatchet with Schnied. He would call a Christmas truce. He'd go to the police station and have a little talk with him, man to man.

He walked several more times up and down the room. Maschka raised an eyebrow at him, gave an exasperated snuffle, and settled down to sleep.

It was no good, he wasn't going to be able to do likewise. He may as well go down to his office and get some work done. He'd neglected a good number of his clients over the last few days. He certainly had plenty to do.

He gave Maschka's ears an affectionate tousle and plodded down the stairs to the basement. He turned on the TV, just to have something on in the background while he was working, and emptied a big packet of Erdnussflips into a bowl. They were delicious, like peanutty Wotsits. He could work his way through a whole packet of them, no trouble at all.

Waiting for his laptop to start up, his eye was caught by one of the missing person posters still sitting in the printer's out-tray. Amin's haunted face. And that was all it took – every thought of work went out of the window. He logged into Facebook and started posting messages on all the local groups of which he was a member. *Can you help? Have you seen this boy?* He posted a copy of the drawing they'd used on the poster. *Missing at Christmas. Help reunite him with his family.* That's right, tug on their heartstrings. Cast the net as wide as possible. The image and the words began to swim in front of his eyes, and his head sank slowly towards the desk…

He woke with a start. He sat up. He was suddenly fully awake.

Had it happened again? No. This time there'd not been any noise to wake him. No echo sounded in his head.

And yet something had changed. The world was different now, or he was looking at it in a different way. He didn't know what, exactly. The TV was still on, the light from it flickering in the glass panel of the door. He could see his own face reflected there too, pale and distorted, his hair standing on end.

He realised suddenly what the difference was. The whirligig in his head had stopped. Instead of a ceaseless reel of disconnected images, there was now only one.

Strange, though. It was hard to make sense of it. There was a group of old ladies, sitting at a table in a café. Knitting little woollen bags and stuffing them with lavender.

The knitting circle. Frau Kaiser's 'Stitch and Bitch' Club! Why had that come back to him now? He could hear their needles clacking away, the continual chatter of their voices and the tinkle of their laughter. He could feel Emma's coarse woollen jumper on his arm as she drank the milk from the bottle. He could even smell the lavender, and that other smell – or was it the same smell? It had reminded him of hashish. It was drifting over to him now from their table…

No wait, it *was* hashish! He hadn't thought it possible when he'd smelled it in the café. He'd dismissed it out of hand. But it came back to him now with the force of a revelation. He *knew* it was hashish!

His mind was racing. What if those little bags the old ladies were knitting contained something more than lavender? If the lavender was only there as a cover, to disguise the smell of hashish?

It was absurd. It just wasn't possible. Those little old ladies, pushing drugs?

No, that couldn't be right. But what if someone was hoodwinking them? Getting them to do the dirty work, without the old dears even realising it? It would be the perfect disguise, a nice little innocent bag of lavender, ideal at Christmas time – and of course a variety of alternative options for other times of the year. A stroke of genius! Who'd take a second look? He'd not even done so himself. And Hannes Schnied would never stoop to investigate an item of knitwear – not even if it was shaped like a balaclava and being used to rob a bank.

Was he losing his mind? He thought perhaps he was. But things that had seemed unconnected were now sliding into some sort of pattern. It was like he was looking at a large pinboard in his head, and everything joined together with pieces of brightly coloured thread. That green woollen jumper Amin had been wearing at the Museum, the one that was far too big for him... it wasn't so very different from the one Frau Kaiser had knitted for Emma. Was it fanciful to think they were connected? He'd known Frau Kaiser for years and felt a good deal of affection for her, but it was perfectly possible someone was taking advantage of her. She was certainly rather fragile and other-worldly. And wasn't she always going on about doing things for the church? Perhaps, if she thought it was for a good cause, she'd willingly help sew little packages of hashish into lavender sacks.

His hand went to his shirt pocket, and he fished out the evidence bag with its tiny deposit of white powder that Nadja had said was cocaine. What if it didn't stop at hashish? What if the 'Stitch and Bitch' Club was busy packaging up doses of ecstasy, cocaine, crystal meth? Where would it end? Heroin? Once you'd found a way to evade the police, why limit yourself? A local drug-pushing empire, hidden behind a group of sweet little old ladies with a passion for knitting, right here in Hofheim…

It was ridiculous. But now that he'd thought it, he couldn't stop thinking it.

And there was that phone call he'd received while he and Nadja were at Metro doing the shopping. The elderly man who'd seen a few foreigners hanging about the place and was convinced the area was under invasion. Where did he say he lived? The Kapellenberg, that was it. What did that have to do with anything?

He reached for his box of index cards, the ones he used for storing all his clients' details. It was an old-fashioned method, but it never let him down. He riffled through it, looking for one particular card. Some had coffee rings on them, and some were so faded with age they'd become illegible. But not this one. This one was clear and perfectly legible. It had been written with a ballpoint pen that hadn't faded. It was Frau Kaiser's address.

There it was. Another connection. She lived in a nice big house in the Kapellenberg.

He must tell Nadja right away. At least she'd be able to tell him if he was going mad. He reached for his phone, and then remembered it was out of battery. Damn. He plugged it in. What a nuisance.

He glanced at the clock. It was well after two in the morning. Still, he had to go now. If Frau Kaiser was being held captive by a gang of human-trafficking drug pushers, there was no time to lose. He could have a snoop around in the dark without anyone noticing, and then go to the police in the morning with the evidence. No one would believe him if he just told them. He had to have proof.

His phone lit up. Four per cent battery. He ought to let it charge a few more minutes before calling Nadja, but he just couldn't wait. He'd text her instead. *Somthing fishy abt Fr Kaiser. Going 2 invesrigate Kapellenbrg. Will report bak asap.* One or two typos. Doesn't matter. Press send.

Climbing the stairs, he realised there was another problem. How was he going to get there? It was too far to walk. Would he be able to drive with his injured shoulder? Perhaps, if he took the Jaguar XJ6 with the automatic transmission. He could probably get away with it. He eased his arm into the sleeve of his coat, gritting his teeth. It took him a while to do it, inch by inch, but it went in eventually. It was all the reassurance he needed. If he could put his coat on, he could certainly drive. And there was no better car for going undercover in the Kapellenberg than a Jaguar XJ6.

He decided not to take Maschka. She needed her sleep, now more than ever. He crept past her in the corridor, jamming on his hat, and went out through the front door.

TWENTY-NINE

No stars in the sky

It took Philipp a little under ten minutes to reach the Kapellenberg in his Jaguar. The night-time streets were deserted. It was a prosperous, sedate neighbourhood on the outskirts of Hofheim, close to the woods where he sometimes went for a Sunday walk. There were plenty of little restaurants and Gasthäuser dotted around, but they were all closed now. It was nearly three o'clock, and a cold, overcast night, not a single star visible in the sky. Everyone was tucked up in bed.

He drove past Frau Kaiser's house and parked a few doors down. The Jaguar, in contrast to the MG, made very little noise. It practically purred. If anything, it seemed to drive itself. His left arm was stiff and a little sore, but it was bearing up fine.

He got out of the car and walked back to the house. In the light from the streetlamps, he could see that it was a large white townhouse, impressively large for a single elderly occupant. There were two little turrets at the front with slate roofs, and even in the dark he could see a trail of something leafy framing the huge, studded oak door. The place certainly had delusions of grandeur. It was like the suburban cousin of a Bavarian castle.

There was a light on in a downstairs window to the left of the door. Just to deter burglars, he thought. He'd discussed Frau Kaiser's security arrangements with her several times, and knew there was no burglar alarm, no guard dog, no decent locks on the windows – nothing to help bring her insurance premiums down. 'Don't worry, Philipp,' she'd said. 'I've got nothing worth stealing.' 'That may be true,' he'd replied, 'But how does the burglar know that?'

He reached for the latch on the wrought-iron gate, and it swung open invitingly. He'd certainly have to have a word with her about this when they next met.

There was a car parked on the drive, which he recognised as the one that had been waiting for her outside his house the last time she'd come visiting. His shoes made a scrunching sound on the gravel, so he veered off onto the lawn and headed towards the side of the house. The grass was crisp with frost beneath his feet. Now he could see another light on at an upstairs windows, one that wasn't visible from the roadside. Interesting. She couldn't be entertaining anyone at this hour, could she? The 'Stitch and Bitch' Club couldn't still be at it. Perhaps Frau Kaiser was a nightbird. He remembered now what Nadja had told him when they'd first met, that she herself had trouble sleeping. She'd mistakenly thought that he was an insomniac too – well, perhaps he was proving her right after all. He wondered if Nadja might still be awake now. Perhaps she'd seen his message and was on her way? So much the better if she was. He considered sending her another message but thought better of it. It was too cold to wait around out here. At the very least he needed some evidence to present to her, a photograph or two to show her in the morning, along with some freshly baked Brötchen for breakfast.

His mouth began to water at the prospect of breakfast, and he pressed on around the side of the house. The only light here was coming from the upstairs window. From this angle, he couldn't see if there was anyone awake inside. There was silence all around him, except for an owl and the wind blowing in the treetops. He had to feel his way carefully along the uneven terrain, not daring to turn on the torchlight on his phone. And anyway he didn't have enough battery for that.

Fleetingly he wondered what he would say if someone – the chauffeur, perhaps – caught him out here, snooping around in the middle of the night. He could hardly say he was sleepwalking, not this far from home. He chuckled at the thought. No, he'd have to come up with something better. Could he say he was carrying out a security appraisal maybe, in his capacity as Frau Kaiser's insurance broker? It would be more convincing if he'd brought a clipboard – he'd have to remember that for next time. He imagined the expression on the chauffeur's face as he sold him that line, and the thought made him chuckle again. *Look at this, I can walk in here like I own the place! Frau Kaiser needs to do something about this, she really does.*

But of course it might not be the chauffeur who accosted him. It might be someone less inclined to ask questions. More inclined to, say, shoot him on sight.

The thought wiped the smile from his face, and as he came to the far corner of the house, he shrank back behind a large evergreen bush from where he could take a good look at the rear of the building. There were no lights on in the windows here, but a single exterior bulb cast a pallid yellow light over the paved terrace, which was raised above the garden by a set of wide stone steps. Three large French windows gave access onto the terrace, but he couldn't see anything at all through them – they were simply black cavities in the house's pale façade. The garden stretched away into the darkness on his left, the shadows broken only by the outlines of a few pine trees and what looked like an outbuilding on the far side of the lawn.

Something light and cold landed on his hand. It felt wet. He looked up and saw in the light of the outside lamp that it had begun to snow. Thick wet flakes were whirling down out of the black vault of the sky. Everything seemed suspended for a moment in some child's vision of Christmas, the snow settling on the black turrets of the house and in the tops of the pine trees. It was beginning to settle even on Philipp's coat and on his clogs. He was glad of his hat. It was, he had to admit, all rather beautiful. Maybe they were in for a white Christmas after all! He thought of the beds lying ready in his house, waiting for his children and his grandchildren to arrive in the morning, and of all the things they'd do together, decorating the tree, going up to the cemetery to place candles on the family graves, handing out presents, and sitting down around the dining table as he brought in one dish after another, all laden with their favourite things. And suddenly he felt it was absurd to be here in Frau Kaiser's garden, lurking behind a bush in the middle of the night. What was he thinking? It was all down to a stupid hunch about an old lady being exploited by a gang of crooks. The whole thing was ludicrous. He'd be better off in bed. He just needed a good sleep.

He took a step out from behind the bush… and stopped.

Over by the outbuilding on the other side of the lawn, there'd been a movement. A door had opened. A light shone out.

He shrank back behind the bush, hoping he hadn't been seen. He peered out through the branches, and saw someone moving across the lawn, from the outbuilding back towards the house. They were wearing thick clothing, and it was hard to tell anything much about them, except that it didn't look like Frau Kaiser. They were too tall and broad-shouldered. If anything, it looked like a man, though he couldn't make out any features. Their back was turned to him now as they went up the steps onto the terrace, and then through one of the French windows, into the house.

Philipp felt his heart beating wildly. Was there a chance he'd been spotted? He didn't think so. The person, whoever it was, hadn't seemed in any hurry. It looked like they were going about some ordinary, routine business that just happened to be in the middle of the night, while it was snowing. He waited for his heartbeat to settle, and watched for any movement inside the house. Nothing. The only thing moving was the snow falling, settling now on the grass. The silence intensified. He thought he could hear his breath forming little ice crystals that tinkled in the air.

So there was a man in Frau Kaiser's house! He was pretty sure it was a man. Perhaps it was only the chauffeur. But what was he doing in that outbuilding, at this time of night?

Philipp knew immediately that he would have to go and see for himself.

He took one more look at the house, checking for any sign of movement at the windows. Nothing at all. They were all as black as the night sky above the wheeling snowflakes.

He stepped out from behind the bush and began to make his way in a wide arc across the lawn, keeping to the shadows beyond the reach of the security light. He felt terribly exposed, and crouched down low as he went, moving as quickly as he could. In the end he broke into a run, risking the loss of his clogs just to reach the safety of the darkness on the far side of the lawn. He stopped to catch his breath at the side of the outbuilding, feeling a sharp pain again in his shoulder. He must have jolted it while he was running.

He put his hand against the wall of the building. It was long and low, about the size and profile of a large greenhouse, but clad in thick, plastic panelling that was fixed to metal struts. There was a low hum coming from inside, like a powerful air conditioning unit. He noticed that the snow wasn't settling on the roof. And in fact the wall did feel slightly warm to the touch. What on earth could they be keeping in there? She hadn't mentioned anything like this when he'd been discussing her insurance with her. He had a brief, flickering vision of shackled prisoners hunched in the dark, and tried to cast it out of his mind.

He felt his way along the wall, towards the end of the building that faced the house, where he'd seen the man emerge from a door. He would have to move quickly once he turned the corner, as he'd be in the full beam of the light, visible to anyone who happened to be looking through a window. It was a risk he'd have to take. He drew a deep breath… and took the plunge.

The door opened as willingly as the gate had. Three seconds and he was inside. He closed it softly behind him.

The humming was much louder inside, and he was bathed in warm air and a pungent smell. It was almost tropical in here, despite the snow falling outside. And there was a dull red glow emanating from some huge lamps hanging from the ceiling. Not quite enough to see by, just enough to make out some huddled forms crouching under the lamps.

'Hello?' he said.

He fumbled for his phone and flicked on the torchlight.

One look, and he almost burst out laughing. There in front of him, in rows running the full length of the building, stood hundreds and hundreds of cannabis plants. And there was that smell again! That sweet, intoxicating smell he'd noticed in Venezia.

So his instincts had been right! Something was going on right here on Frau Kaiser's property. How had they managed to persuade her into this? Did she even know what was going on? It bore all the signs of a sophisticated operation. There was enough cannabis growing in here for... well, he had no idea, but it looked like an awful lot. The little spiky leaves went on and on, row after row, in all stages of development – some barely poking out of their pot, others reaching almost to the level of the lamps suspended above his head. And the smell was so intense, it was making him feel woozy. He wondered if you could get high from the vapours alone. In any case, he didn't have long. He'd just get a couple of photos and then he'd be off. They had enough now to go to the police, and then they could tell them all about Amin. The boy was connected to this somehow, he just knew he was.

He took out his phone and checked for battery. Two per cent. There was a notification too – his message to Nadja hadn't been sent. He tapped resend, and this time it went through, but now the battery was down to one per cent. He should have waited. There was enough maybe for one photo if he was quick. He held the phone up over his head to get in as many of the cannabis plants as possible, and pressed the button. The flash went off and there was a satisfying click. He checked the photo, and as he did so the phone went dead. Never mind, he had what he needed. The clock had said it was twenty past three. Time to get going. On his way to the door, he stopped to tear off one of the cannabis leaves and put it in his pocket, just in case. Belt and braces. You never knew when technology might let you down.

As he slipped silently through the door, the cold night air hit him in the face. The light from the security lamp was right in his eyes, dazzling after the gloom inside, intensified by the snow on the ground.

He felt his hat slip from his head. And then it went dark. No garden. No snow. Just a heavy blackness and the rough sensation of sackcloth wrapped tight around his face.

THIRTY

A big mistake

Philipp was sitting in a rickety chair with his hands tied behind him and a sack over his head, while people seemed to keep popping in from the corridor, and then popping out again.

It felt like there were several people coming and going, though he couldn't be sure. It might just be the one. He could hardly see anything at all through the thick weave of the sack, only that there was a light on in the room. He was shivering, more from the shock of being apprehended and the pain in his left shoulder than from any actual sensation of coldness. He had no idea if it was cold in this room or not. He could only feel pain.

It had probably been a mistake to struggle. He should have bided his time, protested his innocence, and demanded to see Frau Kaiser. But instinctively he'd lashed out at his captor and tried to tear the sacking off his head. It had only led to his arms being pulled roughly behind his back. He'd felt something give again in his injured shoulder, and he'd cried out, but it made no difference. His wrists were bound together, and he was bundled up the steps, into the house.

He'd tried to pay attention to where he was being taken. He knew this was crucial, so that he'd be able to find his way out again if he had the chance. But after the first turn he became disorientated. He was pushed through one door after another, up some stairs and down some corridors. He lost the ability to distinguish left from right, up from down. He didn't even know if it was one pair of hands that had taken hold of him or more.

And then he was shoved into a flimsy chair and left to wait.

From the way it sounded when they came and went, it was a

small room. The door was over to his right, almost within reach. The floor was bare concrete. It was likely to be a basement, he thought, though he couldn't remember coming down any stairs. Perhaps he had. How did anyone without eyesight get around or do anything, he wondered. He'd never really appreciated how difficult it was.

Right now, there didn't seem to be anyone in the room with him. He couldn't be sure. He wasn't going to take any risks, not after what they'd done to his shoulder. It didn't feel quite as bad as it had in the Krebsmühle, but he knew it wasn't good. And Nadja wasn't here if it did need popping back in.

How had he let this happen? He was furious with himself. He should have left when he had the chance, as soon as he'd seen the man go back inside the house. It had been enough to know that someone else was there in Frau Kaiser's house, going about things furtively at night. He could have come back in the morning with Nadja. It was reckless to go rushing in like that. Reckless, and stupid. Annelie's words came back to him now, 'You'll get yourself killed one day.' Perhaps that day had come already.

The silence now was terrible. How long had he been waiting? He was trembling all over, probably from the adrenaline. His mind was playing tricks on him. He had to think straight, work out how to play this. Their first mistake was giving him all this time to plan. Take advantage of it! Think!

But all he could think of was Maschka, asleep in her basket, and the pups inside her, tumbling this way and that, one over the other in a ceaseless hypnotic dance. He might never get to see them now. Nor any of his own children, who'd be waking up soon, starting their journeys, eager to arrive, not knowing the calamity that was about to engulf them.

The door opened again, and someone came in. There was the scrape of another chair on the floor – perhaps they'd brought this one in with them. Maybe all this coming and going was merely a matter of arranging the furniture.

He swallowed hard. 'Now look,' he began. 'There's been some mistake. My name is Philipp von Werthern. I'm Frau Kaiser's insurance broker. She knows exactly who I am. Something urgent has come up, and it's very important that you let me speak to her, right away.'

There was a further silence. Not a flicker from the chair opposite. What now? He'd played his trump card, and it had failed miserably.

There was a movement, he flinched, and then the sacking was lifted from his head. He blinked in the harsh neon light.

When he was able to focus again, he looked at the man sitting in the chair opposite him. He seemed familiar. Broad-shouldered, with dark hair and a beard. Deep-set eyes with a hard glint to them. In his hand was a pistol. It was pointing straight at him.

Philipp swallowed again. His throat was tight. He'd never had a gun pointed at him in his entire life, and he wasn't the sort of private eye who took this in his stride. The room was windowless, he noticed. The walls were dingy. He didn't feel at ease about any of it.

'You're making a mistake,' he said in a trembling voice. 'I came here to speak to Frau Kaiser. Where is she?'

In all the films and TV programmes he'd seen where someone gets taken captive, the most successful strategy always seemed to be to assume authority. To demand answers to questions. It didn't matter how unlikely or unreasonable the questions were, the important thing was to ask them, and to sound like you meant it.

Unfortunately, the words came out of Philipp's mouth in a hoarse croak that carried about as much authority as Kermit the Frog's.

The man stirred. His eyes flickered about. 'Later. Now she is sleeping. We must let her sleep.' He spoke German with a thick accent. The gun was still pointing straight at Philipp's chest.

'And who are you?' said Philipp, trying to inject his voice with disdain. 'You don't live here. Frau Kaiser is the sole registered occupant of this property. I don't know what you think you're doing.'

'You,' said the man, waving his gun about. 'I know who you are. You're the crazy one who threw a pie at the Chancellor.'

Two thoughts went through Philipp's head in quick succession. The first was: in all my obituaries, I shall be known as the man who threw baked goods at the Chancellor.

The second, hard on the heels of the first, was that he knew where he'd seen this man before. Knew it without a doubt. This was the man with the beard that he'd seen at the Museum with Amin. The one standing at the back with the detonator.

He'd been wrong-footed for a moment, and his brain scrambled to seize back the initiative.

'How could you send a poor, innocent boy to his death like that?' He glared at the man. 'Yes, I did throw the pastry. I threw it to prevent you blowing us all sky high. You'd have killed everyone, including Amin. I don't understand people like you. Have you no humanity?'

'Amin? I would not kill Amin. No. Never.' The man was waving the gun around alarmingly. Philipp wished he would put it down.

'But I know exactly what was in the teddy bear,' he said. 'You think I don't? I saw you holding the detonator!'

'Detonator? There was no detonator. It was mobile phone!' The man reached into his pocket and pulled out his phone. 'Here, see? Mobile phone.'

Philipp had to admit, the phone in the man's hand looked a lot like the thing he'd been holding in the Museum. It didn't mean it wasn't a detonator though. Far from it.

'You wanted to attack the Chancellor,' he cried. 'You'd have got away with it too, if I hadn't been there to stop you.'

'No, no. You are wrong. Amin was supposed to give the bear to the Chancellor. A present for her. I take a photo. A nice photo. After that, the photo is in the newspapers, and they will not try to send him back to Syria. Everything okay. Amin can stay here in Germany, have a good life.' The man stood up and started pacing up and down the room. 'Now, not okay. Now, Amin has to stay hidden. All because of you. Because you throw a pie at the Chancellor.'

'But,' cried Philipp, 'But, no! But you snatched him from my car. You kidnapped him!'

The man shook his head. 'Amin is my nephew. My brother's child. He is like a son to me. I look after him, not kidnap him! It is you who kidnap. You take him from the lorry!'

'He nearly died in that lorry! You think that's how you look after a child?'

'There was no other way. His parents are dead. His brothers, sisters, all dead. It was the only way to keep him alive.'

Philipp no longer knew what to say. He didn't know whether to pity the man or fear him. He was beginning to think the best strategy might be to stay silent.

The man had put the gun down on the floor and was scrolling through something on his phone. 'All I wanted was one photo. Amin with the Chancellor, that is all. Then you throw your stupid pie and the photo is *kaputt.*'

He thrust the phone under Philipp's nose. What he saw there made him think that the man might have a point. It would have been a striking image, a small boy giving a huge teddy bear to a beaming Chancellor. A poster boy for asylum seekers. The human face of immigration. But what he'd captured instead was the Chancellor in shock, the canapé splattered all over the side of her face, and a young boy looking absolutely terrified.

'You think you are hero?' said the man, snatching his phone away. 'You are no hero. Not to Amin.'

Philipp hung his head. He was devastated. The idea that what he'd done had changed things for Amin, changed them for the worse, was simply appalling. How could he have been so mistaken?

He looked up at the man. 'If what you say is true, then I'm sorry. I only wanted the best for Amin. I didn't wish him any harm.'

The man looked down at his gun, lying on the floor at his feet. He kicked it over towards the door. Then he turned back to Philipp and raised his hands, palms outwards. It looked like some kind of peace gesture, though Philipp couldn't be sure. Maybe he intended to strangle him.

'Amin speaks about you,' the man said. 'He says you are a good man.'

The words fell on Philipp's ears like the sweetest song ever written. 'Amin? Is he here? How is he?'

'He is fine. Do not worry. He says you looked after him. I am grateful.'

'It was the least I could do.'

'I'm sorry about your dog.'

'So it was you who drugged her?' The anger started boiling up inside him again. He fought against it. 'You nearly killed her.'

'She is good dog. She wanted to stay with Amin. Protect him.'

'Of course. She is fond of the boy.' Philipp felt a little misty-eyed. 'And she's pregnant, you know.'

'Really? I didn't know this.'

'No, well, what you did was…' Philipp felt powerless to express his rage and frustration. He felt exhausted. His shoulder ached.

'I'm sorry,' said the man.

Now the guy was apologising to him. It felt like the world had been tipped on its head. Was this the man who'd locked them in the Krebsmühle? The one who was behind the whole drugs operation? Was he keeping Frau Kaiser captive too? Philipp didn't know what to think.

The man stood up and came over. Philipp watched him warily as he knelt down behind the chair and, quickly and efficiently, untied his wrists. Philipp felt his bonds slip away. He lifted his hands, flexed his fingers. They tingled where the blood came rushing back into them.

He turned to look at the man. 'Will you at least tell me your name?'

'My name is Abdul.'

'Abdul.' Philipp nodded. 'I'm Philipp.'

'Yes. I know this.'

'I thought you were a terrorist, Abdul. The papers are full of these stories. I should have known better, but I was very worried about Amin.'

'I know this too,' Abdul said.

Just then there was a sound outside the door. They both looked round as it opened. There, in an elegant turquoise dressing gown with a peacock feather design, her white hair gleaming in the harsh neon light, stood Frau Kaiser herself.

THIRTY-ONE

A pleasant surprise

Frau Kaiser swept into the room, her peacock dressing gown billowing out behind her. She stepped right over the pistol that was lying on the floor.

'It's you, Philipp! Well, well, what a pleasant surprise.'

He looked up at her, startled. She seemed quite unharmed, and not constrained in any way.

'I see you've met Abdul,' she went on. 'That's good. Saves us the bother of introductions.'

'Frau Kaiser,' Philipp stuttered, struggling to his feet. 'I owe you an explanation. You see, sometimes I like to carry out a little security test, an extra service only for my most valued clients, you understand…'

'Poppycock!' Frau Kaiser interrupted, waving her hand dismissively as if swatting a fly. 'We both know that's not true, Philipp. But never mind. I thought you'd turn up one of these days. And here you are.'

Philipp was taken aback. What had happened to that sweet old lady – the one who took such a kindly interest in his daughter, and who liked nothing better than to sit around in a café all day, knitting and gossiping? There was no sign of her now. The Frau Kaiser who stood before him was formidable. She held herself proud and upright, the folds of her gown shifting and shimmering around her in the doorway. Her hair shone. Her eyes glittered. She owned the room and everything in it. It was hard to imagine her being exploited by anyone. She gave the impression she knew everything that was happening on her property, and that nothing whatsoever took place in any corner of it unless she'd expressly given orders.

'It's rather cramped in here, don't you think?' she said, bending to scoop up the pistol and slipping it into a hidden pocket in her gown. 'Why don't we all go upstairs to the salon? We'll be more comfortable there.'

She didn't wait for a reply. As she turned on the spot, Abdul dashed over to hold the door open for her, and she went out.

Philipp followed her along a corridor and up a spiral ramp – no wonder he hadn't remembered coming down any stairs – which eventually emerged into a large hallway. There in front of him was the other side of the studded oak door he'd seen from the driveway. Frau Kaiser clicked her fingers and Abdul opened a smaller door leading off the hallway. He waited for them both to go through.

The salon, it turned out, was really just a parlour or drawing room, though there were some sizeable paintings on the walls that hinted at an artistic sensibility. The room was too dimly lit for him to be able to make out their subjects. There was a baby grand piano in the far corner. One wall was lined with a walnut bookcase bearing a great many leatherbound tomes. There was a pale blue chaise longue, a Louis XIV armchair in powder pink, and a good deal of chintz.

Philipp became aware that Frau Kaiser was studying him, and he went towards the piano to escape her scrutiny.

'Oh, do you play?' she asked. 'I imagine you do.'

'Not at all,' he said, noticing the music on the stand. Handel's *Messiah*, open at the *Hallelujah* chorus.

'I trained at the Conservatoire in Paris, you know. But all that was a long time ago.' There was a studied wistfulness about how she spoke that made Philipp think this a downright lie. 'Why don't you come and sit down? We have matters to discuss.'

She was lowering herself stiffly into the armchair, so he took the chaise longue.

She beckoned to Abdul. 'We'll have champagne. Make sure to bring the flutes this time.' Abdul nodded and left the room.

Philipp had no great desire to drink champagne at this hour of the morning, and certainly not in Frau Kaiser's company. But she didn't seem inclined to take his wishes into account.

'You're very kind,' he said.

'Well, it's Christmas after all. Let's spoil ourselves.'

He had the impression that she was accustomed to spoiling herself, whatever the season.

'It's so nice of you to drop by, Philipp.' She regarded him with a wry, challenging expression. 'I don't expect you have those documents ready for me to sign?'

'I'm sorry, no.' He'd not given them a moment's thought. 'I'll have them for you first thing after Christmas.'

There was a long and awkward pause while Frau Kaiser continued her scrutiny of him. Finally, Abdul returned with the champagne and set about pouring it into two flutes. He didn't seem at all comfortable with the task, and the silence must have made it no easier. Philipp wondered if he'd been working there as Frau Kaiser's butler for long, or if he was on her books in some other capacity. He came over to Philipp with one of the glasses. It contained very little except bubbles.

'Thank you, Abdul,' said Frau Kaiser. 'Please stay.'

Abdul nodded. He went and stood by the bookcase.

'Now, Philipp. You have questions, I'm sure. About Amin. Is that right?'

She'd caught him off guard yet again. 'Well, yes. Okay. I'd like to know where he is. And if he's all right.'

'He's living here for the time being. With his uncle Abdul. And yes, he's perfectly happy.' She took a sip of her champagne. 'Abdul is his only surviving relative. So naturally I was pleased to be able to reunite them. No small thanks to you, of course.'

'What do you mean?'

'Well, you rescued him from the lorry. You kept him safe. And instead of handing him over to the police, which would have caused a great deal of bother and heartache, you gave him back to us!'

Philipp put his glass down on a side table. 'I did no such thing. You snatched him from my car, and nearly murdered my dog!'

'Yes, we're sorry about the dog, Philipp. Abdul has already apologised to you for that.'

Abdul, still standing in the shadows, cleared his throat, but said nothing. Philipp wondered if Frau Kaiser had been listening at the door throughout their conversation in the basement room. Or perhaps the room had been bugged?

'There's such a lot you don't know, Philipp.' She took another sip of champagne. Her lips were so pale and thin they almost vanished, leaving a blank in the lower half of her face. 'You know about the cannabis, of course. You've seen my little enterprise for yourself.'

'Yes, though I'd hardly describe it as "little".'

She chuckled. 'Well, it's certainly grown over the years. You have no idea, Philipp. The demand is quite extraordinary.' She looked at him with those glittering eyes. 'Or perhaps you do know. You have several children yourself, don't you? Besides Emma, I mean.'

He didn't like to think what she was getting at. He resisted giving her a reply.

'It was my own nephew, in fact, who gave me the idea. I'd been suffering from arthritis for years – you probably noticed it yourself. And nothing the doctors could give me ever really helped. Well, one night, when the whole family were here celebrating my birthday, I came across my nephew smoking a joint in the garden. He was only seventeen at the time. It gave him quite a shock, to be caught red-handed by his fuddy-duddy old aunt. I made him hand it over. I smoked the rest of it in front of him. I tell you, Philipp, it opened my eyes. It's amazing what good, pure marijuana can do for your joints. It was the best birthday present he could have given me!'

She chuckled again and lifted the glass to her lips to drain the last of her champagne.

'It took years off me, that night. I felt young again. Invincible.

The pain fell away. I started going to a Zumba class. Everyone said I looked years younger. Imagine, Philipp, if people knew the truth about it! Everyone would want some. Everyone!'

She held out her empty glass without a word, and Abdul sprang forward to replenish it. He came over to Philipp too and topped his up with more bubbles.

'Well of course, friends started asking questions. Of course they did. They all wanted to know what I was taking. I could hardly refuse. "Love thy neighbour" is what the Lord said, and that's what I did. I gave them a helping hand. That's all I've ever done.'

'I see,' said Philipp. 'And were your friends all suffering from arthritis too?'

Frau Kaiser did that shooing thing again with her hand, swatting flies. 'Oh, you know, the older you get, the more these little niggles keep cropping up. If it's not one thing, it's another. You just wait, Philipp. It comes to us all.' She smiled at him, thinly. 'And anyway, we missed out on the whole hippy experience, didn't we? Or maybe you didn't, I don't know.' She looked at him with a teasing glimmer in her eye.

'From what I could see out there, Frau Kaiser, you're growing more cannabis than you can possibly share out amongst friends.'

'You're right. To begin with, it was whatever my nephew could get hold of through a few contacts of his. Never very satisfactory. The quality was just too variable. I thought, why not grow it yourself? It's not difficult. It's like growing tomatoes. You just need a bit of space in the garden. Some good compost. Protection from the frost. It's all perfectly organic too, of course. And I can harvest it all year round. There's no let-up, even when it's snowing!'

There was a triumphant twinkle now in her eye. Philipp wondered if she was a little tipsy.

'Do you know what the real challenge is? Let me tell you. It's not production. No, no. Production's a doddle. The difficulty lies in distribution. That's the hard nut to crack.'

She tapped the side of her glass, and Abdul came to her assistance once again.

'Distribution is absolutely key.'

'And that's where your "Stitch and Bitch" Club comes in, I imagine.'

She looked a little crestfallen, as if he'd stolen her punchline. But she recovered quickly. 'Precisely. I see we're on the same wavelength. Who would ever suspect some old ladies knitting little bags of lavender? It was my masterstroke, I hope you agree. In fact, I think I can say we've got the whole market very nicely sewn up!'

Philipp watched her giggle gleefully. So, she'd kept a punchline in reserve. He wondered if she'd told this story before, to her lady friends.

'I'd have thought you could do it all online these days, Frau Kaiser. And it would be less risky too. But what do I know?'

'Oh, we are indeed online, Philipp. We move with the times. But at the end of the day, it's little packets pressed into sweaty palms. That's all it is. I'm sorry to be crude.'

'But you haven't got your "Stitch and Bitch" ladies doing drug deals on the streets, have you? I don't imagine that would appeal to them.'

She tittered at the idea. 'Such a wag, Philipp! Of course not. I soon realised what was required. A nice, loyal, discreet workforce. But where could such a thing be found?'

Philipp had a pretty fair idea, but he was beginning to think it wise to let her tell the story in her own way, without interference. He gave her a shrug.

'Oh, Philipp, how disappointing. Well, let me enlighten you.'

She stood up, unexpectedly, and went over to the large bay window, which was behind a pair of heavy, reddish-brown curtains. She drew the curtains aside by pulling on a concealed cord. He could see now that it was still dark outside, and he wondered what the time was. Was it nearly dawn? He glanced at the old-fashioned carriage clock on the mantelpiece, but it didn't appear to have any hands. The room remained as gloomy as before.

'There are many people in the world less fortunate than we are, Philipp. You have only to look out of the window to see them. The poor. The destitute. Those who've lost their way. Those who have ended up far from their homes.'

Philipp looked at the window. There was nothing at all to be seen through it, only their own faces reflected dimly in the glass.

'The Lord spoke to me, Philipp. He said, "Open your house to those in need". And so I did. I opened my house.' She spread her arms wide, like a priest offering a benediction. There was a fierce glow in her eyes. 'As you can see, my house has plenty of rooms. I don't need all of them myself. So I opened the door and I welcomed them in. From Syria. From Iraq. From all kinds of places. Abdul was one of the first. Others followed. None of them pay any rent. They work for me willingly. They're free to go, whenever they like. But where would they go? Back on the street? To their own country? Go if you want, I say to them. Nobody's keeping you here. Please. Leave whenever you like.' She smiled grimly at him. 'Or stay, if you prefer. There's a room for you here. A roof over your head. I ask very little in return. It's all up to you.'

Philipp was shocked at her crazed intensity. His shoulder was throbbing again, and he shifted uncomfortably on the chaise longue.

'What exactly do you ask of them?' he said.

'They help out with the business, of course. On the distribution side mainly, though there's other work they can do if they're inclined. Abdul, for instance, is very useful about the house. Carlos is an experienced driver. There are others who have useful skills. And the business keeps growing. There's such a lot to do. It's an arrangement that benefits everyone, Philipp, I hope you can see that.'

To his alarm, she started back across the room towards him, then veered off unsteadily towards her champagne glass, which she'd left on the armchair. Abdul was inveigled into topping her up again.

'How many people do you have living here?' he asked, trying to keep his voice as neutral as possible.

'There are eight just now,' she said. 'Nine if you include the boy.'

'Nine in this house?'

'Yes, and there's room for plenty more. Most of them live in the basement – I don't know why. They seem to think it's safer down there, that they won't be seen. Well, it's up to them. They could have some of the nice rooms on the upper floors if they wanted. I don't begrudge them that.'

Philipp tried to suppress a shudder. The woman seemed to think she was genuinely their benefactor.

'My business is growing, Philipp. It's growing faster than I could have imagined. Once I'd solved the distribution problem, it was obvious what the next step was. Diversification. Why limit myself to supplying cannabis to old ladies? There's a huge market out there, if you can reach it. And the youngsters want more than plain old garden-variety weed. They have a taste for something stronger. They want choice. And we can give them that. The market is there for the taking.'

'So it's cocaine now too, is it?'

'Yes, you stumbled across that at the Krebsmühle of course. You and that policewoman friend of yours. Nadja Bernstein.'

There was triumph again in her eyes. He remained silent.

'That was a mistake. Our mistake – we had to find a storage facility at short notice. But your mistake too, Philipp. It might have ended badly. You were lucky not to be shot, you and your girlfriend.'

'Why are you keeping me here, Frau Kaiser?'

'What? Keeping you?' She looked appalled. 'My dear Philipp, I'm not keeping you. We're simply having a little drink together. Abdul!' She waved him over, and he came to top up Philipp's glass.

'No more, thank you.'

But Abdul went ahead anyway. The bubbles rose quickly to the rim and overflowed, running down over Philipp's hand.

'We're old friends having a drink on Christmas Eve. What could be nicer!' Abdul returned to his position by the bookcase, taking the empty bottle with him.

'And besides,' she went on. 'You want to know all about Amin, don't you?'

He did, though it didn't seem like he was being given a choice.

'I think you'll find it an interesting story.' She settled herself back in the armchair, her gown falling open a little to reveal the lower part of one leg. 'Until this summer, Abdul's brother – this is Amin's father – was living in Syria with his wife and three children. But life was difficult. They belonged to a Kurdish minority and were being badly persecuted there. He lost his job. He was beaten up. His wife was told that if they didn't leave the country, much worse things would happen. What choice did they have? They left Syria, of course. It was a difficult journey. The risks were very great indeed. They tried to cross to Europe on a boat, but it capsized. No one came to rescue them. Amin was one of the few survivors. The rest of his family drowned. His mother, his father, his two little sisters. He managed to cling to the wreckage of the boat while they all went under the waves. He watched them go. Poor thing, he was in a terrible state. The coast guard found him. He ended up in Greece. He had no papers, of course. Fortunately, Abdul's brother had told him something of his plans, and with my help he was able to locate the boy. We paid someone off. A number of people, in fact. It was all quite costly. It didn't matter, he was family, and we'll do anything for family. We arranged for Amin to be brought here in a lorry. Abdul knew how to make the modifications to the back of the vehicle. He's a highly skilled carpenter, amongst other things. But of course, the lorry never arrived. The driver was incompetent, or a drunkard…'

'I know for a fact it wasn't the driver's fault.'

Frau Kaiser glared at him. It was obvious she hated interruptions.

'That's as may be. It happened outside your house, you know more than I do.' She pulled her gown back over the exposed bit of her leg. 'However it happened, it was unfortunate. The boy was lucky to survive. The police got there before us, so we had to bide our time. It was difficult. Abdul was distraught. And when we eventually got into the back of the lorry, the boy was gone. It was a calamity. Abdul didn't know what to do. He wanted to go to the police, of course, but we couldn't let him do that. A lot was at stake. Not just for him, but for all the others living under my roof. He was very upset, but he understood in the end. I had his best interests at heart. And I took it upon myself to find Amin. He was like family to me too, the dear boy. It wasn't difficult to track him down to your house. I knew if it wasn't you who'd taken him in, you'd at least know something about it. And of course, there he was. I knew perfectly well he wasn't your grandchild, as you pretended. I knew everything, Philipp.'

Philipp bit his lip and allowed her another moment of triumph.

'The rest you know already. We arranged for Amin to be taken off your hands. I hope you didn't mind too much, Philipp. He doesn't belong to you.'

'Nor you, in fact.'

'We're all family here. One big happy family, doing God's will.'

'Frau Kaiser, if you think holding people captive in your house, and using them as labour in your little drugs business, is doing God's will, I think you're very badly mistaken.'

'No, Philipp, it's you who's mistaken!' Her eyes blazed, and she leaned forward in her chair. 'I keep none of the profits. Not a penny. Everything goes to good Christian causes. It is God's work we're doing here. Everything I do is done with His blessing.'

'I'm sorry, Frau Kaiser. I cannot believe that.'

She seemed about to launch herself into another tirade when there was the muffled sound of a commotion from the hallway outside. Philipp heard heavy footsteps, and then sudden scrabbling, and a voice shouted 'No! No!'. It sounded like a boy's voice.

'Amin?' he cried, jumping to his feet.

In a flash, Frau Kaiser had signalled to Abdul, who dashed across the room and slipped out through the door. For the briefest of moments, Philipp heard what sounded like a struggle going on – and then the door was firmly closed, and all fell quiet.

He turned to look at Frau Kaiser. She was holding the pistol in her hand, and it was pointing right at him.

THIRTY-TWO
Abide with me

'Your concern for the boy is endearing, Philipp,' said Frau Kaiser, still pointing the gun at him. 'But it's entirely misplaced. He's among family here – all the family he's got in this world. Where else can he go? If he leaves my house, he'll be taken into care or returned to Syria. And I don't think anyone can truly say which of those two things is the more terrible.'

There was no noise coming from the hallway now. It had fallen silent. If it had been Amin out there, he'd been hauled away somewhere else.

Philipp couldn't bear looking down the barrel of the gun any longer. He turned and looked out of the window. It wasn't yet light, but it wasn't entirely dark either. The silhouettes of some tall pine trees were now visible, a smattering of snow clinging to their outer branches. The road lay just beyond them, and safety.

'I'm afraid I must be going now, Frau Kaiser,' he said as breezily as he could, and started walking towards the door.

'Sit back down!' Her voice was cold and furious. He stopped.

'You're not going to shoot me,' he said. 'Not in here. You'll spoil your carpet.'

'I'm perfectly willing to. The carpet can be replaced.'

He took another step towards the door. Two steps. Three...

The door opened and Abdul walked in. He closed the door softly behind him and stood there, guarding it.

'Why don't you take a seat again, Philipp?' Her voice was lighter now, as if she'd suddenly rediscovered her geniality. 'We've still got things to discuss.'

Philipp turned back. She was smiling at him, the gun in her

hand. He went back to the chaise longue.

'I'm sorry, Philipp. I know it's Christmas, but I can't let you go just yet. I don't want you hurrying off to your precious Nadja Bernstein. You probably think I'm a bit senile, but I promise you I'm not.'

Not senile, Philipp thought. Deluded. Deranged. Absolutely crackers. But not entirely senile, he'd give her that.

'What do you want from me?' he said.

'It's quite simple. I have a business proposition. You've always been an excellent businessman, Philipp. So charming. Such a personal touch. I've appreciated everything you've done for me. Now, since you know so much about my business, why don't you come and work for me?'

'For you, Frau Kaiser? Doing what?'

'You'd look after the books for me. Handle the accounts. I thought I could do it all myself, but it's got too much for me now. I'll admit it, I'm not very good with accounts.'

'You keep accounts?' He couldn't quite believe what he was hearing.

'Of course. It all needs to be recorded. Incomings. Outgoings. It's a considerable amount of work. I have a substantial household now, Philipp. The cost of feeding them, clothing them, getting them medicines when they're ill. All the rest of it. You wouldn't believe how much it costs.'

'But surely you have enough money? You're not even paying them.'

'Oh, I have plenty of money. We're making far more than we spend, of course. But the accounts still need to be kept, or how do I know what's mine and what's God's? We're doing God's work here, Philipp. We must render to God what belongs to Him, right down to the very last penny.'

Now he saw that she was deluding herself. There was a righteous fervour burning deep inside of her, and he knew she wouldn't hesitate to pull the trigger. He looked from Frau Kaiser, sitting in the armchair with the gun, to Abdul standing guard by the door, and weighed up his chances of getting out of the room alive. He didn't fancy the odds.

'It's a kind offer, Frau Kaiser. I'll give it some thought. May I get back to you straight after Christmas?'

'I'm sorry, Philipp. It doesn't work like that. You can't just leave. Think of it like this – you'll be spending Christmas here with your dear friend Amin.' She tilted her head to the side and gave him a smile.

'And if I don't agree?'

'Then Abdul will take you outside and shoot you in the back of the head. And your body will never be found.'

He nodded. 'That's what I thought.'

'There you go,' she said. 'We're on the same wavelength again!'

So much for 'Thou shalt not kill', he thought. It seemed Frau Kaiser's knowledge of the scriptures was partial at best. Perhaps she felt it was okay to kill, so long as someone else did the messy business on her behalf.

He couldn't think what to do. He had to play for time.

'Can I have a moment to think it over?'

'Of course,' she said. 'Take a minute or two. This is an important decision.'

'Thank you. I wonder if I could have some more champagne?'

There was a pause. Would she send Abdul to fetch it? Philipp was counting on it.

'Not now, Philipp,' she said. 'We need a clear head for matters like these.'

Very well. He'd take his chances anyway. He went over to the baby grand. Play for time, play for time. He'd even play the damned piano, if that's what it took. He sat down on the piano stool and put his fingers to the keys. Handel's *Messiah. And He shall reign for ever and ever*. He was willing to bet she'd never been able to play it. He certainly couldn't.

He turned to look out of the window. The light had grown stronger, and he could just about make out the gate he'd come through. It was only twenty yards away. Presumably unlocked still. Twenty yards across the gravel, and a light covering of snow. He put his hand in his pocket, and his fingers brushed his car key. Would he make it to his car in time? He couldn't count on it, but he had to hope. He glanced at the window latch. No good. They'd be on him before he'd ever get it open. And he certainly couldn't leap through solid glass. There must be a better way.

Out of the corner of his eye he checked the sightline. The lid of the baby grand was propped open, blocking Frau Kaiser's shot. There was just a chance…

'Come now, Philipp,' she said from the armchair on the far side of the room. 'Have you made your decision? I do so hope you'll be joining us for Christmas!'

It was now or never. He stood up, grabbed hold of the piano stool, and swung it hard at the window.

Instead of shattering the glass as he'd expected, it bounced off it with a dull thud and landed at his feet. At the same time, he felt a tearing sensation in his left shoulder. He collapsed to the floor in pain. Almost instantly, Abdul's hands took hold of him, and set about tying his wrists behind his back.

With his face pressed firmly into the carpet, he heard Frau Kaiser's voice above him, dripping with venom. 'What a shame. Well, you've made your decision. I should've had you shot at the Krebsmühle. I thought I'd give you a chance to come to your senses, but I see now you're too ignorant for that. Or too obstinate.'

Philipp felt himself being lifted to his feet. The strength of the man! There was no resisting him now. He had the pistol in his hand, anyway. Philipp's shoulder was pulsing painfully. His whole body was shaking. Frau Kaiser had turned away from them, as if the matter was all quite distasteful.

'Take him away,' she hissed.

'Listen,' he said to her back. 'What you're doing here is wrong. You're not helping these people. It's not God's work you're doing. You're nothing but a drug dealer. A criminal. A human trafficker. A slave driver.'

Frau Kaiser kept her back turned. 'I said take him away! Get rid of the body. Make sure of it this time.'

Philipp was half-shoved, half-marched over to the door, and out into the hallway. He considered calling out for Amin, but what good would it do? It would only terrify the boy even further. As Abdul took him to the back of the house, out through the French windows and onto the terrace, down the steps into the garden, he thought of what lay in store for Amin. What a shining future Frau Kaiser had planned for him. Spending the rest of his childhood hidden away underground. Coming out only to help sell drugs on the street corner, or in the playground. With someone like Amin, she'd be able to reach a whole new clientele without raising suspicion. It was all part of the plan, no doubt. The woman was sick and depraved. Clothed in righteousness. He wondered how he'd not seen it before. He'd failed to see a lot of things.

He was shivering helplessly. At least he could put that down to the cold. Abdul had a firm hold of him by the collar, and was walking him briskly through the snow, towards the outbuilding.

It was still fairly dark. The sky was a gun-barrel grey, with a lighter patch creeping up in the east. The snow underfoot seemed to give off its own illumination. He could see the footprints they'd left earlier in the night, leading the other way. There on the ground by the end of the outbuilding lay his hat, crusted with snow. It must have fallen off in the struggle. His old hat. His hat-wearing days were over now.

They were carrying on down the side of the outbuilding, towards the back. Out of sight, presumably. Hidden away.

There was no point appealing to Abdul. He'd gone through worse than this to get where he was. His family had nearly all perished. He'd do Frau Kaiser's bidding, whatever it was. Doing otherwise was too great a risk.

They'd reached the back of the outbuilding. The air pumps were thrumming away. There was a cordon of bare ground around the building where the snow had melted. Inside, the plants were all busy growing. Life carrying on regardless.

Out here, a different story.

Abdul pushed him down onto his knees in the snow. Some words were going round in his head. *As black as ebony, as white as snow, as red as blood.* He heard his mother's voice reading to him, remembered the words of the fairy story, remembered lying in his warm bed, safe and happy. He closed his eyes.

There was a click. He held his breath. A shot rang out, vanquishing the world.

THIRTY-THREE

While mortals sleep

Nadja sat up in bed with a start. Something was wrong.

She looked at her bedside clock. Still only seven o'clock, and more or less dark outside. She'd been awake most of the night, tossing and turning in her bed as usual. She knew the alarm hadn't woken her, as she hadn't even set it. It was Christmas Eve. She had nothing to get up for.

She rolled over and pulled the blankets over her head.

There was a bleep from her mobile phone. If that was Sven again…

She stuck her hand out from under the blankets and groped for the phone. Yes, damn it! Five messages from Sven! That was it, she was going to have to block him. She couldn't have him hounding her like this, night and day. It had to stop.

Wait. There was one from Philipp. What time was that one? Twenty past three! What was he doing texting her at that hour? She sat up and looked at the message.

Somthing fishy abt Fr Kaiser. Going 2 invesrigate Kapellenbrg. Will report bak asap.

Frau Kaiser? Wasn't that the old lady who ran the knitting circle? What had she got to do with anything? And why was Philipp going to investigate an old lady at twenty past three in the morning? Had he gone completely mad?

'Found out anything?' she texted back.

She put the phone down on her bedside table, pulled the blanket over her again, and tried to get back to sleep.

Five minutes later she was fully dressed and climbing onto her motorbike. There'd been no response from Philipp, but she knew she wasn't going to be able to get back to sleep.

THIRTY-FOUR
No chance to say goodbye

So this is what it feels like to be dead.

It had been quick, too quick to feel any pain, and Philipp was grateful for that. All he felt was a great sadness that it had happened just before Christmas. It had come so suddenly he hadn't had a chance to say goodbye. He thought of his children and his grandchildren, all starting their day, all looking forward to what lay ahead. He thought of Emma and Annelie, no doubt up and about long ago. He thought of Maschka too, waking up hungry, not knowing where he was. And Nadja. Had she got his message? Too late, if she had.

He felt a tear streaking down his cheek. Wait a minute... a tear?

He opened his eyes. He was still in Frau Kaiser's garden. There was snow on the ground. He could feel it seeping through his trousers, under his knees. This wasn't at all what he'd been expecting.

He felt a hand on his collar, lifting him to his feet. Abdul's hand.

'I will untie you now,' said Abdul in a low voice. 'And then you must run. Run away. Do not come back.'

Philipp nodded. He didn't seem to be able to form any words.

'You run that way,' he said, pointing away from the house, towards the back of the garden. 'You must not be seen. Understand?'

Philipp nodded again. He felt the rope fall from his wrists. His left arm hung loose at his side, but the other one seemed to be working okay.

'Why?' he croaked, looking into Abdul's deep-set eyes. 'Why didn't you shoot me?'

'For Amin,' he said. 'Now go.'

Philipp didn't wait to be told again. He loped off through the snow, away from the house, keeping to the edge of the garden so he wouldn't be seen from the house. When he reached the stand of pine trees, he turned and looked back. The security light was still on over the terrace, but the windows were all black. Abdul was still there by the outbuilding. He was holding a spade. He waved to Philipp. It was more of a 'Get lost' than a 'Cheerio', but to Philipp it seemed like the sweetest thing he'd ever seen.

He turned and headed deeper into the shadows beneath the trees. There was hardly any snow underfoot here, the branches were so thick overhead. He soon came to a fence. It was sturdily built and about six feet high. Impossible to climb over in his current state. Why had Abdul sent him this way if it was a dead-end? It was too dark to see very much, so he began working his way along the fence, hoping he'd find a way through. It wasn't long before he came to a gate. He tried the latch. The gate sprang open. Bingo! Another security lapse. He wouldn't be having a word with Frau Kaiser about it any time soon.

He found himself at the end of a row of allotments. Nobody working on them, not at this hour, at this time of year. He could see streetlamps lit on the far side, so he headed towards them.

What should he do? Could he go around the block, back to his car? He wasn't sure he was going to be able to drive, even with the Jaguar's automatic transmission. His left arm still hung slack at his side, and he had an awful feeling that his shoulder was out again. He couldn't call anyone since his mobile was dead. Nothing for it, he'd have to go home on foot.

He set off along the road at a brisk trot in the direction of town. His shoulder jarred agonisingly with every stride, and the cold air made his lungs burn and his breath rasp. But he was alive. Gloriously alive.

He emerged onto the main road that headed downhill

towards the centre of town. He could see the onion-domed Catholic church down there, glinting in the early morning light. And the streetlamps along his own street, the Zeilsheimer Road. Everything spread out under a light blanket of snow. What a beautiful Heiligabend it was going to be!

There was the sudden roar of a motorbike approaching from behind. A Yamaha SR400, if he wasn't mistaken. He turned to see Nadja pulling up at the kerbside, lifting the visor of her helmet.

'Philipp?' she shouted.

He smiled at her in grateful disbelief.

'What's happened to you?' she said, dismounting. 'Look at your shoulder. You can't walk around like that! What were you thinking?'

Philipp sat down on the kerbside. In truth, he hadn't been thinking about very much at all.

THIRTY-FIVE

And this shall be the sign

Half an hour later, Philipp and Nadja were sitting side by side on the pavement at the front of Frau Kaiser's house. Nadja had chosen a spot where they could keep an eye on the house without being seen.

Philipp's arm was in a makeshift sling that she'd made with her scarf. He was in considerable pain, but he hadn't blacked out this time, and he'd refused to go home until Frau Kaiser was safely in custody. He wanted to be there when it happened.

Nadja had made some phone calls. Now they just had to wait.

'Why don't you go and sit in your car?' she said. 'You'll be warmer in there, and I can keep watch.'

'I'm fine. It's perfectly warm.'

'You don't feel the cold?'

'Not really. Not with my shoulder like this.'

She smiled at him, not without concern. 'You were crazy to come on your own. Why didn't you call me?'

'I did send you a message.'

'You should have called.'

'I'll know next time. Besides, it was only a hunch.'

'Your hunches are good ones.'

He didn't think there was much truth in that. Mainly he just got lucky.

It was getting lighter now. The streetlamps were still lit, but if anyone was looking their way from the other side of the road, they could be plainly seen.

'Have you made your mind up about Christmas?' he asked.

'What do you mean?'

'You're still very welcome to come to mine. I mean, if you're not going to your mum's, or… whatshisname's.'

'Thank you,' she said. 'I'm definitely not going to whatshisname's. Not a chance.'

He smiled. 'Why don't you come to mine then?'

'I'll think about it.'

He wondered if she would. He hoped so. But of course she had other things on her mind.

'Did they say if you can have your job back?'

'What, Rabbinger? I didn't speak to Rabbinger.'

'Who, then?'

'Who do you think?'

'Was it Schnied himself?'

She nodded.

'What did he say about it?'

'Not much. We didn't really have time to discuss it. And anyway, I'd never tell Schnied anything.'

'I hope you told him to get here soon.'

'Straight away, I said.'

'He's probably just putting the tree up first.'

She laughed. 'It did sound like he was half asleep.'

'Did you tell him there are others being kept in the house? And not to sound the siren when they come?'

'Of course.'

They stopped to listen. From a long way away came the faintest sound of something shrill. It was coming closer and closer, piercing the cold morning air. They could hear it clearly now, a single siren, varying in pitch and intensity as it sped through the snow-laden streets towards them.

'He never listens,' said Nadja.

They remained there, crouched low on the pavement, as the police car drew up, blue lights flashing, siren blaring. Sufficient to wake the dead.

Out of the car stepped Hannes Schnied, his uniform buttoned

tight over his portly frame. He was accompanied by two other officers.

'Is this the house then?' he said, addressing Nadja, doing his best to ignore Philipp.

'That's right,' said Nadja. 'Shame you've given her such a lot of warning.'

Schnied led the two officers through the gate and up the drive. One of them was carrying a small sledgehammer.

'They'll never get through the door with that,' said Philipp. 'It's solid oak.'

'Is there a way round the back?' she asked.

'Follow me.'

While Schnied knocked on the front door, Philipp led Nadja round the side of the building, retracing his steps of the night before. It felt very different in the morning light, and he almost didn't recognise the bush he'd hidden behind at the back of the house.

'What's that noise?' she said.

There was a scraping, digging sound coming from the other side of the lawn, behind the outbuilding. For a moment, he thought it might be the heating system, but it was too irregular for that. Then he remembered Abdul, standing there with the shovel, waving him off. Poor man, he was still hard at it.

'Don't worry about that,' he said. 'It's only someone digging my grave.'

Just then there was another noise, this time from the house itself. It was the sound of one of the French windows being opened. Nadja gasped. Frau Kaiser had stepped out onto the terrace. In one hand she was clutching Amin by the wrist. In the other was a large, serrated knife.

Instantly, Nadja stepped out from behind the bush.

'Drop the knife!' she shouted. 'The house is surrounded.'

Frau Kaiser looked startled, but she quickly regained her composure. She put her arm tight around Amin, holding him close to her body, and pressed the knife to his neck.

'Stay back!' she shouted in a shrill voice. 'Or I'll cut his sweet little head right off his neck!'

Philipp watched from behind the bush, not daring to move in case it made her do something stupid. He could see Amin trying to stay on his feet, unbalanced by her grip. There was terror in his eyes. One slip and the knife would slice through his throat.

Nadja had advanced to the foot of the steps leading up to the terrace. She stopped there and spoke more softly now.

'Don't be foolish, Frau Kaiser. You won't get anywhere by hurting the boy. Let him go, and we'll talk about this.'

'Nadja Bernstein?' said Frau Kaiser. 'I might have known. Well, you're too late to save your beloved Philipp.'

Abdul had appeared around the corner of the outbuilding. He was holding the spade in his hand, and his trouser legs were soaked and spattered with mud.

'Is it done?' Frau Kaiser called to him.

Abdul nodded and threw down the spade.

Frau Kaiser broke out into a hellish, high-pitched laugh. Amin began to sob, his body shaking with fear.

'It's not too late for you though,' said Nadja. 'We can talk about this. Just let the boy go.'

'Poppycock!' said Frau Kaiser. 'You can't trick me like that.'

Philipp couldn't bear it any longer. He stepped out from behind the bush, onto the lawn. Frau Kaiser spotted him straight away. She went rigid. The colour drained from her face.

'It's over,' he shouted. 'Let Amin go.'

She stared at him like he'd risen from the dead. The hand holding the knife began to tremble.

'So they've betrayed me,' she said. 'All of them. That's all the thanks I get.'

There was the sound of running feet along the side of the house, and Hannes Schnied appeared, red in the face, followed by one of the officers. He took a moment to assess the scene, and then fumbled for the gun in his holster.

'Easy now,' called Nadja, holding her palm out towards

Schnied. 'Take it easy.'

Schnied had his gun out and was pointing it at Frau Kaiser. He was twenty-five yards away at least. His hands were shaking.

'Tell him to back off,' shouted Frau Kaiser. 'Or the boy gets it.'

Nadja spoke softly. 'It's no good, Frau Kaiser. He has a clear shot. The boy's just too small for you to hide behind.' She took a step up towards the terrace. 'Why don't we swap me for the boy? That way it's much more difficult for him to get his shot.'

Frau Kaiser looked from Nadja to Schnied, and then back again. She seemed confused. Nadja had taken another step. She was only five yards away now.

'It's an easy shot. He's a good marksman. One of the best. He can take out your left eyebrow. Or your right one. Your shoulder. All the way down your left-hand side. Anywhere he chooses. It would just be target practice for a man like him.' She took the last step up onto the terrace. 'Why don't you let the boy go? Take me instead.'

As Nadja took one more step, Frau Kaiser shoved Amin aside and lunged at her. Philipp couldn't tell if she was going for Nadja with the knife or trying to take her hostage. Either way, Nadja sidestepped the thrust, caught hold of her assailant's wrist, and in one fluid movement slammed her arm down hard onto her knee. The knife fell the floor, and Nadja kicked it away. Frau Kaiser collapsed in a heap. Philipp had never seen anything happen so fast.

As Schnied rushed forward, waving his gun around wildly, Amin ran headlong down the steps and threw himself into Philipp's embrace.

'There now. You're safe.' Philipp put his good arm around the boy and let him sob. 'It's all over.'

There was snow again in the air as Frau Kaiser was led in handcuffs to the police car at the front of the house. Philipp stood on the pavement and watched her go past, flanked by two officers. She didn't meet his eyes. She hadn't spoken a word since she'd collapsed on the terrace. Those lips of hers seemed to have sealed themselves up for good.

There was a flurry of activity in the street. People had come out of their houses to see what was going on, and he wondered if any of them knew Frau Kaiser, or anything about her. They'd probably turned a blind eye. They were interested now, suddenly. It was so often the way.

Another police car had pulled up, and he spotted a man in uniform with a moustache talking to Nadja. The man was familiar from his pictures in the newspapers: it was Commissioner Rabbinger. Philipp was too far away from them to hear what was being said, and he couldn't see Nadja's face. He hoped she was getting all the praise she deserved. Schnied was busying himself, he noticed, ordering people around. The man was a downright scoundrel!

Two ambulances had now arrived, and paramedics were leading a procession of young men out of the house. They all looked exhausted and dishevelled. Some of them needed help just to walk. Philipp wondered how Abdul had managed to stay so healthy and strong. What deals had he struck with Frau Kaiser? But then what would he have done, in Abdul's position? All the same, he'd noticed that Amin had come running to him rather than to his uncle. Should he read anything into that?

He turned to look for the boy. Had he been taken to one of the ambulances too? No, there he was, standing off to one side, his alert eyes watching everything that was going on. Nadja was there with him, holding his hand. She must have finished talking to Rabbinger. He went over to join them.

'Philipp, I've been telling Amin he's going to the hospital. He seems to think he's going to prison.'

'No, Amin. Of course not. You'll be looked after very well, I promise.'

Amin looked up at him, his eyes full of questions he couldn't express. Philipp smiled and rumpled his hair.

'Philipp!' said the boy. 'Maschka!'

'That's right,' said Philipp. 'You'll see Maschka again soon. You'll see all of us, I promise you will.'

He gave him a one-armed hug, and then Nadja led the boy away by the hand to the waiting ambulance.

'Did you mean that, what you promised him?' she said, when she returned.

'Of course,' he said, wiping a tear from his eye. 'What did Rabbinger say? Have the two of you ironed everything out?'

'Not exactly.' She flashed him a look. 'He said I can resume my position in the police force. He's willing to overlook my insubordination.'

'That's good then. Isn't it?'

'But he won't be putting me forward for Commissioner, even if I pass my exams. I'll be remaining as Sergeant.'

'Okay.'

'And none of this must come out in the press. Schnied gets the credit, as the officer in charge of the case.'

'Ridiculous. Who'd believe that?'

'Also, he'll be promoted above me.'

'Schnied will?'

She nodded. 'He'll be my direct superior. I'll be reporting to him from now on. Hannes Schnied.'

She couldn't meet his eye. Philipp didn't know what to say. Perhaps it would all be okay in the end?

'Nadja…'

'Don't. Don't say anything.'

'Okay.' He reached out and touched her arm.

'Come on,' she said, shaking off her torpor. 'I'll drive you home in your car.'

He smiled. 'Thank you.'

'The snow's getting heavier,' she said. 'We'd better go.'

'Can you wait just a minute?'

He'd remembered something. He went once again down

the side of Frau Kaiser's house, across the lawn, towards the outbuilding. He wondered what would happen to all the cannabis growing in there. He hoped it would be put to good use.

He bent down and picked up his hat, knocked the snow off it, and put it on his head.

Standing there, he had a momentary feeling that Nadja was standing just behind him in the falling snow. He would turn around and she'd be right there, the snowflakes dancing around her, sparkling in her loose dark hair and on her jacket. He would step towards her, and she'd smile and touch the brim of his hat, and everything would be settled between them.

But when he turned around, there was nobody there.

THIRTY-SIX

Tidings of comfort and joy

Philipp woke in his own bed. The clock said it was half past four in the afternoon, but that couldn't be right. He'd only come upstairs for a minute.

After Nadja had brought him back from the Kapellenberg in the Jaguar and got him safely in through his front door, he'd gone upstairs, sat down on his bed, and thought through everything that needed doing before his children and grandchildren arrived later that morning.

He needed a shower, a shave, some painkillers for his shoulder, and a fresh change of clothes…

Maschka needed feeding and walking, and generally a great deal of fuss making of her to atone for his recent absence…

His horse Schimmi needed feeding and grooming, and the chickens would also need feeding (though not so much grooming as Schimmi)…

The tree decorations needed fetching from the cupboard in the basement, ready to be put on the tree…

Some dirty mugs in the kitchen needed washing up. Or at the very least they needed putting away in a box until after Christmas…

Food needed to be prepared for his twenty guests…

Drinks to be chilled…

Presents to be brought downstairs ready for the Bescherung, and carefully laid out in individual piles on tables and chairs, one for each of the guests…

Candles to be found, and fitted into candlesticks…

Matches located…

Wood chopped for the wood burner…

And so on and so forth…

He'd only put his head on the pillow for a moment. How was it half past four already?

Sheepishly, he rolled out of bed and opened the curtains. There was snow on the roofs, although the roads were mostly clear of it. The streetlamps were lit. It was difficult to say what time of day it was, since there was nothing to either confirm or deny what the clock was telling him. He pulled out his mobile phone. It was still out of battery. He shuffled to the top of the stairs.

'Hello?' he called out. 'Maschka? Anyone?' There was nothing but silence in reply.

He plodded down the stairs, feeling more and more gloomy with each step. Either he'd slept all the way through Christmas and everyone had gone home… or they hadn't even bothered to come.

Maschka wasn't in her basket in the hallway. Where'd she got to? Had she given up on him and gone to someone else's house for Christmas? It was all he deserved after abandoning her for so long.

He pushed open the living room door…

'Surprise!' The cry went up from twenty different mouths, young and old, all packed in around the living room. He nearly fell back into the hallway in astonishment. Everyone was there, his four grown-up children, all his grandchildren, Annelie and Emma, his ex-wives, his housemate Michi… even Maschka, who added an enthusiastic woof to the hubbub.

'Happy Christmas, Papa!' said his eldest daughter, the first to come over and give him a hug.

'Hello, Schlumpa… Ow! Mind the shoulder, please.'

'Schlumpa! Shoulder!' shouted Emma, jumping up and down.

'What's happened to you?' said his daughter. 'Have you hurt yourself?'

'Long story. I'll tell you over dinner.'

'Philipp!' cried Michi, his eyes beaming.

'So you're back, are you? How was Lanzarote?'

'Hello, Papa!' said his middle daughter over Michi's reply. 'I brought that bag of clothes you wanted. I've put it in the blue cupboard on the landing.'

'Clothes?'

'Yes. For a nine-year-old boy, like you said.'

'Oh yes, right. Thank you!'

'I'm glad to see you took my advice,' said Annelie, giving him a kiss.

'Did I?'

'I said you needed a good rest. Though to be honest, Philipp, I didn't expect you'd actually have one!'

Philipp was more than a little dazed by it all, and he had to sit down on the sofa while someone fetched him a cup of tea.

He went on sitting there while the tree was brought in and decorated, the candles lit, the food prepared, and all the presents brought down and set out on the Gabentische ready for the Bescherung. Nobody seemed to mind him putting his feet up in the middle of it all. They knew where everything was kept just as well as he did. Better, in some cases. Emma ran around directing everything, showing people where things had to be put, even though this was her first proper Christmas. Children, in fact, were not supposed to enter the living room once the presents had been laid out there. It was a firm tradition. They were supposed to stay upstairs, playing boardgames. But not all of them observed this as solemnly as they might. Emma was the chief offender, and she kept putting her head around the door to giggle at her papa.

Out in the corridor, someone had started singing, '*Morgen, Kinder, wird's was geben, morgen warden wir uns freun*', and the children all joined in with the bit that went, '*Welch ein Jubel, welch ein Leben wird in unserem Hause sein*', which means more or less: 'Such a joy, so much life there'll be in our house', followed by an almighty cheer from all around. Philipp found it difficult to take everything in.

When he eventually got around to charging his phone, he found he had thirty-seven messages waiting for him. Mostly from family saying they'd arrived at the station, and when was he coming to fetch them?

One message he left unread, hoping there'd be a knock at the door and one last guest to welcome in. But the knock didn't come, and just before they sat down to eat, he allowed himself to look at that final message.

'Dear Philipp, I hope your shoulder is feeling better. I shan't go on about it. I know you won't listen anyway. I wish you'd look after yourself. I know this is what all your ex-wives and partners say, so I'll stop saying it now. I hope you have a wonderful Christmas. I was touched to be invited, but as it turns out my mother has just called. She's taken a tumble and bruised her hip, and I really must go and look after her. Besides, Christmas is a time for families, isn't it? Like them or loathe them, we're stuck with them. Oh well, it's only one day in the year. I'll light a candle for Amin. And another one for you, Philipp. Happy Christmas! Nadja'

He put his phone away in his pocket and went to join everyone in the dining room.

On the Zeilsheimer Road, Christmas was soon in full swing. They talked and ate, drank and sang festive songs, and generally made merry in a most satisfactory way until late into the night.

THIRTY-SEVEN
The hopes and fears of all the years

It was a dank and dismal January morning, the rain hanging in the air like a fine, cold spray, penetrating whatever layers you'd put on to keep it out. Philipp was wearing his long coat and his trusty hat as he made his way up the winding path towards the chapel. But he was wet through already, and the funeral hadn't yet begun.

The cemetery was on the hillside west of Hofheim, surrounded by enormous spruces and Scots pines, and it felt sombre even on a sunny day. There were clusters of mourners standing around outside the little chapel, huddling under umbrellas, which were largely ineffective against the pervasive damp. There was a hushed reverence about the proceedings, even before they'd entered the chapel.

Philipp had come with Abdul and Amin, picking them up from outside the hostel where they'd been given temporary accommodation pending Frau Kaiser's trial. It hadn't yet been decided what would happen to them after the trial, but there'd been a special dispensation to accommodate them together, and this meant that Amin didn't have to go into care. He seemed happy enough. He was getting to know his uncle, who'd practically been a stranger to him until now. Abdul was even teaching him German, and each time Philipp visited – which was almost every day – he showed signs of improvement.

'Will there be dead body?' he whispered, tugging Philipp's sleeve as they approached the chapel.

'Don't worry,' he said. 'He'll be in a coffin.'

'He'll be coughing?'

'No, in a wooden box.'

'Oh. When we bury, we put body in *kafan*.'

'In a coffin?'

'He means a shroud,' said Abdul. 'A *kafan*.'

'Oh, I see.' Philipp put his good arm around the boy's shoulder as they went inside.

They sat discreetly at the back and watched as the other mourners filed in. It wasn't a big crowd. Jürgen Fischer, the man who'd driven the lorry and died in the crash, had been a private man. A lorry driver for the whole of his working life, he'd lived on the road – and died on it too. Philipp shuddered at the memory of Jürgen's body lying flat on the pavement outside his house while the paramedic tried to revive him.

The service was brief and to the point. Rather perfunctory, Philipp thought. He'd been to a funeral not very long ago for a man he'd known in the fire service, and his colleagues had all got together and performed 'Stairway to Heaven', a cappella. It had brought tears to everyone's eyes.

He didn't recognise any of the mourners. Jürgen had lived in Diedenbergen, out on the other side of Hofheim, towards Wiesbaden. One or two people glanced over at them, especially at Amin and Abdul. They probably didn't know very much yet about the circumstances of Jürgen's death. Philipp was glad the funeral was happening now, before the trial, before it all came out in public. It felt important for them to attend. The man had died bringing Amin here.

Afterwards, at the interment, the three of them stood well back from the graveside. They didn't want to intrude. The rain had eased up, thankfully. The soil made a dull thudding sound as it was scattered on the coffin. Amin gripped his hand. He was wearing a green cagoule that had belonged to one of Philipp's grandsons, one of the items his daughter had brought. Philipp gave the boy's hand a gentle squeeze in return.

As they turned to go, Philipp spotted his neighbour Beatrix – the woman who'd thrown the pot of skin cream – standing amongst the trees, watching. He gave her a little wave, and she dabbed her eyes with a tissue. He'd make sure to go and call on her later, take her some biscuits. The trial was going to be an ordeal for her as well.

Walking back down the path to his car, he wondered why Nadja hadn't been able to come. She hadn't returned any of his calls. Perhaps she was just busy preparing for her exams. He knew how important they were to her.

'Would you like to come back to my house for some cake?' he asked Amin. 'I know Maschka would be happy to see you.'

'Maschka!' cried Amin, smiling. 'Cake! Yes please!'

'You too, Abdul. If you like.'

Abdul seemed surprised to be asked. He blinked his deep-set eyes uncertainly, and finally gave a nod. 'Okay, this sounds good.'

They all got into the car, Philipp easing himself in behind the wheel. His shoulder was a lot better now, but he was still glad he'd come in the Jaguar.

They sat around the kitchen table and Philipp served up slices of New Year's cake. This was a traditional round cake with three layers of different fillings, each with its own symbolic meaning that Philipp was happy to explain.

'Poppy seeds for a year of plenty, nuts for new life, and apple for… I can't remember what apple's for. Michi, can you remember?'

Michi had his head inside the dishwasher, trying to work out why it had stopped working again.

'Apple's not for anything,' he said. 'It just tastes nice.'

'What is wrong with your dishwasher?' asked Abdul. 'It's broken?'

'It hasn't worked properly for years,' said Philipp. 'It's mostly there to stack plates in, until someone can be bothered to wash them up.'

'It was working over Christmas,' said Michi, giving up on it. 'Maybe having so many people in the house has finished it off.'

'I can take a look, if you like?' said Abdul.

'Please do,' said Michi. 'It doesn't get on with me.'

Amin had taken his slice of cake out into the hallway on a plate. He wanted to sit beside Maschka, who was spending most of her time committed to her dog basket.

Abdul rolled up his sleeves and ducked inside the dishwasher. Philipp worried that he might find something unsavoury lurking at the bottom of it. Strange, he thought. What was making him so house-proud, all of a sudden? Was it the effect of having come so close to death at this man's hands? He'd been wary of Abdul to begin with, and worried that he might not be a good influence on Amin. But the more he saw of him, the easier he felt about it. The guy wasn't so bad. He was gentle and kind. And if he managed to fix the dishwasher…

There was a shout from the hallway. It sounded like Amin. Philipp dashed out, his heart thumping in his chest.

'Maschka!' cried the boy, his face pale with anguish. 'She poorly!'

Philipp knelt beside the basket to see what was wrong. The dog did seem a bit off-colour. Her breath was coming in snatches, her flank rising and falling in great heaving pants, and she wouldn't look at him when he called her name.

'No, no!' cried Amin, growing hysterical.

Philipp put his hand calmly on the boy's shoulder and held him still. 'It's okay. She's fine. You'll see.'

They crouched there, side by side, and watched as Maschka pushed herself into position against the side of her basket. Her tail lifted and suddenly something appeared, wet and slippery, like a baby otter.

'You see?' said Philipp. 'She's having her puppies.'

Amin watched wide-eyed as another appeared, and then another. Each tiny creature tumbled out onto the old towel that Philipp had put in the bottom of the basket, their eyes shut tight, their noses pink. Maschka gave each of them a series of firm licks, and then they began squealing, almost like piglets, before latching on for a drink. Soon there were five of them crawling around, scrapping for pole position. One of them was blond like Maschka, but tiny. The others were all black.

'Is it all of them now?' said Amin.

'Four more,' said Philipp. 'You wait, the biggest one usually comes last.'

It was well after dark when the ninth pup made its appearance. The cake had long since been polished off, and the dishwasher restored miraculously to working order by Abdul. Maschka was exhausted, the job of delivering her pups now complete. Philipp didn't like to mention it but, in his experience, this was the moment the hard work really began – although he had to accept that he'd never actually given birth himself.

For the moment, there was a bit of peace and quiet as nine healthy puppies – all black except the single one that was blond – suckled away contentedly in the basket.

'Well done, Maschka,' said Philipp, giving her head a good scratch.

'Maschka!' echoed Amin. 'Well done!'

When it was time for going back to the hostel, Amin looked up at Philipp with baleful green eyes. He seemed to be making a silent request.

'Of course,' said Philipp. 'Which one do you want?'

Amin pointed to the small blond one, the one that looked most like Maschka.

Philipp nodded. 'Then, if Abdul agrees, that one will be yours.'

EPILOGUE

Now it is Christmas again. A lot has happened since that last Christmas. Some things you'll be able to guess, others perhaps you won't.

Philipp has some new housemates. Yes, that's right, they're called Amin and Abdul. After long talks with the local authorities – and of course with people rather closer to home – he came to the decision that he wished to adopt Amin. It would give the boy an easier pathway to German citizenship, he reasoned. But it wasn't only that. Philipp discovered that he felt about Amin the same way he'd felt about his own sons. Not exactly the same, since he'd missed out on the first nine years of Amin's life – but no different in any essential respect. He very much wanted Amin to be a part of his life, and when he enquired about the boy's feelings, he discovered they were just the same.

So in July, soon after the conclusion of Frau Kaiser's trial, the papers were signed, and then Amin and his uncle both moved into Philipp's house on the Zeilsheimer Road. For the time being they're sharing Youssef's old room, although the plan is for Philipp to do up another room – with Abdul's help – so that Amin can have his own space. He will soon be eleven, and a boy of that age needs a room he can call his own, ideally with a bed, a bookcase and a solid wooden door.

Amin goes to school at the Pestalozzi School, which is just around the corner on Ostend Street. His German is coming along nicely. In fact, he now knows so many words in German that he's teaching some of them to Abdul. He's like a big brother to Emma too, and the two of them dote on each other. They spend a lot of time playing games that Amin can remember playing when he used to live in Syria, and it turns out that many of them are very similar to the ones that Emma has learnt from her cousins. There's an infinite number of games that children can play in this world, yet strangely there are never really any new ones you can teach them.

Of Frau Kaiser's trial, there's little more to be said. It's Christmas time, after all. Suffice it to say that it ended satisfactorily for almost everyone concerned. The knitting circle won't be seeing her any time soon.

What of Nadja? Philipp didn't hear from her for quite a while, and when he did, he got a big surprise. She'd decided not to sit her exams after all, but to take a break from the Police Force and go travelling around the world. It was probably the thought of taking orders from Hannes Schnied, or perhaps seeing Rabbinger every day, twiddling his moustache. Besides, her mother had made a full recovery after bruising her hip and had taken up Taekwondo – so there was really nothing holding her back. Now and then he receives a postcard from her: 'Greetings from Rio de Janeiro', 'Just arrived in Bora Bora', 'Quite cold in Moscow'. He sticks each of them up on the fridge door alongside Amin's school timetable and Emma's handprints.

Maschka is the same as ever, though she now shares her basket in the hallway with Max, who officially belongs to Amin. The two dogs get on perfectly well, even though Max is now bigger than his mother. He's still just as blond as she is. The fact that all of Maschka's other pups had black fur convinced Philipp that the father must have been the black Labrador she'd taken a shine to through the fence at the animal hospital – though of course their acquaintance must have preceded that day for him to have been so closely involved. Philipp doesn't know where the Labrador resides, but he wishes him well.

And now, since it is Christmas Eve, all the numerous members of Philipp's family have assembled once again. Philipp has been cooking all day. After his Christmas off with the injured shoulder, he's gone the extra mile this time and thrown everything at it. Michi has been busy too, baking Christmas biscuits: those lovely half-moon-shaped almondy Vanillekipferl that he's famous for, and also some Zimtsterne, which are cinnamon-flavoured stars covered in glossy lemon icing. Abdul and Amin, not wanting to be left out, have made a batch of milk *barfi*, a fudge-like delicacy studded with pistachios. The whole house smells wonderful.

Since it is Amin's first real Christmas, he's been watching everything carefully with wide eyes, and taken his lead from the other children. They've all been up to the cemetery to put candles on the family graves, and Amin put one on Jürgen's too, so he wouldn't feel left out. Right now, they're sitting on the stairs waiting for the grownups to finish doing whatever they have to do behind the closed door of the living room. The older children know perfectly well what's going on, but they can't believe how long it takes the adults to do it. Why can't they just get on with it, and then they can all start opening presents? Instead, they have to sit here on the darkened staircase, listening to the footsteps going to and fro across the living room floor, back and forth, on and on, endlessly. They simply can't bear it. It's the most exciting time of all.

Soon the little Christmas bell will ding-a-ling to announce that everything's ready, and then the Bescherung will begin. The living room door will be thrown open, and they'll all leap up and make their way through, singing '*Ihr Kinderlein Kommet*' as they gather round the tree. That's when they'll see all the presents laid out in their little piles on tables and chairs around the room. And then, at long last after all the waiting, they'll be led one by one to their own pile of presents.

But wait, what's this? It's not the tinkly little Christmas bell but the doorbell that's ringing. Someone go and open the door quick, or we'll never get to the presents!

Philipp pops out of the living room and, before he closes the door, all the children try to steal a look at the presents. But they have to wait a little longer. Who can it be at the door? As Philipp opens it, a wave of cold air rushes in along the corridor and up the staircase, making all the children shiver.

There on the doorstep is a woman they've not seen before, except Amin and Emma who maybe remember her. She has loose dark wavy hair and bright eyes. She's got a motorcycle helmet under one arm, and a big bag of presents in the other.

'Merry Christmas,' she says, giving Philipp a kiss on the cheek.

'Are you back then?' he says. 'Very good. Come in. We're just about to start.'

ACKNOWLEDGEMENTS

Thank you to everyone who made this book possible…

To my family in Germany and my family in London, and all my many friends who supported me during the writing and translation process – you know who you are!

To James, Marlene and Luka, for giving me the space and the time.

To all the great people working at independent bookshops who helped to get *Only the Lonely*, the first book in the series, out into the world. A special shout-out to everyone at Pages of Hackney, the Notting Hill Bookshop, Word on the Water, Stoke Newington Bookshop, Jam Bookshop and Broadway Books, and to Homerton Library and Shepherd's Bush Library, who have all supported me in any number of ways.

To everyone at Nick Hern Books, especially Jodi Gray who typeset this book and Sarah Lambie for proofreading.

To Stone Bros for giving me a home from home to write in.

Thanks, also, to Ana Ilic and Queen Mary University.

Thank you to my agent, Sissi Liechtenstein, who read all the German versions and advised on this translation.

Huge thanks to my wonderful editor Robin Booth, and to Andrew Davis who came up with the series design, and to the brilliant illustrator and artist Sam Green for the beautiful cover of this book.

Already available in the
Accidental Detective series:

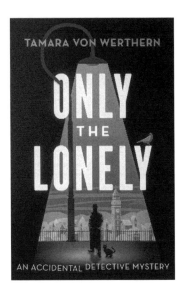

In *Only the Lonely*, detective Philipp drives a number of
battered old cars, chases the woman of his dreams and gets into
some seriously tight spots.

'A wickedly funny, wildly imaginative thriller that is as gripping
as it is entertaining' *CrimeFictionCritic.com*

'I love it! The world would be a better place
if we were all a little more Philipp' *FranMcBookface*

'Thoroughly enjoyable' *Number9reviews*

'Absolutely delicious' *Bobs and Books*

Coming soon in the Accidental Detective series:

In book three, Philipp is drawn into a dark fairy tale at a ball at his cousin's castle, when the daughter of a family friend disappears. Has she run away with an unsuitable lover, or has something even worse happened to her? Worried about a potential scandal, the family asks Philipp to take on the case. And when he discovers that his good friend Nadja Bernstein is in the neighbourhood investigating a series of murders, the two of them join forces once again to solve the mystery.

Tamara von Werthern is a German-British writer who lives in Hackney, London, with her husband and two children. *Silent Night* is the second in a series of crime novels that were originally published in German under the titles *Ich glaub, es hackt!*, *Ach Du liebe Zeit* and *Adel auf dem Radel*, all revolving around the character of Philipp, the accidental detective. The whole series is set in her hometown, Hofheim am Taunus in Germany, where she grew up before relocating to the UK, and the character of Philipp is based on her own father. She also writes for stage and screen and is represented by Sissi Liechtenstein of International Performing Rights Ltd. Her plays are published by Nick Hern Books. She won the Best Screenplay award at Lift-Off Film Festival's Season Awards 2019, translated the National Theatre musical *Hex* for its German premiere and is co-artistic director and founder of the Fizzy Sherbet Podcast (www.fizzysherbetplays.com).

For more information, visit www.tamaravonwerthern.com